2 Timers:

Love Sisters Series

2 Timers:
Love Sisters Series

Amaleka McCall

www.urbanbooks.net

Urban Books, LLC
300 Farmingdale Road, NY-Route 109
Farmingdale, NY 11735

2 Timers: Love Sisters Series

ISBN 13: 978-1-62286-895-7
ISBN 10: 1-62286-895-1

First Mass Market Printing April 2017
First Trade Paperback Printing December 2016
Printed in the United States of America

10 9 8 7 6 5 4 3 2 1

Distributed by Kensington Publishing Corp.
Submit orders to:
Customer Service
400 Hahn Road
Westminster, MD 21157-4627
Phone: 1-800-733-3000
Fax: 1-800-659-2436

Chapter 1

Melody

Light music played softly in the background, like an angel strumming harp strings. The warm orange glow cast over the room from the wall-embedded fireplace brought a smile of relaxation to Melody's lips. She was free falling, like strips of golden ribbon floating in the sky. Her heart thumped steadily to the rhythm of the music. She squeezed her eyes shut and giggled when a rainbow appeared inside her eyelids. Is this what love felt like?

"I make you feel good, don't I?" he whispered roughly against her neck.

It was him. He was the reason she felt so good; the owner of that familiar voice that had whispered in her ear hundreds of times.

Melody kept her eyes closed, folded her bottom lip between her teeth, and nodded her head.

Yes, yes, you do!

"Damn, girl," he said. Without warning, he crushed his mouth over hers. Grabbing her tightly, he forced his tongue between her lips. Melody lifted her arms in weak protest. She didn't want to appear too eager for more.

"Don't stop me, baby," he panted out each word as he forced her arms above her head. The heat of his breath danced over her lips. Everything about him was intoxicating. Melody felt light-headed.

"Stop," she gasped, overwhelmed by her desire for him. She moved her head from side to side, but he found her lips every time.

"I missed you. I love you," he murmured between kisses.

The words *I love you* softened Melody. The tension in her muscles began to ease.

He pressed his body into hers until she was sandwiched between her bedroom wall and his muscular chest. He smelled and felt so good. His touch, his scent, their chemistry—it was all familiar. The combination was heady, causing her insides to warm and her body to ache with need.

"Let me love you, Melody. Let me take care of you. Let me stop all of your pain. You don't have to be in control all of the time."

Melody relaxed as a tsunami of lust rushed over her. She was drowning and did not want to be saved. Her entire body trembled.

He moved his mouth from hers and trailed his tongue down her neck, sending a shockwave of electricity to her loins. She didn't know how much longer she would be able to stand upright.

"What about T—" Melody started, the throbbing between her legs growing stronger.

"Shhh. I love you," he interrupted before she could finish.

Melody couldn't understand why her body was betraying her like this. Logically, she knew this would end in heartache.

"You are with someone else now. You told me you love her. You're having a . . ." Melody struggled to get the words out.

"Hush. I love you," he said with a nip on her neck.

"I love you," he repeated as he moved lower, taking in a mouthful of nipple.

Melody gasped and moaned. An explosion of pleasure shook her small frame.

He sucked on her breasts, gently cupping each one like a precious treasure. Melody panted through her mouth, breathless with want. She parted her legs, inviting him inside. He lifted his head and smiled.

Then he slipped his pointer finger into his mouth and pulled it back out slowly.

"You ready?" he whispered, moving his moistened finger below her belly button. Melody shivered as he rubbed her clit with his wet finger until her juices flowed freely over it.

"Shit," Melody huffed. "Keep going . . . don't stop."

He added his middle finger, stretching her wide. He slipped both fingers inside and out, increasing the pressure.

Melody felt her pleasure mount, and she groaned in ecstasy. Tears welled in her eyes. She writhed her hips until she got his fingers to touch her just in the right spot.

"Yeah. That's what I like to see. Now, look at me," he urged.

Melody's eyes slowly fluttered open. She watched as he licked the nectar from his fingers.

"Oh God," she said, breathing heavily.

"Stop . . . no . . . wait," Melody huffed trying to push him away from her again. "What about her?" The words came out in a hot rush.

"I want you. I want to taste you. I fucking love you," he said with urgency. Melody closed her eyes again. Heat engulfed her body.

He moved his head further south, licking all the way to his destination.

Melody's heart beat erratically, and her vagina pulsed.

On his knees, he put his hot mouth over her clitoris and blew on it. Melody's body bucked with pleasure as she neared her peak. Her back arched sharply against the wall.

In a flash of light, she floated to the ceiling and watched herself and her lover from above. She could see his face, but couldn't feel him anymore. She reached out and tried to grab him. He was fading away, and she could no longer hear the words that he uttered. She couldn't smell his essence or taste his lips. She wanted to scream his name. She wanted him to see her, to hear her. She wanted him to touch her again. She tried in vain to grab his muscular chest, but he slipped away like a phantom.

Come back. You said you loved me!

Melody felt herself falling into a vortex. The floor seemed to spin beneath her. She opened her mouth to scream, but no sound came out. She threw her hands up right before she was about to hit the floor.

Melody awoke with a start, her chest heaving. Sweat drenched the front of her nightgown, and a chill seemed to permeate the air. She whipped her head around, but there was no sign of Sly.

Melody touched her face, then her chest. It had seemed so real. She lowered her right hand to her crotch, and it was soaked with her juices. She didn't realize women could have wet dreams too.

Her shoulders slumped, and her lips curled down. She sighed and turned to the left. Her face immediately folded into a frown.

"I hope that nasty dream you were having was about me," Ron said, chuckling over his shoulder. "You were moaning and groaning like you was getting a good old back-breaking fuck."

Melody glared at him. In just two weeks, he had gone from gorgeous to hideous. Ron's skin was ashen, his lips were dark, and the unkempt, overgrown hair on his head and face made him look like he was homeless. Her eyes darted to the nightstand where his cocaine, straw, and stem lay on top of her expensive, gold-trimmed handheld mirror. How could she have thought being with him would make her happy? Clearly, he was a weak man, and nothing disgusted her more than weak men.

Melody sucked her teeth and flopped back down on her pillow. The dream had seemed so real. Sly's touch and the sensations she'd experienced were almost palpable. She shook her head wishing she could go back to sleep and pick up where the dream had left off.

The sound of Ron snorting at her bedside brought reality crashing down on her. Sly was gone. Forever. Period.

After he took in a nostril full of coke, Ron turned toward Melody and laughed. "No? So the dream wasn't about me?"

She groaned. This man was a disgusting addict. If she had something handy to throw at him, she would have.

"Damn. I guess not. That must've been some hot loving you was riding in that dream, though. You're not going to tell me who you were dreaming about?"

Melody closed her eyes and exhaled. Her jaw rocked. "Have you been up all night getting high?" she grumbled, turning her back on him. "Is that all you do, day and night? Don't you ever sleep? Or think about other shit? Other shit besides who I'm having a wet dream about? Ugh, get a life."

"Get a life? I had a life, remember? I thought you wanted this," Ron replied, touching his chest. "Me being here with you, instead of being home with my wife and daughter. Wasn't this all part of your plan? I mean, you did go to great lengths to get me where you wanted me, no?"

Melody shot up in the bed and threw her legs over the side. "Fuck you, Ron."

"Answer me. *You* wanted *me*, right? Let's just clarify that I didn't go chasing after you, Melody. You wanted to take me away from her. You knew my weakness, and you exploited it. Didn't you?" he shouted. Since he'd been holed up in her SoHo penthouse, she noticed that Ron rarely took responsibility for his actions.

Melody shrugged into her bathrobe in a fury and tied the belt so tight it squeezed her stomach. She turned around to face Ron, her eyes squinted into dashes.

"If you didn't want me, you wouldn't be here either. And, for the record, you gave in to your own weakness. It was going to happen with or without me. Once a fiend, always a fiend," Melody taunted.

She stormed into her bathroom en suite and slammed the door; then she leaned her head against the door and closed her eyes. Her temples were throbbing. The reality of her situation and the truth of Ron's words hit her like a hammer to the skull.

It was true. When Melody first met Ron at her mother's funeral, he appeared to be a loving, attentive husband to her sister, Harmony, and a dedicated father to her baby niece, Aubrey. It burned Melody up inside with jealousy. Melody remembered watching Harmony walk into the funeral chapel with her little family—baby in hand, husband at her side. Melody had noticed right away how Ron supportively held onto Harmony with love in his eyes, and how, when they sat down, Harmony had so easily and lovingly lay her head on his shoulder and how Ron, in response, wrapped his arm around Harmony, holding her close. It was clear to Melody then that her sister had found a good man to love. Real love.

As she watched Harmony and Ron from behind her dark shades that day, Melody had actually become nauseated from the rough waves of jealousy swirling inside of her. Even then she had thought, *I was supposed to have everything. I was supposed to be the happiest. I am the only one worthy of a perfect life.* These same words had been uttered by the girls' mother throughout their lives. Melody had always been their mother's favorite, and no matter what Melody wanted, she could have it—even if it belonged to Harmony and Lyric. It was a fact they all had accepted very early on in life.

Melody had the mansions, the cars, the jewelry, the money, and anything else she could buy. Melody Love was the megastar, but Harmony seemed to have something that all the money in the world couldn't buy—love.

Melody decided that she deserved a man like Ron. She convinced herself that it was her mother's fault that she was lacking in the love department.

Melody swiped her hands over her face, trying to get rid of the sharp pangs of guilt that occasionally swamped her.

"You were so wrong, Melody," she whispered to her reflection, looking into the large, custom-made beveled glass mirror that hung over the bathroom sink. "You should go to hell for what you did. When Harmony finds out, she will never speak to you again."

Nauseated, Melody held the sides of the sink, her body bowed over. She closed her eyes and took a deep breath, trying to steady her emotions as she thought back to what she'd done.

"Did you think you were being smart? Did you think you were being funny?" Ron had growled, slamming Melody against the wall.

His hand was a vise on her throat, cutting off her air supply until her lungs burned.

Her vision blurred for a few seconds. Melody hissed and spit, trying to gasp for air. Her hands clawed at the fingers wrapped around her neck.

"You thought you would be more important to me than my wife, huh?" Ron used his free hand and dangled the tiny bag in front of Melody's face.

"You fucking tried to set me up?" he accused, biting off each word and spitting them in her face. "You know damn well I'm in recovery. Why did you leave this in my jacket?"

He held the damning evidence in front of Melody's bulging eyes. She tried to shake her head, but the movement sent a shock of pain straight down her spine.

Ron clamped down harder. His pupils were ringed with a fiery, orange tinge. He was the devil incarnate.

Melody's eyes burned with tears. The memory made her shudder with disgust. In a fit of jealousy, Melody had set a trap, and it worked. As solid as Ron and Harmony's relationship had seemed, Melody was able to snag him. Like a fish on a hook, he'd taken the bait. The bag of cocaine in his jacket pocket was how she managed to finally reel him in.

Not even a week after that violent encounter, Ron returned to Melody looking for more coke. The drugs made him weak, a shell of his former self.

Melody wasn't doing so well herself. She had just found out that her longtime boyfriend, rapper, and music mogul, Sly, was having a baby with Terikka, a young superstar who was signed to his Diamond Records label.

Melody felt abandoned, weak, and alone. So when Ron approached her car and slid into the backseat, she didn't protest. She let him in willingly, despite his unpredictable behavior.

"Driver, please move the car," Melody instructed, wanting to get away from the cameras.

Ron appeared relatively calm, almost despairing. She was no longer afraid that he would beat her up. Instead, she almost felt sorry for the bastard. She pretended not to be sexually attracted to Ron, but she was lying to herself. Faking, as usual.

"I didn't put the drugs into your jacket pocket," Melody asserted.

"It doesn't matter now. I've lost Harmony forever," he said. "One bag of dope and she's gone."

"What are you talking about? What do you mean you've lost—"

Before Melody could finish, Ron lurched over and forcefully put his mouth on top of hers. Melody's mind went blank, and her body tingled in places she hadn't felt in a long time, even with Sly. In that moment, Melody wanted to be loved so badly, she didn't care where she was.

Ron pushed her against the door, his hands moving all over her body.

"Wait," Melody whispered over his lips. She tried to push him away before things went too far, but he was more determined than she.

Ron ran his tongue down her neck. His hands worked feverishly at the buttons of her jeans. He was skillful and had her pants off in mere seconds. He tossed them into a heap on the floor, an unspoken challenge.

"C'mere," he wolfed, almost breathless.

Melody screamed out as Ron grabbed her upper arms and forced her to straddle him. She closed her eyes as she felt his erection pushing against her stomach. She couldn't bring herself to look at him.

Ron used his powerful hands to clutch her hips and force her up and down on him.

"Oh God," she grunted, digging her nails into his shoulders as she rode him hard.

Melody covered her mouth to keep herself from screaming now. What a fool she had been. Petty. Pathetic. She lowered her head in shame.

It had all been a game to her—Harmony had something that made her happy, and Melody wanted it—like a spoiled child who was denied a shiny new toy. Melody had gotten so used to taking everything from Harmony that it had become second nature to her. Even now after their mother, Ava Love, was dead, her wicked influence still lingered like a dark cloud over the sisters.

"Your phone is ringing!" Ron yelled from the other side of the bathroom door, interrupting Melody's thoughts.

Melody lifted her head and curled her hands into fists. She inhaled and squeezed her eyes shut, praying for patience.

Ron pounded on the door.

"I heard you! Now get the hell away from the door!" Melody yelled, her temper barely in check.

Since Ava's death, Melody had gone from the most beautiful, sought-after star in the world, to this ghost in the mirror. She hadn't seen dark circles under her eyes in years. Her hair had gone untouched for longer than a week.

Tears streaked down her cheeks. *Bastard! Sneaky, lying, snake-in-the-grass bastard! You did this to me, and I'm going to make sure I pay you back.*

Sly should've loved her like she needed to be loved. He should've been like Ron was to Harmony—in the early days at least.

She hunched over the sink and dry heaved. Thinking about Sly and Terikka together made her physically sick. Melody imagined the young girl's beautiful, smooth, caramel skin intertwined with Sly's velvety dark skin as they made love. Her stomach muscles clenched as she thought about Sly touching, licking, and fucking Terikka. The same way he did in her dream last night.

She missed him. There. She admitted it to herself.

"It's Lyric. She left a text. Says it's an emergency," Ron called from the bedroom, interrupting her pity party. Melody exhaled and swiped at the remnants of tears. Her patience was all but gone. Ron had to go. She'd come up with another master plan to get rid of him.

Ava used to say, "You only think you want something until you actually get it." Truer words were never spoken.

Melody snatched the bathroom door open and prepared to curse Ron out.

"Find out if Harmony and Aubrey are okay," he urged, pushing the phone into Melody's face. She grabbed her phone and narrowed her eyes at him.

"If you were home with them, instead of being here on a weeklong drug bender, you'd know if they were okay, now, wouldn't you?"

Ron threw his hands up in frustration.

"Yeah, that's what I thought. Now please move out of my way."

Melody scanned her phone. There were six missed calls from Lyric and four text messages. She sucked her teeth. Lyric's definition of an "emergency" was much broader than the average person's. Lyric was a pesky, opportunistic, drug-addicted baby sister that always needed money to get high.

Melody thought about ignoring her sister, but something told her to go ahead and call her back. Lyric knew something about Melody that she wasn't proud of at the moment. If the price was right, she knew Lyric could remain quiet. Melody couldn't afford for any salacious information to get out in the media about her.

Melody's fans had no idea that she lived a double life. When she was performing and in the public eye, she made sure her reputation was pristine. Whatever the price, Melody wouldn't let her image be marred with scandal. The Sly and Terikka baby announcement would drop soon and Melody already had her PR team working overtime on casting her as the victim of a two-timing boyfriend and home-wrecking whore.

When her team was done, Melody hoped her album would go double platinum. In the meantime, she would completely destroy Terikka's image and, hopefully, her singing career. Melody didn't like to lose in any aspect of her life, love life included.

She dialed her sister's number and waited for her to answer.

The words came out faster than her mind could process.

"Homicide? What? How? I'm . . . coming."

Melody's phone dropped to the floor. Her entire body grew cold.

Chapter 2

Lyric

"Shit," Lyric grumbled as she stumbled, nearly twisting her ankle. She paced in front of the building that housed New York City Police Department's Brooklyn North Homicide squad.

She folded down the top of the brown paper bag that concealed her Olde English 40 Ounce. A good old forty—the old-school way to get buzzed. It was the easiest and quickest medicine she could afford. She had to get her mind off of what was going on. Lyric wished she could forget everything she'd seen in the past two weeks. She wanted to call her boyfriend Rebel and beg him to come back to her. She missed him so badly. She replayed in her mind the last time she saw him. She wished she had fought harder to make him stay. Lyric blamed herself for losing him. Just like everyone else in her life, he had left her when she needed him the most. Another sip of beer and it didn't hurt as much.

Rebel visited Lyric in the hospital after her overdose in the club. She was so happy to wake up and find him at her bedside that numbers on her heart monitor almost doubled. Within no time, things were like old times with them.

"Come on. Open up for the airplane," Rebel joked, making airplane noises and waving a spoonful of applesauce in front of her mouth.

"Get out of here," Lyric giggled and turned her head away. They both laughed. He usually put up a hard, tough-guy act, but Lyric knew he had a softer side, which few had witnessed.

"Yo, you scared the shit out of me," Rebel confessed, putting the spoon on the hospital tray.

Lyric lowered her eyes, embarrassed by her actions.

"I know. I scared the hell out of myself too," she confided. "But I remember that high, yo. It was like nothing I ever had before, Reb. I was wishing I could share that shit with you the whole time. I mean, I was flying so fucking high," she said, her eyes lighting up with excitement.

*Rebel reached out and squeezed Lyric's hand,
halting her words. Lyric looked down at the
skull and crossbones tattoo on the top of his
hand, and then at his face.*

"What?" she asked softly.

*"I want you to kick, Lyric," Rebel said seri-
ously. "This is the end of the line for you and the
life. You gotta get yourself clean."*

*Lyric pulled her hand away, put her head
back on the pillow, and stared up at the ceiling.*

*"Not you too. I don't know how many lectures
I can fucking take," she groaned. "My sisters
are going to be on that rehab shit. I already
know . . ."*

*"This shit ain't for you, Lyric. You almost died,
and for what? Going on tour with your sisters,
singing and dancing, being a beautiful young
girl, and living, enjoying life . . . that's for you.
That's what you been trying to get back to all
this time. You got the support right here." Rebel
opened his hands, driving home his point.*

*Lyric sucked her teeth and closed her eyes.
She wasn't a child, but she felt so helpless in life.*

*"I'm serious, Lyric. Your sisters are in your
corner . . . for once. You should've seen how
Harmony was ready to kick my ass when she
thought I was the reason you overdosed. Man,
she was ready to rip me apart with her bare*

hands. That means something, Lyric. That means you're loved, even more than you know. Don't blow it," Rebel said with more feeling than she'd expected. Lyric swiped at the tears leaking from her eyes. Thinking about rehab and having nothing to help ease her pain made her stomach knotty. She couldn't imagine life without getting high.

"I don't want to lose you," she said honestly. "So if kicking means I can't be around you, then I'm not going to fucking do it," she said firmly, squaring her jaw.

Rebel sighed loudly. "Look at me," he demanded. She reluctantly met his gaze.

"Did I ever tell you how I got hooked on this shit, Lyric?"

"No," she murmured.

"I was a kid when I took my first hit. I was just a twelve-year-old child. My pops gave me my first one," Rebel said, swallowing hard.

Lyric's shoulders quaked with emotion. She didn't know if she was capable of handling her own pain, let alone his.

"That fucking coward told me it was for my own good. But, really, he forced it on me because he was afraid. He was afraid to be alone in his fucked-up, miserable world. When my moms overdosed and died, he didn't have

nobody else to get high with. So, I was the next best thing. I had just started dabbling in music with a couple of my friends at school. My pops told me the smack would make me better at my music. I was too curious to say no to that kind of promise." Rebel's voice cracked. He blew out a long, hard breath, like he was trying hard not to cry. Lyric noticed the dagger tattoo on Rebel's neck moving in and out with the pulsing of his heart.

"It did, for a while, you know? I was flying high all of the time. I could perform for a couple days straight, nonstop. The record label and my pops benefited off that shit. Everybody was collecting checks. I would get high and go like the Energizer Bunny, show after show. My pops kept the drugs coming, and I kept going. When my single blew up, I was riding fucking high, literally. But then, I started crashing. My body needed the smack to stay regular and not just for performances. I needed to hit it more and more often. I didn't care about shit else but a hit. I started seeing the little bit of money they gave me disappear faster than I could blink. My brain got all fuzzy. I couldn't write rhymes. I couldn't go onstage. I couldn't get into the studio. Fuck, I couldn't even remember where the studio was half of the time. All I wanted to

do was chase the high and keep myself from being sick. Then that stupid fuck-head pops of mine up and dies. Endocarditis the doctors said." Rebel shook his bald head, lowering his tattooed skull into his hands.

Lyric cried hard for him. She had no idea that he had been through this before. She was genuinely sorry to have reawakened his demons.

He lifted his head abruptly and parted an awkward smile. "Then, I met you. From the gate, you were the best thing that ever happened to me. I know I did some foul shit to you, Lyric. It was because I'm sick. It was because I didn't know how to fucking love someone as innocent and pure as you. I grew up around shitheads all my life. But, you, Lyric, I have loved you from the day we met. It's so fucked up that the only way I learned to express love was to get a person high. I thought by giving you that first hit I was showing you what my father showed me . . . love. I know it sounds like pure bullshit."

Rebel's resolve finally broke. His bottom lip quivered, and hot, angry tears danced down his face.

"I know you love me, Rebel," Lyric offered, extending her hand to him.

"Don't you ever believe that me fucking up your life with this poison meant that I loved you," he said through his teeth.

Lyric could see that he was angry at himself, not her. She looked down at the big, silver skull head ring on Rebel's left ring finger.

"I love you, Rebel."

"I want you to kick, Lyric. I want you to know real love . . . but it can't be with me. I'm not capable of giving that to you," he said, pulling his hand away.

Lyric's eyes went wide with surprise. Her heart beat erratically, sending off the monitor. He wasn't serious, was he?

"We can do it together. I'll only do it if you do it with me," Lyric said, anxiety lacing her words.

Rebel stood, shaking his head.

"I'm never going to get better. But, you have to, Lyric." Rebel backed away from Lyric's bed, his mouth turned down. The jingling from the chains hanging from his pants pockets sounded ominous. Like a prisoner walking to his execution.

He couldn't leave her like this. Alone. Afraid.

"Rebel. Don't leave me," Lyric begged, trying to muster enough strength to go after him. *"I won't stay here. I won't kick. I'll find you. I'll*

fucking hunt you down," she screamed, her face flushed.

"You have to stay and get the help you need. I can't help you. I can only hurt you," he said with finality.

Lyric threw back her hospital blanket and tried to disconnect her IV. The monitors next to her bed began to chirp loudly. Her heart was pounding so hard, she felt light-headed and weak. She was going to vomit on the sheets.

"Rebel," Lyric cried, her arms tangled in the tubes and wires as she fought to free herself.

"I'm no good for you," Rebel said through his tears as he quietly closed the door to her room.

"Reb! Reb! Don't do this to me! Please, Rebel!" Lyric sobbed as the nurses rushed to her bedside.

Lyric scrubbed roughly at her tears. "Oh my God. I fucking hate these flashbacks," she grunted under her alcohol-laden breath. She took another swig of her forty. Her sister needed to get her ass here soon, or she wouldn't be responsible for what happened next.

"Lyric. Lyric, what's going on?"

For a minute, the shrill voice sounded eerily like her dead mother's. Angry and judgmental.

Her sister, Melody, was the next worst thing to their mother.

"Thank goodness you're out here. What the hell is going on?" Melody rushed over, fake concern creasing her brow. As usual, Melody was flanked by a phalanx of goon-squad-looking security guards.

Lyric shook her head. She was finally feeling the effects of her libation.

"Damn, need security much?" she slurred a little, rolling her eyes at Melody. Thank God Lyric had enough foresight to run to the bodega and grab that beer before Melody arrived. There was no way Lyric could ever deal with her sober. In fact, Lyric still wanted to tear Melody apart with her bare hands for what she'd done to Harmony. The bitch had no moral compass.

"You're drunk," Melody declared, waving her hand in front of her face and scrunching her nose.

"And, you are correct," Lyric said, simulating an ovation clap with her hands. "You should probably have a drink too. I mean, it's what I would do if I was evil like you." Lyric raised her brown paper bag to her lips again.

"Is there ever a time you don't find yourself escaping into a bottle of booze or a baggie of drugs?" Melody asked with her arms crossed.

"Do . . . do . . . not start that bullshit, Mel-o-dee," Lyric slurred, pointing a wavering finger at her.

"Where's Harmony?" Melody cut to the chase.

"Talking to the DTs. It's been almost twenty-four hours now," Lyric hiccupped. "First, they spoke to her, then me, then her. I . . . I . . . guess they think one of us murdered the great Av . . . Ava . . . lub," Lyric garbled, raising her drink. "I should pour some out for our good ol' mother. Yeah, pour some out for the wicked bitch."

Melody jumped back as some of the frothy malt liquor splashed on the ground and splattered on her shoes.

"Damn shame, girl. You're a hot mess. So embarrassing," Melody shook her head in disgust.

"Take her into the car before it becomes a paparazzi zoo out here," Melody instructed, nodding at Virgil, her head of security.

A few members of Melody's security team moved to escort Lyric to the waiting Range Rover with dark tinted windows.

"I . . . I . . . can walk on my own," Lyric garbled, snatching her arm away from the goons.

"Melody," Lyric called out, somewhat coherently.

Melody stopped in her tracks, pivoting toward her sister.

"Harmony doesn't know. I didn't have the heart or the chance to fucking tell her," Lyric spat.

"Well, maybe you shouldn't," Melody said matter-of-factly.

Lyric squinted her eyes, her jaw rocking feverishly. She had some nerve to tell her what to do. She was in no position to negotiate.

Lyric had frozen in place, her mouth agape. "Ron?"

"Shit," Ron gasped like he'd seen a ghost. "Lyric, listen to me." He put his hands up, pleadingly. "Let me just explain."

Melody rushed out of her bedroom, just in time to see Lyric and Ron standing face-to-face like they were getting ready to name their seconds in a duel.

"What are you doing here? Didn't we leave you in a rehab in Pennsylvania?" Melody asked, clutching the material of her gown trying to cover her naked body.

"I can't believe you. I can't believe either of you," Lyric gritted, shaking her head. She was sick to her stomach. "Y'all are both fucking

disgusting," she growled, her hands curling into fists.

"Just listen to me, Lyric." Ron reached his hand out toward her. Lyric slapped it away.

"Don't you fucking touch me with those dirty hands!" Lyric screamed, pushing at his chest with all of her strength. "I can't believe that you're such a lowlife. After all Harmony has done for you? This is how you fucking repay her, you bastard?" She jabbed her finger in his chest.

"It was a one-night stand. It happened so fast. I didn't mean for it—" Ron rambled, stumbling backward.

Melody chortled and stepped closer to Lyric. "How much? What's your price to keep this quiet?"

Lyric jerked back as if she'd been slapped. Her sister was one dirty bitch.

"What? What did you just ask me?" Lyric asked through clenched teeth.

"Let's face it, Lyric. You didn't leave rehab because you felt like it. You left because the urge to get high was too much to handle. Everybody has a price," Melody said flatly.

Ron frowned and lowered his head in shame.

"You selfish, conniving bitch. You disgust me," Lyric said, her voice trembling. "Fuck you *and your money. I hope that money and this no-good addict bring you all of the happiness you think your money can buy." She turned her back on them both, ready to leave.*

"Lyric," Ron called after her. Lyric paused but didn't turn around.

"Please, don't tell Harmony. This would destroy her. Let me do it. Let me be the one," *he pleaded.*

Lyric would not let Harmony be made a fool. She owed her sister that much.

Lyric shook her head now, recalling the anxiety that plagued her as she took the long cab ride to Harmony's place in New Jersey, contemplating how she would tell Harmony that their evil sister had slept with her husband. Lyric's stomach cramped up now, the same way it had that day.

Lyric had entered Harmony's dance studio and went straight to the office, where she knew she would find her sister hard at work.

"I . . . I . . . need to talk to you, Harm. It's real important." Lyric's lips trembled.

The chimes over the front doors sounded off just as Lyric sat in the chair opposite the desk. She paused, glancing at the intruder.

"Good afternoon, ladies. I'm Detective Brice Simpson, NYPD, Homicide." A tall, handsome man stepped forward, while his trench coat-clad partner remained a few steps behind.

"Homicide?" Harmony repeated.

"What's this about?" Lyric dropped her bag at her feet.

"Are you the daughters of Ava Love?" Detective Simpson asked.

"Yes," Harmony and Lyric answered in surprised unison.

"Why are you asking about Ava? What is this really about?" Harmony asked suspiciously, concern creasing her brow.

Detective Simpson cleared his throat. The other detective looked uncomfortably at his black, shiny, wingtip shoes.

"Your mother's death has been ruled a homicide by the medical examiner."

"Is that all, Lyric?" Melody's question brought her back to the present.

"No. That's not all. Don't think this issue is over between me and you. It's far from over," she warned.

Melody glared at her before flicking her hair over her shoulder in dismissal.

"It damn sure ain't over. You're going to pay. One way or another, you'll get what's coming to you," Lyric mumbled as she entered the waiting vehicle.

Chapter 3

Harmony

Harmony used the tips of her fingers to massage her throbbing temples. The headache was definitely stress induced, and it made her mind feel fuzzy. The constant rapid fire of questions from the detective had her patience at an all-time low. She wasn't going to "break," but she guessed Detective Brice Simpson thought the long hours of interrogation would somehow yield useful or incriminating information. She wished they would just waterboard her and be done with it.

Now Harmony understood how the NYPD got so many forced confessions. If she was some poor, young girl sitting in a dank and drab room for hours on end with two men rotating in and out to badger her with the same questions, she probably would have sung whatever tune they asked her to sing. If they wanted a singer, they had picked the wrong sister to question. She chuckled sarcastically to herself at the irony of it all, then glanced over at the two-way mirror and hoped no one was watching her. She must've looked crazy.

Harmony sighed and swallowed hard. She was exhausted. It had been almost twenty-four hours since the detectives had barged into her performing arts school and told her that her mother's death had been ruled a homicide. It was just one more thing to deal with now.

Harmony and her sisters had already been struggling to deal with all of their buried hurt, pain, jealousies, and the demons of their past that surfaced after finding out that their mother had been found dead in her house. But to learn that Ava might have been murdered—this made Harmony feel like she'd been pushed into traffic with cars speeding at and around her from every direction.

She looked at the papers spread out on the table. The medical examiner's words started to swim in front of her tired eyes.

"Let's go over it one more time, Ms. Love—" Detective Simpson started.

"*Mrs. Bridges,*" Harmony cut him off. "I'm married." Chills cropped up on Harmony's arms as soon as she uttered the statement.

She was angry at her husband Ron, but she missed him terribly. She wondered every night if he had gone back to sleeping in the streets. Harmony rubbed at her temples again. She couldn't help but rehash the pain of their last encounter.

Harmony had doubled back to the hotel room. Ron said he'd forgotten something, but his behavior seemed odd, which made her suspicious. Living with a recovering drug addict was not easy.

At the hotel room door, she slowly stepped inside, balancing her daughter on her hip. A fire burned in her stomach and chest. Her instincts told her not to call out to Ron. She moved through the suite slowly, her breath coming out rough and fast.

Harmony approached the bathroom door on unsteady legs. The door had been left slightly ajar. She craned her neck, trying to see through the small sliver.

Harmony heard loud snorting from inside. She stumbled back a few steps. Her heart felt like it had stopped. There he was—her husband, the love of her life, the man she had supported for the past three years—bent over the sink, sniffing white powder.

Cocaine! Her knees nearly gave out, and she came close to dropping baby Aubrey. The baby giggled, like she did when Harmony was being silly with her. Harmony's heart seized, and her hand flew up to cover the baby's mouth.

"Harm?" Ron called from the bathroom.

She could hear him fumbling around. Glass shattered, followed by low cursing.

"Harm, is that you?" he called anxiously.

She could hear him sniffling. She whirled around, not sure what to do next. Harmony felt untethered, like she'd just slipped off the side of a mountain and was freefalling to her death.

"Harm?" Ron emerged, a tiny dot of white powder still rimming his right nostril. Harmony's eyes bulged at the evidence of his crime. She moved backward, no longer recognizing the man who stood before her.

"Harm, wait," Ron said, his left hand extended. "Let me just tell you what happened." His eyes were watery. His brow was dripping sweat. Harmony had seen him in this condition before. It was not something she hoped to repeat.

Harmony stumbled into the small hotel room desk. Her baby laughed joyfully, oblivious to the seriousness of the situation.

"Just hear me out, Harm," he pleaded.

Harmony opened her mouth to speak, but no sound came out. She couldn't find the words. She couldn't cry. She couldn't yell. She couldn't do anything. The devastation she felt was like nothing she had ever experienced in her life. Harmony stood on proverbial quicksand—there was no hope for escape.

"I got it under control, Harm," Ron said. "I promise you. I was a little stressed out with everything that was going on with us, um . . . with you, but I know once things are back to normal between us, I can stop."

Ron was blaming her for his relapse? How dare he!

Harmony turned swiftly and sprinted to the door.

Ron was quicker than she anticipated; his large chest blocked the door and her exit. She tried to go around him, but he shifted sideways to stop her.

"Harmony, wait."

"Da-da," Aubrey cooed, stretching her chubby arms toward Ron. It was the first time she'd said the word. Harmony felt a sharp pain in her stomach. One of her worst fears realized—her daughter would grow up fatherless, just like she did. This wasn't what Harmony had envisioned for her life when she started

rebuilding it after the Sista Love breakup. Anything but this type of disappointment and pain.

"Harmony, just listen to me. I promise I can handle it. I swear it won't be like before," Ron begged. "It's not like you didn't drive me to this point."

Without thought, Harmony slapped him across the face with every ounce of strength she had in her body. Ron's head swung to the left; his hand flew up to his cheek as he stumbled sideways from the impact.

Aubrey started crying. Without a word, Harmony yanked opened the door and stormed out, screaming baby in tow.

"Harmony, please wait," Ron called after her. "Just give me a minute to talk to you."

Harmony didn't bother to turn around. Her legs felt as heavy as lead pipes, but she forged ahead as fast as they would carry her.

"Harmony," he called after her again, but stopped at the doorway to the hotel room. She knew that Ron wouldn't chase her. The cocaine in the bathroom was far more enticing than Harmony would ever be to Ron at that moment. Of that, she was sure.

***

"Ms. Bridges? Are you okay?" Detective Simpson asked. Harmony blinked a few times, focusing on the present.

She cleared her throat and feathered her hands nervously through her hair.

"I've looked at it over and over again. My answers are still the same. I don't know anyone who would want my mother dead, and I damn sure wouldn't know anyone who could get close enough to her to poison her. Who knows, maybe she did it to herself."

"Suicide by poison?" Detective Simpson seemed to contemplate her theory. "Not a likely MO for a woman her age."

"There wasn't much that was likely for Ava. She wasn't your typical 'woman of her age,' Detective. My mother was alone these past few years. Perhaps she wanted to die alone as well. Maybe all of the cruel things she did finally caught up to her." Harmony looked up at Detective Simpson wearily, the truth pressing against the roof of her mouth.

The detective nodded for her to continue.

"My mother wasn't some little sweet old lady who baked cookies and looked forward to visits from her three daughters. Far from it. She had no friends except Murray Fleischer, and he's so old he probably couldn't make a cup of tea much less prepare a killer concoction. Like I told you already, I hadn't seen her in three years, but I would bet my life that Ava didn't make any close friends in that time. To put it lightly, my mother was an evil bitch of a woman. She didn't even allow us to call her mom."

As soon as the words left Harmony's mouth, her lips started trembling. Harmony had lived through years of Ava's cruel treatment and name-calling: *You jiggaboo, tar baby. You nappy-headed run-away slave. How did I give birth to such a black, ugly spook?* She had endured vicious beatings as well—*leather belts to the palm of her hands, wet towels to the back, closed-fist punches to the soft parts of the body that didn't leave bruises.* She had attended every cruel and merciless rehearsal too—*up at 5 a.m., eating only one meal a day until the routine was perfect. Never allowed to eat candy or sweets to make sure she didn't gain any weight.*

Ava had also stolen millions from Harmony and didn't bat one false eyelash about it. Sure, Harmony had wished her mother dead on several occasions. But to actually go through with killing her mother? No, Harmony wasn't that type of monster.

"I know I've asked you this a couple of times . . ." the detective persisted.

Harmony threw her head back in exhaustion. "No. Not a couple of times. You've asked me the same things over and over again since you dragged me down here. And, trust me, despite this constant barrage of questions, my answers will remain the same."

Detective Simpson sighed and removed his already loosened necktie. He pinched the bridge of his nose and paced the room.

He was an attractive man, with smooth skin, broad shoulders, perfect teeth, and tight, dark, scalp-hugging curls. Harmony could tell that the bags cropping up under his eyes and the strain lines around his mouth were a product of his profession and not his age. She pegged him to be roughly thirty-five years old.

"I know this all seems redundant, but Ms. Lov . . . I mean Bridges, we are trying to figure out who would want your mother dead. Who could have gotten close enough to add poison to her food and drink? But most importantly, why?" Detective Simpson leaned his back against the wall and crossed his arms in front of his chest.

Harmony met his gaze and stared him down.

"So I know you've told me that you and your sisters were members of the singing group, Sista Love," Detective Simpson recounted. "My little sister loved your music, by the way," he said with a half smile. "In fact, she dragged me to two of your concerts. It was just as memorable for her as it was terrible for me, no offense. There is nothing worse than being surrounded by throngs of screaming girls. Needless to say, I couldn't hear for a week after the concert," he joked.

Harmony could tell he was trying to lighten the mood. She cracked a weak smile too. Maybe if she played nice for a while, he would let her go home.

"Yeah. Sista Love had many fans. We definitely had a good thing going. It's just too bad that the ugly human side of things got in the way of our success. But, you know humans—we lie, we cheat, and we steal. Success brought the worst out in all of us. They say that sisterhood is a bond that can never be broken. Well, we proved that saying false." Harmony's voice cracked at the end of her statement.

"So, your mother was your manager, but then things went bad. Your mother and her partner, Murray Fleischer, were the reason things didn't work out, correct?"

Harmony nodded. "That's right."

"You found out that she was secretly brokering a solo deal for your sister, Melody, and was also robbing you and Lyric blind. You finally had enough and said screw it, I'm out of here. But before you left, you had a physical altercation with your mother. No charges pressed. No police report. You later sue your mother, the label, your sister, and Murray, and win a lucrative judgment and open up your business. You move away and stay away from your family. No contact with your mother. No contact with your sister Melody, and only sporadic contact with your sister Lyric."

"That's a decent summary, Detective Simpson. I see you've been listening. At least I don't feel as bad knowing these hours of talking didn't fall on deaf ears," Harmony said sarcastically. Detective Simpson rubbed his chin and pursed his lips.

"So you come back to bury your mother, and what . . . face your sisters for the first time in years?" he asked gently.

"Yes, and it wasn't easy. Like I told you before, my sisters and I have never been as close with one another as sisters should be. Ava was cruel to me, and Lyric . . ." Harmony's voice thickened. She closed her eyes and sighed. She hated rehashing so much of the past. She bit her lip hard. Talking about Ava made her feel angry and depressed.

"We were just kids when Ava came up with the idea of making us into stars. Ava was hanging on for dear life to a long dead singing career. The way she told it, back in her day, she was one breath away from a star on the Walk of Fame," Harmony said dryly.

"But she got pregnant with me. From what I've heard, my father was the lead drummer in Donna Summer's band. Ava, of course, was a backup singer. My father was married, and Ava was beautiful and irresistible. Like Lena Horne beautiful. A hot, one-night stand on the road and boom, a baby was on the way. I've always heard that Ava equated being pregnant with a terminal illness diagnosis. She was simply miserable. I apparently ruined her body and her career. Hearing her speak about her pregnancy and about me as a baby, I never understood why she didn't just have an abortion. But I guess back then, it wasn't as easy as it is now. Ava knew my father wasn't going to leave his wife. She knew having a baby on the road would be incompatible with her lifestyle. And she never forgot to remind me of just how inconvenient my presence was in her life. I'm not helping my case here, am I, Detective?" Harmony chuckled despondently, wiping the tears before they could fall.

Detective Simpson handed her a box of tissues and nodded for her to continue. It was oddly comforting to spill her feelings to a complete stranger.

"I never got to meet him—my father. I found pictures, though, and immediately recognized who he was. It was like looking in a mirror, that's how much I looked like him. Same roasted coffee bean complexion, same thick, coarse hair. I didn't need a DNA test to confirm who my father was. But my mother never had the decency to tell me anything about him, except that I looked just like him, and she hated me for it," Harmony said bitterly.

She fell silent for a few minutes. Her words lingered over the room like a thick, suffocating fog.

Detective Simpson grunted in response, and then cleared his throat. "I'm sorry that you had such a difficult mother. It must not have been easy for you or your sisters." For once, Harmony heard genuine compassion in his voice. She twisted the drawstring on her sweatpants around her finger and moved her legs in and out under the table.

"From the time I could remember, Detective Simpson . . . I'm talking about being two years old, and even then, Ava treated me with disdain. I remember sleeping in an old rickety, wooden, secondhand crib with no blankets and

Ava screaming, '*Shut up, you little ugly jigga-boo,*' whenever I cried because I was hungry. She called me that name so often, I once told a lady in the grocery store that my name was 'Ugly Jiggaboo' and she looked at me in horror."

Detective Simpson moved from the wall and folded into the chair in front of her. He patted the top of her hand sympathetically. She smiled weakly at his effort to console her. The mood in the room had definitely shifted from suspicious to sympathetic. Harmony knew it would once she got started.

"Yeah, I know. To other people, it sounds horrible, but to me, that was my normal life. As I got older, it got worse, especially after Melody was born. Melody's father is a famous actor who Ava loved more than any other man—past or present. But as much as she loved him, he refused to put a ring on it. I'm pretty sure he was already married too. I remember him. Boy, do I remember him. He was a good-looking white man—tall, dusty-blond hair, shocking blue eyes. I would sneak a peek at him as he came in and out of Ava's bedroom late at night and early in the mornings. He left all types of sweet treats for Melody. Dolls, candy with fancy wrappings, beautiful dresses with frills and bows, shiny patent leather shoes, gold earrings," Harmony recalled, shaking her head.

Detective Simpson scribbled wildly on his white legal pad. The pen scratching against the paper unnerved Harmony slightly. She didn't know if she was saying too much, but she also couldn't stop talking.

"I always wished he was my father too," she said, her face going stony. "But just like everyone else in our lives, one day Melody's father stopped coming around too. Ava cried for what seemed like months. She was depressed for a long while. Afterward, there was a dramatic change in her behavior toward Lyric and me. She became crueler, if you could imagine that even being possible. But Melody was treated more like a princess—a beautiful, honey-colored, half-white princess," Harmony gritted.

Harmony shook her head and squeezed her eyes shut. She was unearthing deeply buried, painful memories.

"Melody was perfect in Ava's eyes. She was a pretty doll that Ava liked to play with. But me, I got called a worthless, nappy-headed nigger, a black scoundrel, an escaped slave," Harmony rattled off.

Detective Simpson's eyebrows shot up. Harmony met his gaze unashamedly.

"Oh, yeah . . . all types of derogatory names because of my complexion. I died a little more inside every time she uttered those words. Did you know that I had such a complex about my skin color that I tried to bleach my skin when I was fifteen years old? Twice, Ava was forced to take me to the emergency room for skin irritation and burning. I scrubbed my body each night hoping that some of the color would rub off. I prayed to God that when I woke up, I would be just as light as Melody and realize that my darkness was just a figment of my imagination. I just wanted her to see me, to love me."

"Did you ever get to tell your mother how you felt about all of this? Have a sit-down with her, get your pain off your chest?" Detective Simpson asked, throwing his pen down on top of his pad. Harmony laughed at him.

"Sitting down to talk with my mother would've never happened, Detective. When my baby sister came along, I began to hate my mother even more. Lyric was an innocent child, but Ava treated her like garbage. The woman had no maternal instinct. I believe that even her relationship with Melody was more obsession based than love based."

Harmony's jaw stiffened. Detective Simpson sat up straight, his facial expression was serious, but Harmony could see in his eyes that he was saddened by what he was hearing.

"One time, Ava beat Lyric's hands with a belt. I can't even remember what Lyric had done— maybe dropped her sippy cup on the carpet or something. I was so angry at Ava for hitting Lyric that I rammed my little body into her with the force of a wrecking ball. I screamed 'don't hit my baby sister.' I started biting, kicking, and scratching Ava. I got the worst beating that day. I was five years old, but from that day forward, I knew that I needed to protect my baby sister from our mother. I took beatings for Lyric all the time. I covered Lyric's ears when Ava called her names. I never wanted my baby sister to know how much our mother truly hated us.

When Ava would make us wear five-inch heels to dance and sing for hours until our little bodies nearly gave out, I was the one who would comfort Lyric, rub the cramps from her muscles, sneak her little sweet treats." Harmony's voice grew gruff, and the tears fell freely from her eyes now. She didn't even try to wipe them anymore. Speaking about Lyric was the one thing that caused Harmony the most pain. She was still haunted by what Ava had done to Lyric. Harmony regretted that she didn't do anything to stop it or change it.

But she didn't share *that* story with Detective Simpson. Harmony thought telling him that their mother had basically sold Lyric as a sex slave to Andrew Harvey, a perverted record executive that was old enough to be Lyric's grandfather, in order to get them a record deal, would push Lyric to the top of the murder suspect list. Harmony would rather the police tear her apart than harass Lyric.

Harmony never forgave herself for allowing that to happen to her baby sister. Now, she felt like it was her responsibility to protect Lyric . . . to save her.

"I'm very sorry, Ms. Bridges. But you did say earlier that your mother had one redeeming quality. She was the reason you all made it big, right?"

Harmony opened her hands, palms up, and hunched her shoulders. "If you want to look at it that way, yes. All of Ava's cruel treatment was attributed to her desire to see us become the next big girl group. She was the reason we had the work ethic and singing skills to make it to the top of the charts. Ava made us work hard, and she'd crack the whip . . . literally sometimes. We had chart-topping hits and Grammy Awards to show for it. But we lost in the game of life. We had no childhood friends, no school trips, no candy, no sleepovers, no amusement parks . . . none of the things normal children experienced.

We were just one big music experiment—a get-rich-quick scheme that happened to pan out. So, yes, my mother was good at recognizing talent and exploiting it. She gambled with us, and she won. We won too—until it all came crashing down around us."

"And at the height of your success, you just walked out on it all?" Detective Simpson asked, his eyebrows furrowed.

"Yes. When I grew tired of the abuse, the lies, and the cruelty, I left. And you know what? I walked away only with the clothes on my back and a few dollars in my pocket, and it was the smartest thing I'd done in my entire life. I felt strong, independent. Most importantly, I felt free." Harmony used the back of her hand to wipe her runny nose.

"Sounds brave," Detective Simpson said. "You must've been proud of yourself."

"It didn't matter if I was proud of myself because still, only Melody could ever make Ava proud. Only Melody was ever good enough. And you know what? In the end, Melody turned her back on Ava too. I'm not afraid to admit I hated my mother for the things she did to me as a child, Detective Simpson, but it doesn't mean I killed her."

"What about your sisters? Would they have a good enough reason to end your mother's life?" Detective Simpson asked point-blank. Before Harmony could answer his question a loud knock reverberated through the door.

"Harmony? Are you in there?"

Detective Simpson looked at Harmony, his eyebrows rounded into arches.

"Well, Detective Simpson, you've met Lyric, and you've met me . . . Now, brace yourself. You are about to be graced with the presence of her royal highness, Melody Love."

Chapter 4

Melody

Melody was ready to battle as soon as the interrogation room door swung open. Her jaw was set, and her eyes squinted. How dare the police think they could hold her sister and question her without a lawyer!

Melody pursed her lips, ready to unleash a vile stream of curses. But the words she'd prepared went tumbling back down her throat at the sight of the gorgeous man standing in front of her.

Damn! He's fine.

This was no balding old man in a donut jelly-stained shirt like she'd expected.

"Ah, if it isn't the famous Melody Love, here in the flesh," Detective Simpson said, flashing his gorgeous smile. The lone dimple in his right cheek winked at Melody. She was speechless; a first for her.

"Detective Simpson. Brice Simpson. Come on in. We were just discussing you," he said, inviting Melody into the tiny room, gesturing to a nearby chair.

Melody sauntered into the room, her bodyguards in tow.

Detective Simpson held up his hand. "Your secret service detail can stand right outside. There's not enough room in here," he directed, shooing away the bulky men in dark suit jackets.

Melody sucked her teeth, but she nodded for her security team to do as instructed.

Before he closed the door, Detective Simpson stuck his head into the hallway and yelled at the precinct staff that were hovering nearby. "Get back to work. No one is getting autographs or concert tickets. And don't even think about leaking any information to the press."

The staff went scurrying back to their offices. He shook his head in disbelief.

"Boy oh boy, the way these people are acting, you would think it was the Second Coming of Christ," he said as he stepped back into the room.

"You must not know 'bout me," Melody said indignantly, flipping her long, sandy-brown hair.

"Trust me, I know about you. In fact, I know more about you than you think," he said confidently.

Melody blushed at his brazenness. "Well, if you know me, then you know I came to get my sisters. Neither they, nor I, will speak to you or any of your people without our attorney present," she said, obstinately lifting her chin and folding her arms across her chest. "Let's go, Harmony. We're finished here."

"Everyone has a right to have an attorney, but most of the time, people request them when they're under arrest or guilty of something they don't want us to find out about. I'm simply trying to help you ladies find out who could've harmed your mother," Detective Simpson said evenly.

"Like I said, you've probably heard more than you should have without an attorney present," Melody shot back. "Let's go, Harmony," she said, tilting her head toward the door.

"I don't need your attorney, Melody. I was done here anyway. I have a baby at home that needs my attention. Besides, you're the only one they haven't interrogated," Harmony snapped, standing up and heading for the door. "I will see myself out, Detective Simpson."

Melody rolled her eyes and sucked her teeth as she watched her sister storm toward the door. That was the thanks she got for trying to come to the rescue. As usual.

"This is always what I get for trying to help you and Lyric? Attitude. Ungratefulness," Melody huffed, shaking her head. "I'm leaving too."

"Ms. Love," Detective Simpson said, holding his hand up. "You might want to reconsider that. I have information you'd be very interested in," he said cryptically as he slid a yellow folder across the table.

"And just what the hell is this? A court order? Some kind of trumped-up evidence? You don't have a right to detain me and question me without . . ." Melody stopped midsentence after Detective Simpson opened the folder in front of her and leaned back in his chair to gauge her reaction.

"This change your mind?"

Melody froze. She swallowed hard. Almost immediately, sweat beads cropped up at her hairline. Suddenly, the incident flashed across her mind's eye like it was happening now.

"Let's go. No distractions and no more stopping . . . period," Melody had ordered as she slipped into her stilettos. All six of her dancers fell in line and proceeded to perform the first set. Melody swung her head up and down, gyrated her hips, and moved to the music. She got to the

fourth count, and before she knew what was happening, her face collided with the hardwood floor. A sharp pain shot from her nose straight up to her brain. It felt like all of the bones in her skull had shattered. She tasted blood in the back of her throat and saw small squirms of light invading her peripheral vision.

Melody opened her eyes slowly. Pain reverberated through her skull. The dancers gathered around her, their faces contorted into different stages of shock and horror. Someone bent down and helped Melody to her feet. The pain intensified as she stood. The room spun.

"Ms. Love, I'm . . . so sorry. My leg caught a cramp, and I almost fell. I didn't mean to use you to break my fall. Oh my God, I am so sorry," the clumsy dancer apologized, her hands stretched to help Melody to her feet.

Melody blinked rapidly as the room came back into focus. Blood pooled under the skin near her eyes, and her temples pulsed with pain. She lifted her hand to her face and touched the bridge of her nose. An explosion of pain made her see fireworks. A fucking broken nose three weeks before the tour kicked off. Just what she needed . . . another damned distraction!

White-hot fury engulfed her body, causing her blood pressure to rise. She squinted her eyes and scowled at the faces gathered around. The adrenaline coursing through her veins seemed to temporarily numb the pain. The dancers' eyes were wide, and some trembled visibly. No one dared move.

Melody calmly stepped out of her stilettos, then bent over to pick up a lone shoe as if to examine the heel. "I'm fine," she said in a low growl, her heart beating wildly in the base of her throat, embarrassment tingeing her skin an unbecoming shade of red.

"Yes, I'm perfectly fine," Melody said in a voice devoid of emotion. Before anyone could move, Melody spun around and drove the five-inch heel right into the side of the guilty dancer's head. The girl emitted a bloodcurdling scream and crumpled to her knees.

"You're fired," Melody panted, blood dripping from her nose and spit spraying from her lips. "You're fucking fired." Melody couldn't even feel the pain from her injuries anymore. Everyone in the room froze. There were agape mouths, eyes the size of saucers, hands clasped over lips, and arched eyebrows.

"You're fired!" Melody shouted as she used her fists to punish the girl. Screams rose and fell, echoing off the studio walls.

"Please," the victim cried.

Melody could not control the demon that had been unleashed. Sweat pooled over her face and neck, and blood leaked from her nose, but she continued to pound the helpless girl, like a nail driven into a piece of wood.

"You're going to kill her," someone screamed.

Melody shivered now, unable to pry her eyes away from the pictures of the bloodied girl. The words on the papers next to the picture: ARREST WARRANT.

"Like I said, Ms. *Love,* I thought you would be interested in what I had to show you," Detective Simpson smiled. Melody swallowed hard, and her hands fell at her sides.

"Good. Have a seat. Get comfortable. Let's talk."

Melody took a seat and folded her hands neatly in front of her like an obedient schoolgirl.

"What would you like to know, Detective?"

He smiled and reared back in his chair. "Tell me about your mother, Ava Love. Why do *you* think someone would want her dead?"

Melody sighed and closed her eyes. "There are a lot of possibilities, Detective Simpson. Ava . . . my mother . . . She was different."

"How so?"

"Look, you know you don't have to play games here. I can see in your eyes that you know things and you're trying to get me to corroborate them. I know my sisters have probably already told you all about how they felt abused as kids and how I was the favorite," Melody said, glaring.

Detective Simpson nodded.

"You do this for a living, so I know that you know there's always three sides to a story: theirs, mine, and the truth. What really happened will probably fall somewhere in between the three."

"You're right, Ms. Love. Since I have theirs, why don't you tell me yours," he replied, his gaze serious.

"My mother grew up in the South, Detective. She left the South as a teenager with nothing but a bus ticket and the clothes on her back. The one thing my mother had that set her apart from the rest of the wide-eyed, young hopefuls who were trying to escape the backward ways of the South was her voice. When Ava arrived here in Brooklyn, New York, in 1979, Ava Love did not have to sell her ass or clean anyone's kitchen to get by. All she had to do was open her mouth and let out the blessed sound. Her voice could capture you and hold you hostage forever. It was just as beautiful as her face," Melody said, her eyes lowered dreamily, and her lips curled into a slight smile.

"Impressive," Detective Simpson said dryly. Melody shot him an evil look; her mood snapped back to reality.

"It was *more* than impressive, Detective. If you know anything about those times, you know that Ava wasn't expected to succeed. And she did. She made something out of nothing. That same year she was singing backup for Donna Summer, and a couple years after that, she was set to record her own album, but . . ." Melody's voice trailed off.

Detective Simpson leaned in closer to the table, his brows arched.

"She got pregnant, and the industry snubbed her. All of that talent gone to waste." Melody lowered her eyes to her fidgeting hands.

"Tell me about your relationship with her."

Melody closed her eyes and sighed. "I won't lie. Ava treated me 100 times better than she treated my sisters. But that doesn't mean it was all good. You have no idea how it felt growing up feeling inferior all of the time," Melody said, looking up at Detective Simpson. His face was crumpled into a frown.

"You think just because I was the favored one, it meant I felt better? Quite the opposite. My sisters had an alliance that I'll never be a part of, Detective. They had each other . . . I had no one. I had nothing but my music."

Detective Simpson nodded his understanding.

"It may sound ungrateful, but there were many times I wished to be the one getting called the names or taking the beatings from Ava just so I could have something in common with Harmony and Lyric. I hurt for them, and because I was always so jealous that they had each other, I did cruel things to them too. I had learned from Ava." Melody's voice cracked. She sat up erect in the chair and exhaled a heavy breath.

"I am not going to dredge up these old feelings," she said, running her hands through her hair. "Let's keep it present, Detective. I was mad at my mother. I hadn't seen her in six or seven months . . . maybe more. In my opinion, Ava had reached a new low, and I just couldn't stand it anymore," she confessed. "I just couldn't stand it." She thought back . . .

"What?" Melody had gritted, her fists curled at her sides. Gary fanned himself like he was about to faint.

"Yes, hunty. You heard me right. Ava said, and I quote, 'If Melody doesn't up my payments and turn over some of the publishing rights to Sista Love's albums, I will go to the tabloids with the story about her and a certain senator,'"

Gary relayed. Melody began pacing around the small studio space.

"But what does she have? Won't it be her word against mine?" Melody said, her voice shaky.

"It would've been had you not taken her to those fundraisers with you back then. Ava has pictures. Oh, and that night you couldn't get me so you called her to talk through the pain of the senator's public shunning for his wife's sake. Ava has all of that, Mel," Gary reminded her. Melody stopped moving and eased down into a chair. She lowered her face into her hands.

"Ugh. I could just kill her," Melody growled. "She can't just be a fucking good mother for once in her life. If it doesn't benefit Ava Love, then it won't happen. I wish she would just disappear forever. The world would just be a better place."

"I hear you. I hear you loud and clear. It is a shame," Gary comforted, rubbing Melody's shoulders.

"When you say 'new low,' what do you mean?" Detective Simpson asked.

Melody shook off her memory. "Um . . . I . . . just mean," she stammered, trying to gather her thoughts before she said the wrong thing.

"Ava was demanding money. She was doing things in public to embarrass me. That's what I mean when I say new low," Melody lied.

"Did it make you angry?" the detective pressed.

"You damn right it made me angry, but not angry enough to kill my own mother," she replied. "I didn't kill Ava, Detective Simpson. But once I tell you more about Ava's relationships with my sisters, you may figure out who did."

Chapter 5

Lyric

When the Range Rover pulled up to the curb, Lyric stared out the window at the familiar building. She took a deep breath and smiled. The nighttime sounds coming from the Harlem jazz club on the corner and the bustling sidewalk made her feel warm and at ease. To her, it was a like a kid coming home from school and walking into a house with freshly baked cookies and a sweet kiss from her mama.

"Damn, Harlem, I fucking missed you," she whispered in the dark as she exited the vehicle.

"I'm good. Y'all can go ahead." Lyric dismissed Melody's security team. The gorilla of a man in the front passenger's seat opened his mouth to protest, but Lyric held up her hand.

"I said get the fuck out of here. I'm fine," she snarled. It was bad enough she had to act crazy, kicking the seat and banging the windows to get them to drive her to Harlem from Brooklyn in the first place.

The man sank back down in his seat and closed his door. Still, the vehicle didn't move. Even with the blacked-out windows, Lyric could tell Melody's goons were still watching her.

"Suit yourselves and sit out here like assholes." Lyric turned her back on them and walked up to the building. It was hard for her to imagine herself being back in her old stomping grounds after her drug overdose, failed stint in rehab, and the horrors of reliving the past during her reunion with her sisters.

Lyric still smiled. It felt damned good to be free though. Now she knew how all her rich friends felt when they got released from drug rehab or what they called—rich-bitch prison.

Lyric shook her arms at her sides, trying to ward off the jitters that made her feel like she was standing on the edge of a skyscraper about to fall off. Her beer buzz was long gone, and she felt unexplainably nervous. She was home and lucky to be back, but that didn't change the eerie feeling creeping up and down her spine.

She finally walked up to the front door and pounded on it. There was no sense in trying the bell; it hadn't worked in years.

"Who?" a male voice boomed from behind.

Lyric didn't recognize the voice, and apparently she didn't answer fast enough.

"Who the fuck is it?" the voice shot again.

"It's me, Lyric," she called out, leaning her face closer to the door. "Where's Rebel?"

Lyric shoved her shaky hands deep into her pockets, shifting her weight from one foot to the other as she waited for the door to open. Her stomach fluttered at the sound of the locks clicking. She wasn't nervous about seeing Rebel; she was nervous about *why* she'd come to see him. She had practiced ten ways to beg him to take her back, although he was the one who had left her. She needed him now more than ever. He had always been her escape. Rebel knew what to do to make Lyric forget her pain.

"Hey, Lyric," Drew, one of Rebel's stoner friends, opened the door and said. He blocked the doorway with his body.

Lyric smiled. "Oh, shit, Drew. I haven't seen your dope-fiend ass in a minute," she chimed. She had gotten some of her best highs from dope Drew had copped. She rushed forward and hugged him tightly.

Drew didn't return the embrace.

"Um, listen, Lyric . . ." Drew stammered, looking over his shoulder, and then back at her.

"What? Why you acting like you don't know me and shit? This is my home," Lyric said, her smile fading.

"I . . . just don't want any problems," Drew replied, hanging his head.

"What the fuck are you talking about?" she snapped, craning her neck to look past him. "Problems? What problems?"

"May . . . maybe I should . . . tell . . . um . . . Rebel that you're here first," Drew said hesitantly.

"Oh, hell no. Fuck you, man. Where *is* Rebel?" Lyric growled, pushing past him and storming inside. "I don't need to be announced. I'm the fucking lady of this house."

Lyric stumbled down the long, dimly lit hallway to the door that led to the home she once shared with Rebel.

Once she crossed the doorsill, Lyric felt like the breath had been snatched from her body. Dumbfounded, she stared at the newly laid dark ebony hardwood floors, the plush Italian leather sofas, the chrome bar stools, modern artwork on the walls, and the large flat-screen television.

"Who did this?" Lyric asked through her teeth, rounding on Drew with fire in her eyes.

"Who the fuck decorated this place?"

Instinctually, Lyric knew that a woman had been responsible for the upgrades. Rebel was a pig and didn't care one bit about fancy furnishings or artsy designs. There was no trace of him in the room—gone were the liquor and beer bottles, old food wrappers, and used drug paraphernalia that usually littered the place.

Lyric glared at Drew. "Where the fuck is Rebel? I want to see him, *now*."

Drew shrugged and looked away. Lyric saw the guilt wash over his expression. Her heart sped up, and her nostrils opened and closed like a bull ready to charge.

A few seconds of silence passed before Lyric started screaming. "Rebel! Rebel! Where the fuck are you?" she stomped through the house.

Drew put his hands up in front of him and stood aside. She started to pass the first door on her right and heard music playing within. Lyric paused and listened at the door, eyebrows dipping low on her face.

"Why the fuck is he blasting love songs?" Lyric could hear the crooning voice of Trey Songz. It wasn't Rebel's choice of music; he was a hardcore hip-hop head. Lyric swallowed hard, her stomach in knots. This did not bode well.

"Rebel!" she called out, jiggling the doorknob. "Unlock this damn door!" Her hands were shaking. She was certain he had female company inside. Then she heard it.

A woman called out Rebel's name in ecstasy—it was clear, even over the music. Lyric felt things around her begin to spin. A flash of anger rose from her feet and climbed up to her chest. Enraged, she rammed her body into the door, sending it crashing open.

The woman screeched and scrambled off of Rebel. "What the fuck?" she gasped, pulling the sheet in an attempt to cover herself.

Lyric shook her head, tears immediately filling her eyes.

"Ki . . . Kim?" she gasped, clutching at her chest, the pain nearly unbearable. Kim had been Lyric's friend for six years. Tears streamed down her face. Kim had been with her and supplied her the drugs the night she had overdosed, but this was beyond unforgivable. All of Kim's words that night, the whole horrifying scene—everything replayed in Lyric's head . . .

Lyric had held her left nostril closed as she used her right nostril to inhale the small mound of white powder laid out on a pocket mirror in front of her.

"*Whew.*" *She flinched as the drugs hit her system. Her eyes snapped shut by themselves, and her body went limp for a few seconds. Then she slumped over, nearly kissing the floor.*

"*Hey. Hey, be easy on this shit, girl,*" *Kim said, grabbing Lyric before she face planted.*

"*Damn,*" *Lyric huffed. "That is the shit!*"

"*I told you,*" *Kim laughed. "This is premium. Not that stepped-on shit you and Rebel are used to. Now be easy, because this is not to be messed with,*" *Kim said, as she stepped between the little mountain of white powder and Lyric.*

"*I'm a pro,*" *Lyric waved her off. "Let me hit that again. That shit is better than sex and chocolate and chocolate and sex.*" *She laughed and pranced around.*

Opening her eyes, she looked in the mirror. She finally liked what she saw. Lyric flipped the long side of her hair and rubbed the lipstick off of her teeth. "I'm ready for the next one." Lyric loved how she felt. Invincible. Beautiful. Happy. She'd finally found that high again.

"*Lyric, I'm telling you, girl, you have to get used to the kick of this shit. You can't be blowing through it. You're lightweight when it comes to this straight-off-the-boat product. Take one more quick sniff and that's it. I mean it,*" *Kim warned. "I am not trying to pick your ass up off*

the floor or have you be in the damn morgue,"
Kim joked.

"You worry too much, girlie. We came to have
a good time. Shit, if I end up in the morgue, at
least you can stand up at my funeral and say,
'That bitch went out hiii-gh as a motherfucker,'"
Lyric replied, raising her hands above her head
for emphasis.

Kim laughed. She had been Lyric's friend
for six years, and she had watched Lyric's
entire life change. And not for the better. Lyric
told Kim all about how the singing group had
broken up and how Lyric desperately wanted
to still be famous, but Lyric had never told Kim
everything that she was battling inside.

"One more. Dead ass," Kim said sternly, stepping aside to give Lyric access to their little
party stash.

"One more," Lyric acquiesced. "I promise. Just
one more." That was the famous drug addict
line—it was always "just one more" or "one last"
hit.

This time, Lyric held her right nostril closed
and vacuumed up the powder with her left
nostril. When the tiny line of white powder was
all gone, she threw her head back and shook
her shoulders. The pure, uncut cocaine hit her
central nervous system with a bang. Lyric saw
colorful fireworks erupting behind her eyelids.

This was better than any heroin high she'd had in years. Lyric's drug addiction had taken on a life of its own over the years. It had started with the pills Andrew Harvey fed her every time she was forced to be with him. At first, Lyric tried to resist, but she quickly learned that the pills made it, and him, easier to deal with. Then, after he died with his dick inside of her, Lyric had graduated to using heroin; her first time was with Rebel. When that high wasn't strong enough for her to escape reality anymore, Lyric began mixing things and using whatever she could get—alcohol, pills, meth, cocaine, and heroin. She didn't care so long as she didn't have to feel any pain. So long as she didn't have to live with reality.

Lyric let out a high-pitched squeak and cackled somewhat maniacally. Her head hung down until her chin was touching her neck, causing her hair to spill forward wildly. She could feel the vibration from the club's music pounding in her chest. Lyric felt good.

"That's some primo shit," she giggled.

She kept complimenting Kim on her new drug because she couldn't get over how good it was. Lyric swayed her body to the sound of the loud music filtering through the club's bathroom.

"It's a celebration, bitches," Lyric joked. She danced over and planted a playful kiss on Kim's cheek. "Thank you for celebrating with me, best friend. That's my best friend. That's my best friend," Lyric sang. Kim giggled.

"Well, you getting back out there, making moves, is cause for celebration," Kim said. "And a tour with Melody Love is fucking big. I mean, she's your sister and all, but to the world, she's like a god. I've been waiting for you to patch things up with her so I could just meet her one time. I think if she shook my hand, I wouldn't ever wash it again. I am definitely part of the Melody Army."

Lyric had told Kim all about the fact that she was going back out on tour. And how it wasn't going to be long before she had her own money, her own big house, and Tribeca loft.

"Naw, forget Melody. That good shit you got right there is cause for celebration. That's what we should be worshipping. You can change the world with that," Lyric replied joyfully. She felt damned good. In fact, she didn't think she had felt this great in years. She danced around some more.

"I told you," Kim said, bending down and sniffing up her own dose of her supply. "My guy told me this is what his richest clients use. He hooked me up. I mean, I had to give him a little something, but it was worth it."

"He hooked you up for real. That shit so good, I'd give him some ass too. I'm ready to take on the world now," Lyric cheered, raising her hands over her head and clapping.

"You just graduated, chick. This is better than that depressing-ass smack. That shit is a downer, and it makes you look terrible too. Uppers, girlfriend, you can't beat this high. This is the new wave shit, and I made sure you had it first. You can't be stopped now," Kim said, cheering Lyric on even more.

"Let me have one more hit," Lyric begged, spinning around like a ballerina, her dress riding up her thighs.

"No more hits yet. You need to take it slow. You can't hit this like it's that regular half-pure street junk," Kim warned again for the third time.

"Let's go party. Shit, you know I can get us into VIP. I mean, you are celebrating, right?" Kim said, leaning over the bathroom sink so she could apply another coat of lip gloss to her full lips.

"Ah, VIP. We big time again?" Lyric giggled, holding her fist up as a show of power. "I can definitely dig it. I could really dig it if I could hit again," she winked.

"Okay, look. One more tiny line before we go get our party on," Kim said, dumping a tiny hill of drugs on the mirror.

"Hell, yeah," Lyric cheered, rushing over to the sink.

She quickly snorted the line. Within seconds, she was ready. Kim watched as Lyric's eyes rolled back in her head. Her back went straight and stiff for a few seconds.

"Lyric? You all right?" Kim shook Lyric's shoulders. Suddenly, Lyric seemed to come back. Her eyes returned to normal. She sniffled and brushed her nostrils off.

"I'm good! I'm real good!"

Kim's face eased with relief. "C'mon. Let's go have some fun. Let's go celebrate your rebirth," she said, pulling Lyric's arm through her own as they exited the bathroom and headed into the bowels of the club.

Lyric and Kim sauntered through the club, attracting a lot of attention. Lyric hadn't felt attractive or beautiful in a long while. But now, with the drugs giving her a newfound dose of confidence and courage, she stopped on the dance floor and began dancing up on several strange men. She let the music reverberate through her body and soul while she made herself forget about Rebel, Ava's death,

Harmony, Melody, her past . . . everything. As Lyric bucked her body vigorously to the beat, she remembered all of the times she and Melody had partied in their girl group days. Harmony had never been one to go out and party, but Lyric and Melody had done enough for all of them. When Ava finally let them out, they were like animals out of a cage. Industry parties had been everything back then—the expensive drinks, the high-grade weed, the special treatment from club owners, and just the rush of the nightlife had been a form of escapism for Lyric. She used it to escape thoughts of Andrew Harvey touching her. She used it to escape the fact that her mother hated her. When Melody went solo, she focused on her career and left Lyric behind like she never mattered. Lyric had missed the fun days after that. She had missed the days when she didn't have to worry about having money or when people still recognized her as Lyric Love and not as Melody Love's sister. Lyric had missed being able to say she was actually a celebrity. Those days were the only times she could put the abuse out of her mind. Lyric needed the attention like she needed air, food, and water.

Now, Lyric was getting all of the attention. She closed her eyes and let the music soak into her soul. "Ow!" she sang, rocking and letting all of her problems fall away, even if just for that moment. She shook her hips and sandwiched herself between two dudes—one grinded her from the front, and one grinded her from the back. She was loving it. She didn't care about their hands on her thighs, on her ass. It was the attention she craved. Lyric pulled the dude behind her in closer, and she threw her arms around the neck of the dude in front of her— until Kim rushed over and grabbed her arm like a parent chaperone at a high school dance.

"What? What's the matter? I'm having fun," Lyric's eyes popped open. Kim clutched onto her tightly and dragged her off of the dance floor. "I'll be back, cuties," Lyric flirted with her two confused dance partners.

"Girl, no. You are about to be a big name again. You can't be dancing with the local yokels looking like a thot out here. We fuck with VIP-status dudes only. Did you even look at those lames you were dancing with? Had their damn hands all up your dress and on your ass. Yuck, Lyric," Kim scolded. "You and I have a reputation to uphold, and it is of style and class. Not ratchetness. Do I have to teach you everything? Better start getting back in that A-list celeb mind-set. You think Beyoncé would

be out here on the dance floor grinding up with some lames with her ass all out?"

"First of all, I'm not Beyoncé . . . more like Solange or not even Solange. Shit, right now, I'm more like that washed-up ass Michelle." Lyric busted out laughing at her own joke. "And, why the hell else did we come to the club if it wasn't to get our dance on? I damned sure didn't come to sit around and be cute, acting like some stuck-up celebrity prude like my sister," she replied sassily.

Lyric loved to party hard. Her idea of coming out was to dance and have fun, not sit like a princess on her throne, decked out in the latest fashions with a high-priced purse in her lap, just to make other women jealous.

Kim sucked her teeth and continued dragging Lyric toward the VIP.

"I came to the club to listen to the music, have a few drinks, and do a few lines. In VIP." Kim stressed the VIP part.

"Stuck up," Lyric mocked. "You could've been Melody in another life."

"Yes, call it what you want. But I keep it classy all the time. I don't let people make me sweat, and I certainly don't dance with club regulars who come to the club with five dollars in their pockets and try to get a free feel," Kim answered. "Shit, they ain't even have to buy you a drink and you gave them free feels!"

"Yeah, yeah, mother-may-I. You sound like Harmony with the lectures. I need a hit," Lyric grumbled. "You blew my high all the way. Shit, I might as well have come out with Rebel, the biggest hater of all."

"One more hit and that's it for the night," Kim warned, storming back into the VIP section. "And I mean it, Lyric. Don't ask me for anymore after this."

Lyric followed Kim to a darkened corner in the VIP section like a horse following a carrot. Kim looked around to make sure they were all clear; then she dug into her bag and handed Lyric a small glassine envelope.

"Hit it easy. A little bit at a time," Kim instructed. "I already told you this stuff is not to be fucked with." Lyric waved her hand dismissively.

"You worry too much, damn. If I wanted to be out with my sisters, I would've invited those bitches," Lyric grumbled.

"Just hurry up before someone sees," Kim spoke directly into Lyric's ear.

"Okay. Okay."

Kim turned her back so that she could play lookout just in case any of the club's security guards wanted to get nosy.

"Lyric, I told you a tiny bit. You sound like you took too—" Kim spun around to warn Lyric again about the potency of the product.

"Lyric! Lyric!" Kim screeched at the top of her lungs.

Lyric's eyes hooded over, and her nostrils went wide.

"Lyric! Wait. Just listen," Kim pleaded, stumbling off the bed and tangling in the sheets, trying in vain to keep her naked body covered. "I . . . I can explain everything," Kim stammered.

"What the fuck . . ." Rebel panted, springing to his feet. "Yo, Lyric, what you doing here?" he gasped, his dick still hard and aiming straight at Lyric.

Lyric wished she had a kitchen knife nearby so she could sever his shit in one fell swoop. The heat that engulfed her body was enough to set the entire place on fire. She bit her bottom lip so hard, it began to bleed. The metallic taste of blood on her tongue reminded her that this was all too real, and not just a bad dream.

Rebel recognized the fire flashing in her eyes and slowly backed away. There was an urgency in the air that seemed to have them all trembling.

"Lyric, just listen . . . wait," he said, moving toward her apprehensively. "Let me explain . . ."

Lyric's fists curled at her sides and before Rebel could say another word, she launched herself into him.

"You fucking bastard! I can't believe you did this to me!" Lyric screeched, her arms flying wildly as she landed punches to Rebel's face and chest. Kim tried to slide around Rebel, but Lyric was too fast for her.

Lyric caught her ex-best friend by her long, straight hair and yanked her down hard to the floor.

"You backstabbing bitch," Lyric spat as she wrapped her fist with Kim's hair and tugged viciously. "You tried to kill me, and then you turned around and fucked my man!"

Kim squealed like a stuck pig and crumpled to her knees. Lyric kneed her in the face and blood spurted from her nose. Lyric didn't care about anything anymore. She slammed wildly thrown fists into Kim's face with so much force, she heard cracking noises. She didn't know if it was her knuckles or Kim's jaw breaking. She didn't care.

"Oh, shit! Lyric! What the fuck are you doing?" Rebel hollered.

Lyric spit at him as he tried to grab her. White-hot angry tears spilled from her eyes, and she wavered unsteadily on her feet. Suddenly weak, she tossed Kim like a ragdoll to the floor.

Kim frantically scrambled away from Lyric and cowered in the corner, whimpering in fear.

"C'mon, Lyric. Calm down—" Rebel started, his trembling hands up in front of him.

"Don't you fucking tell me to do anything," Lyric screamed, her index finger jutting in his face.

"Stay the fuck away from me. I never want to see you again. You lying two-timing mother-fucker. I believed you when you said you loved me. I fucking trusted you with everything. I fucking gave up the chance to get clean because I couldn't stop thinking about being with you," Lyric cried, her entire body wracked with sobs. Rebel shook his head, but he didn't say anything.

"You never loved me, Rebel. Just like every-body else in my life, all you did was use me until I had nothing left to give," Lyric said, raising her hands, tears spilling over her lips. "And when you didn't need me anymore, you moved on, just like my mother, my sisters, everybody that I ever loved."

Lyric turned swiftly to leave. She knew that if she stayed another second she would kill Rebel and Kim and maybe even herself, the way she was feeling.

"Wait, Lyric," Rebel yelled as he hopped awkwardly into his pants. "I do love you. Just let me explain," he pleaded.

"You better not leave me like this, Rebel. If you take another step, I will put that bitch in jail," Kim threatened.

Rebel paused, visibly torn between the two women. His hesitation only confirmed what Lyric knew in her heart to be true. The man that she once loved was gone. Forever.

"Don't worry, Rebel. You don't have to choose. I'm out of here. Have a nice fucking life."

"Wait!" he yelled as she swiftly exited the room. Lyric did not respond to Rebel yelling her name. He was dead to her. She raced outside and down the front steps, tears streaming down her cheeks. Life was full of pain and unbelievable heartache. She needed a release, an escape from reality. She needed a hit badly.

Chapter 6

Harmony

The sun was peeking over the horizon when Harmony unlocked her front door and stepped inside her home. She inhaled deeply and sighed with relief. *Home sweet home.*

The house was calm and silent. Sonia, the overnight sitter, and Aubrey were still asleep. Although Harmony was longing to hold her sweet baby girl against her chest and feel her little breaths on her neck, she decided to take the silent time to clear her mind and try to recover from the terrible night she'd had.

Harmony needed more than a few minutes to unwind. She still couldn't shake the fact that someone had poisoned Ava. She had been wracking her brain since she'd gotten the news. She hadn't lied to the detectives when she said Ava was evil, but she had no idea who would actually have the time or opportunity to go through with killing her. And, most importantly, why? Through all of the questioning, Harmony couldn't stop thinking about something Melody had said a few weeks back while they sat together with Murray in Ava's living room making funeral arrangements . . .

"If either one of you think that Lyric, the wild child, is coming here after what she did to Ava, think again," Melody had said. Harmony tilted her head quizzically.

"You don't know about the assault and the attempted murder?" Melody asked with her eyebrows arched. Murray began coughing uncontrollably. Harmony looked at Murray and back to Melody.

"Oh, yes. Your baby sister is completely off her little rocker. I won't even get into the half-shaved head and purple-dyed hair. She looks like a Goth freak with those piercings in the face, neck, and who knows where else. And don't forget the totally insane behavior. I had to send the police over here more than once when she was living here with Ava. Now, you and I may have told Ava on countless occasions that we wished her dead, but your baby sister? Miss Wild and Crazy actually tried to kill her. It wasn't a simple fight, either; it was attempted murder."

***

Harmony shook her shoulders to rid her mind of the incriminating facts about Lyric, although Lyric was the most likely suspect at the moment. It's not like Lyric wouldn't have been justified in killing Ava. Harmony shuddered just thinking about it.

"She gave my life to him. She just gave him my entire life, and I was a baby," Lyric had bawled. *"I sacrificed everything, my entire soul, so that we all could be famous—and look at me. I have nothing. I have nothing left. All of you left me."* Lyric struggled to get out of Harmony's grasp.

"He took my innocence. Over and over again she sent me to him, and when I was all used up, that was it. No more deals. No more fame. No more money. Everyone just left me." Lyric's words were like daggers.

"Your mother . . . your fucking mother made me drink Blackberry Brandy to try to give me a homemade abortion! I didn't even know I was pregnant! She said it would work, and that I wouldn't feel the pain! Do you remember that, Harmony? Huh? When I was deathly ill from being pregnant by the man she sold me

to so that we could be famous! Huh? Does any-body remember that I was seventeen and preg-nant by a disgusting troll that was fucking old enough to be my grandfather? Huh? Does any-body remember how I bled and screamed in pain, and she didn't even want to take me to the fucking hospital, and then lied and made me look like some off-the-hook teenage whore! Do you and Melody remember all of the nights your mother, her mother, grabbed me out of my bed and sent me to him so you bitches could have record deals and fame and so your mother could live out her sick fantasy of being famous? Huh? Do you remember?" Lyric had screamed through her tears while her chest heaved.

"I don't even have shit to show for all of it. Used up. Broke. Damn near homeless. Nothing left. And now she's gone so I can't even tell her how fucked up she was and how I've never been the same since I was thirteen years old." Lyric punched the metal wall of the bathroom stall.

Harmony jumped now just like she had those days she'd relived Lyric's past pain. Lyric had left before Harmony made it out of the precinct. Harmony had left Lyric a voice mail, but hadn't heard from her since they'd been separated for questioning.

Harmony kicked off her shoes and massaged the sides of her neck to relieve some of the tension. Memories, the murder, her rocky marriage, all had her head swimming with thoughts. She headed for the kitchen. A nice hot cup of her favorite chamomile tea was what she needed. She didn't bother to switch on any lights. She knew her way around her modest three-bedroom home well enough to navigate in the dark. Besides, the predawn glow and twinkle of light from the appliances was enough and oddly welcoming. Harmony padded over to the cabinets, humming a tune. Music always helped to calm her nerves. She shrugged. At least Ava had given her something—a love for music.

She was glad to be home after spending three weeks in a Brooklyn hotel after Ava died, sorting through all of her mother's personal possessions and also completing all of the legal paperwork associated with Ava's estate. Not to mention, all of the effort she'd put into trying to save Lyric from herself. Harmony shook her head just thinking about how her marriage had suffered the most through it all.

She reached up into the cabinet and pulled down her favorite cup—a pretty pink and brown mug that read, *Ballerinas Have More Fun*. She smiled. The mug had been a gift from one of

her first dance students in her performing arts
school, Dance and More. The school had been
Harmony's most inspired idea to date. She had
been a singer and dancer all of her life, and
Ron had been a child actor. Both had much success in their careers—Harmony had won several
Grammy Awards with Sista Love, and Ron had
two Emmy Awards for starring in eight seasons
of the hit television sitcom, *Our Family, Your
Family.*

*"That's a great idea, babe. People will flock
to our performing arts school because of our
names alone,"* Ron had said when Harmony first
proposed the idea.

Harmony smiled wider now, just like she did
every time she used the mug and thought about
those days; the happier times in her life. She
and Ron were a dynamic duo back then. He had
been clean and sober and highly motivated after
coming out of drug rehab for what Harmony
thought would be the last time. She had been
awarded over $2 million after winning her law-
suit for back royalties, stolen wages, and song
writing/publishing credits against the record
label, Ava, Murray, and Melody. Suing her own
family had been difficult for Harmony, but in the
end, justice had prevailed. Harmony took her
windfall, bought the quaint little house that she

currently lived in, and opened the school. The rest of the money, she put away in a rainy day fund. She was a self-made woman, independent and in charge of her own destiny.

Harmony had jumped into Ron's arms and kissed him passionately as he spun her around their new studio.

"To forever," Ron pledged, breathless with excitement.

"To forever," Harmony agreed, eyes sparkling with joy.

Harmony felt her throat tighten at the memory. She rolled her shoulders and stretched her back. It was time to accept that things had changed. She went to set her mug on the Keurig coffee machine platform.

"Care to share?"

Startled, Harmony jumped so hard she nearly lost her balance. The ceramic mug slipped from her grasp and crashed to the floor, shattering.

"Oh my God," she gasped, trying to catch her breath. "You scared the shit out of me, Ron."

Harmony's hands shook, and her knees knocked together. She hadn't seen Ron sitting in the dark at the dinette table, just a few feet away.

Even now, his shadowy silhouette reminded her of a scene from a scary movie where the villain appeared half-cloaked in darkness. Her heart pumped wildly.

What is he doing here? I told Sonia not to let anyone in.

"I didn't mean to scare you." Ron stood. Small slivers of light began coming through the blinds as the sun came up. Harmony noticed the nervous grin on Ron's face as he started walking toward her.

She inched backward. "What are you doing here, Ron?" she asked on unsteady legs. "You should've called or something. Arranged to talk to me, not just show up here unannounced. I don't like it."

"I live here, Harmony," Ron answered, his grin fading. He stepped over the shards of the broken mug, moving closer. "I know we are going through stuff right now, but I still live here," he said evenly. He bent down and began picking up the jagged pieces of pink and brown glazed ceramic.

Harmony's back bumped against the far wall of the kitchen. With trembling hands, she flicked on the light, afraid that she wouldn't be able to see Ron's every move. She stared down at him cleaning up the mess on the floor. For a split second, her fear subsided and she saw flashes of the old Ron—her loving husband, the man who had been so thoughtful and attentive, the man that always made her feel safe and wanted.

Ron swept the remains of her favorite cup into the trash bin and walked back toward her. He brushed his hands off on his jeans nervously and turned his attention to Harmony.

"I miss you, Harm," Ron said. "I fucked up, but I miss you and Aubrey like crazy."

Harmony blinked a few times and the good image of him faded like a puff of smoke. She stared at him. His skin was sallow and ashen; his face full of unruly overgrown hair, long and unkempt. Ron's eyes were jaundiced, and she wondered if his liver was failing. He had lost a significant amount of weight, which showed in his scrawny neck and sunken eye sockets. He still wore the clothes she'd left him wearing three weeks ago at the hotel. Only now the once clean T-shirt was wrinkled and stained, and his jeans were rumpled like he'd taken them straight out of the clothes hamper and put them on.

Harmony swallowed hard, her heart breaking. When Ron wasn't a slave to drugs, he took great pride in his personal appearance. It was one of the things she loved about him. He'd always made sure that before he stepped out of the house he was dressed neatly and crisply. And he had always kept a sharply lined up haircut. Ron was a pretty boy that could put his woman to shame with his style and grooming. But not anymore. He had been reduced almost back to the way Harmony had found him—homeless and hopeless.

She stared wide-eyed at this man who now bore little resemblance to her once sweet, sensitive, caring husband. She shook her head at a loss for words.

"I'm sorry for everything," Ron said, lowering his head and shoving his hands deep into his pockets. Harmony averted her eyes to the floor. She had seen enough.

"You shouldn't be here," she croaked, finally looking back up and finding the words. Her heart felt like it would crumble to dust. She wanted so badly to just rush to him, throw her arms around his neck, and tell him she loved him with her entire being. She wanted to whisk him away to rehab again and make those addiction demons vanish from his life forever. She wanted to feel him touch her intimately one more time, and she wanted to touch him. She wanted to do all of those things, but in that moment of powerlessness, she did nothing. Loving Ron hadn't worked to save him before, and Harmony knew it wouldn't work now. She swallowed hard, set her jaw, and silently decided that letting Ron hit rock bottom again was the only thing that might work. But, she wasn't too hopeful about that either.

"I . . . I . . . know what you're thinking," Ron stuttered. "But I'm going to beat it." He moved toward her, but Harmony put her hands up in a halting motion.

"Don't," she said firmly. A pain exploded in her chest. She hated treating him like this. But she had to stay strong. She needed to keep the lines clear.

Ron stopped short. His facial expression pained.

"A lot of has happened, Ron. I refuse to go back to the pain of the past," Harmony asserted, remembering his previous relapses. The uncertainty, the embarrassment, the shame of those times all whirled around her now.

"That'll be one sixty-two, seventy-six," the cashier had said, smiling at Harmony warmly as she transferred the grocery bags into her shopping cart. Harmony smiled back as she extended her debit card. She had been feeling good lately, living like a grown-up. Food

shopping may have seemed like a small thing to others, but to Harmony, it was one of those simple things that signaled her independence from her mother.

"Um . . . I'm sorry, ma'am . . . your card has been declined," the cashier whispered furtively, making sure none of the other customers could hear.

Harmony's eyebrows furrowed.

"Declined? Impossible. It's a debit card," Harmony replied, her voice taking on a slightly higher pitch. The cashier's face turned a bright shade of red.

"Try it again," Harmony demanded, agitation lacing her words. The cashier did as she was told. Hushed murmurs rose and fell behind her.

The cashier's mouth dipped at the corners with pity. "I'm sorry. Still declined."

"Trust me, that card is linked directly to my bank account, and I have plenty of money in there," Harmony said defensively. "Try it again," she commanded, drawing the attention of more customers.

The cashier looked down the line at the faces of several angry customers.

"I'm sorry, ma'am. I've tried five times already. I really need to take care of them," the cashier said, jerking her chin toward the people who

stood behind her. Harmony turned around and saw the judgmental looks being sent her way. Her neck and face felt like they were on fire.

"Just put my things aside. I'm going to straighten this out with the bank. I'm calling them right now. I have plenty of money," Harmony announced, loud enough for the crowd of shoppers to overhear. She stormed out of the store and quickly called her bank. Perhaps a fraud alert had been placed on her account. Either way, she had to straighten this out quickly.

"The joint account holder, Ronald Bridges, withdrew all funds yesterday. With no funds in the account, we closed it," the customer service representative explained.

"What?" Harmony's body went cold. "That can't be right." She collapsed to her knees on the sidewalk because she knew exactly what that meant.

Relapse.

The shame Harmony felt that day was repeated multiple times during the course of their marriage, and always during a relapse. At first, she would make excuses for Ron, but even that had grown old and played out.

"I don't want to live in constant fear that you'll risk everything for drugs again, Ron," she said. "I think you'll agree, I've been through this enough times to know that it will get worse and not better."

Ron swiped his hands over his face. "It won't be like that. I can kick this shit whenever I want. You've seen me do it, Harmony. I can just quit whenever I want to."

"We both know that's a lie, Ron. I mean, look at you. A few weeks in the city and you look like this," she said, gesturing at his disheveled appearance. "My heart can't take it. It's not fair to Aubrey either. We need you, but not like this. We deserve a strong husband and father . . ." Harmony's voice trailed off. "I just think it's best that you go," Harmony said, defeated.

Ron reacted as if she had thrown a bucket of cold water in his face.

"That's it? Just like that? You think you can tell me I can't come back to my own home? I can't be a part of my daughter's life?" he replied, biting down into his jaw until it rocked. Harmony opened her mouth but didn't get a chance to speak.

"It's always about you. Always about Harmony's feelings. Well, we were here living happily. I was clean and *staying* clean," Ron spat, hitting his chest with his right hand. "I was being a man and holding it down. It was *you* who dragged us to the city, not me. It was you, Miss I-Have-to-Save-My-Little-Sister-from-Herself, that turned our world upside down. I told you more than once that I was feeling alone, abandoned, and overwhelmed. Did you care?" Ron's voice grew deeper and louder with emotion. "Did you care about me and how *I* felt? Naw, Harmony. You put them first, and I lost my shit. There. Is that what you wanted to hear? Huh? Me admit that I lost my shit? That I fell and started using again? Well, I'll admit what I did just as soon as you fucking admit the part you played in all of this. Admit it, Harmony."

"Ron, please. Not now. You did this, not me," she shot back, exhausted. "You should just leave. If you feel like it's my fault, so be it. Either way, you can't stay here."

Harmony was growing more agitated by the minute. How dare he mention what she did for her sister. How dare he try to blame her when it was his own stupid decision to sniff cocaine again. She knew over the years Ron had a problem taking responsibility for his actions sometimes, but blaming her for this was a new low.

"So that's it, Harmony? Just like that? You're not going to give me your support? You're willing to just throw away everything we have? All that we've built together?" Ron gritted. "You're going to just toss me away like yesterday's trash? Is there somebody else waiting for you? Is that what this is *really* about? You got your eye on a bigger prize?" Ron spun around as if he were looking for a man hiding in the house.

Harmony's eyes hooded over. He had gone too far, accusing her of cheating. Her breaths came out in short huffs. The look in her eyes was so hard it could split a diamond in half.

"How fucking dare you ask me that. Did you think about throwing away what we had and what we built when you snorted all of our hopes, dreams, and love up your nose in a goddamn cocaine straw?" Harmony exploded. "*You* ruined *us*. And now you want to accuse me of having someone else? Are you blaming me for something that you feel guilty about? You're probably the one sleeping with someone else. Oh, I know you so well, Ronald Bridges—you can't hide from me." She pushed her sleeves up to her elbows, ready for a battle.

Ron opened his mouth to speak, but she cut him off before he could get a word in.

"I don't want to hear any more of your fucking lies. If anyone threw away what we *had,* it was you. I found you sleeping on the steps of a fucking church, homeless, hungry, strung out, and yet I still saw something good in you. Three times, I dealt with your relapses. Dealt with the embarrassment of you emptying *my* bank accounts and disappearing for days to get high. Cried in private after learning that you sold your first wedding band to get high. Still, I was the good wife, holding your hand through the sickness of withdrawal. The mental anguish of not knowing each day if I would come home to find you dead or gone. The constant worry that you would stop going to your meetings or lose your way. I can't do it again, Ron." Harmony's voice cracked. "Correction, I *refuse* to do it again. Over these past few weeks, I've realized a lot. Not just about you and us, but about me," she said, pointing to herself. "I learned that I've spent my entire life trying to please sick, broken people like you and my mother. I made you and her and even my sisters more important than myself. Well, no more."

Harmony felt the tightness in her chest ease after releasing all of her pent-up anger and frustration.

"Give me one more chance, Harmony," Ron said pleadingly, suddenly changing his tone. "It's the last time. I just need a few dollars now. I'll get that last pack, and then I'll go back to rehab. I promise. I'll stay clean after that," he said with desperation in his voice.

Harmony held her stomach trying to stave off the knots. Seeing Ron killed her a little inside, but she had to stand firm.

Harmony shook her head. "I knew there was a reason you came back," she replied, her eyes squinted into dashes. "Just leave, Ron. Please. Make it easier on me and yourself. We don't have to drag this out."

"All I need is one more pack to get me over the hump; then I'll work on getting our life back. I'll give it up just right after this, just to have you and Aubrey back. I need you. Please help me," he groveled.

Ron moved in closer for his final plea. Harmony could smell that he hadn't showered in at least two days. He was making her uncomfortable. She had never been scared of Ron before, but in this moment, something in his eyes—the feral look of a man coming apart—made the hairs on the back of her neck rise.

"Harmony, you have to give me one more chance. You know that I can do this. You've seen it before. You know that I'm not lying. I did all of it for you. I didn't want to live anymore when you found me at the church. I was fine with dying high and happy. But when I met you and fell in love, I fought against it all. I wanted to live again. I fought like hell to get clean. Not for myself. I did it all for you. I have lived for you all of these years."

Harmony could feel herself softening at his words. The sound of their daughter crying in her crib was exactly what she needed to snap her back to reality. She needed to protect her baby.

"Ron, just go," she rasped, swiping her hand over her face, emotionally drained. "It's just not the right time. There's a lot going on, and I just can't right now."

"You have some fucking nerve, Harmony," Ron barked, his face turning deep red. Sweat ran down the sides of his face, and his flaring nostrils were wet with mucous.

Harmony startled at his sudden outburst. She recognized those signs. She remembered that in this condition, Ron got desperate, out of control, even. She'd once watched him break up everything in their first apartment—he tossed dishes out of the cabinets, pulled drawers out of the dresser, dumped clothes on the floor, shattered picture frames, and punched holes in the walls when he couldn't get money for drugs.

She shuddered now just thinking about how she had locked herself in the bathroom with a knife, so scared he would harm her. When he finally calmed down, it had taken him six hours to convince her to come out of the bathroom.

"Ron, I really think it's time for you to go," Harmony said evenly, trying her best to keep her tone from riling him up any further. She took a few sideway steps toward the kitchen doorway. She figured if she remained calm, he would too. But if not, she would try to get away from him.

"So that's it? That's really it? You're not even going to consider what I'm asking you to do?" Ron growled, moving closer. "You won't even fucking consider helping me out?" His mood had taken a swing from *husband desperate to win his wife back* to *crazed addict in desperate need of money for drugs*.

"No. I've done this all with you before, Ron. This time, you have to do it for yourself. Until then, I'm done. Now, like I said, you should—"

Ron lurched forward and grabbed the collar of her shirt and pulled her close to his face. She let out a weak squeal. His dilated pupils were tinged with red, and his wet nostrils flared. Harmony's heart pounded until the veins in her neck corded against her skin.

"I fucking asked for your help," he snarled, jerking Harmony again until her face was mere inches from his.

"Ron, get the fuck off of me," she gritted through her teeth, putting on a brave face although the fear was nearly strangling her.

"You enjoy making me feel like less than a man, right?" he growled, baring his teeth. "Always nagging me about NA meetings and searching through my pockets to see if you find any pills or coke or dope. You think I didn't know about all of the checking behind me that you do? You think I didn't see you secretly counting the money in the register at the school every time I went into it?" He tightened his grasp on her.

"Get the fuck off of me," she rasped, close to a scream. He was too strong for her to fend off alone. She tried to get out of his grasp, but her efforts were futile.

"Just listen to me, Harmony. For once, I need you to let me be the man in this relationship. I need you to trust me," Ron said, a manic gleam in his eyes. He eased his grasp on her ever so slightly.

"I want us to be okay," he said softly. Another mood swing. This time he tried to pull Harmony into him for an embrace, or maybe even a kiss. Mortified, Harmony turned her face away, the strain causing sharp pains in her neck and back.

"Please let me go; you're hurting me." Harmony dug her nails into the tops of his clenched hands.

Ron clamped down even harder. He jerked her roughly against his chest. "Just listen to me."

"Get off of me," she cried out with urgency. She lifted her knee and tried to connect with his balls, but she missed and hit his upper thigh.

Ron laughed, but there was no amusement in the sound.

"Oh, now you want to hurt me even more, huh? Stop fighting me, Harm. I came here in peace. I came here so we could fix what you broke," Ron whispered like a madman, putting his face against hers until the sharp, coarse hairs of his wild beard roughly scraped her cheeks. Harmony writhed and groaned, continuing to dig her nails into his hands. The harder she pierced him with her nails, the harder he gripped her.

"Let me go, Ron," she growled. "I am not playing anymore. You're just making things worse for yourself. This is not going to do shit to win me back." Her entire body was engulfed in heat now—a mixture of adrenaline, fear, and anger. "If you hurt me, I'll never be with you again. Is that what you want? I'm sure that's not what you want, right? Just let me go." Harmony tried reasoning now, since nothing else had worked.

"Let you go? Let you fucking go? Is that what you really want? For me to let you go, forever? Is that what you're saying? That you'll never be with me again, and I can't see my fucking baby? Is that what you just fucking said?" Ron raged.

Tears began streaming down Harmony's face. She couldn't believe he was doing this to her. He had never roughed her up like this before. Ron's bipolar mood swings told her that she was in danger. Fear was choking her. Her breathing became labored. Her chest felt ready to explode.

"Please," she whispered. She dropped her arms and decided to stop fighting hoping that Ron would release her from his powerful grip.

"I won't let you go," he spat. "I won't fucking let you go—ever."

Still holding his face close to Harmony's, he tried to force her mouth to his. Harmony moaned and moved her head side to side.

"Fucking love me, Harmony. Fucking love me," he hissed. Harmony felt like vomiting. His musty body odor overwhelmed her senses. She needed a breath of fresh air or she would actually pass out.

"Let me have what I came here for," he growled in her face, his breath burning her lips and nostrils.

"Let me go," Harmony whispered, her eyes closed, trying to breathe through her mouth alone. "Please, I'll give you whatever you want. Just let me go." She kept her voice steady even though her nerves were unraveling.

Ron chuckled evilly.

"Oh, now you're playing a head game on me," he said.

"You heard her. She asked you to let her go."

The voice shocked both Harmony and Ron.

Harmony opened her eyes. Ron loosened his grasp slightly and turned around. They stared wide-eyed at Sonia. She held the tan baseball bat that Harmony usually kept by her bedside menacingly in front of her.

"Let her go or I *will* use it," Sonia threatened, her accent growing thicker with each word. "I'm serious," Sonia said, rolling her *R*s.

Ron released his grip on Harmony and chortled before he rounded on Sonia. "And just what the hell you planning on doing with that?" he asked, smirking as he gestured toward the bat.

In response, Sonia raised the bat, gripping the handle so hard her knuckles paled. She rocked on the balls of her feet, her legs slightly bent. She was clearly ready to swing at the slightest movement.

"So now she even got the damn babysitter in on it?" Ron said, raising his hands in surrender and shaking his head.

"She asked you to leave. I'm sorry, but you will have to go," Sonia said firmly. "I will not let you hurt her. Now go. Or else," she warned, moving the bat slightly.

Ron raised his hands higher. He turned back toward Harmony.

"Is this what you want?" he asked. "The fucking babysitter putting me out on the street?"

"Just go," Harmony croaked, wrapping her arms around herself to try to stop trembling.

"Remember something, Harmony. This time, it wasn't all my fault. You're to blame for some of this. You're not always as innocent and perfect as you pretend. This is not over. I won't let you throw me out of my daughter's life just because you grew up without a father."

"Please just go," she said, barely above a whisper.

Ron took one long look at Sonia before he walked calmly to the front door.

Once he left, Sonia lowered the bat, her shoulders slumped with relief. She placed her free hand over her heart and released a long, heavy breath.

"Oh my God. Thank you so much," Harmony hugged her tightly.

Both women stood in the middle of Harmony's kitchen, locked in a tight embrace as tears ran down their faces.

Chapter 7

Melody

"You want something to eat? Tea? Anything?" Gary asked as he fluffed the pillows on the couch inside of Melody's Saddlebrook, New Jersey estate. "You must be starved after the long night you've had, Miss Thang," he said jokingly, trying to lighten the mood.

"Ugh. I have absolutely no appetite," Melody replied, flopping down on the spot her BFF and manager had made for her. "That damn detective is so lucky I wanted to get that warrant taken care of on the spot or else he would've been speaking to my attorney, and that would've been it. There's no way I would've told him shit otherwise."

"He's also lucky you have money at your fingertips for bail and could get out as soon as I got down there, or else he would've really been short. Imagine those poor people that can't afford to buy their way out like that," Gary commented, flamboyantly fanning himself with his left hand. "I guess it's better to be rich than lucky."

"Yeah, and I bit the bullet and answered his questions about Ava on top of that. All to get him off my back about the damn assault. It's a good thing I did, though. Goodness, you could only imagine the picture Harmony and Lyric painted of Ava. Pure evil let them tell it. I set the record straight. Yes, she had her moments, but she didn't have it easy in life. I mean, really. That detective probed all into our childhood. Asking me about beatings and nonstop dance rehearsals. Just invasive. Very invasive."

"Whaaat?" Gary sang, simulating himself clutching his pearls.

"Yes. I mean, how old do we have to be for them to get over how Ava treated them? Okay, Ava showed me favoritism. Get the hell over it. She also didn't put those two in a boiling vat of water or make them kneel on rice. No, she made something out of those two nothings, for Christ's sake. I guess I just don't have the same horrendous memories, you know. Maybe I can appreciate the fact that the reason I have all of these luxuries now is because my mother instilled hard work in me. Harmony acts like she forgot that our mother didn't have such a grand life growing up. No one is perfect. You do the best that you can with what you have. Period."

"Well, you were born a star. Ain't nothing wrong with owning that." Gary smiled and unlaced Melody's shoes for her. "But back to that detective . . . He was fine and all, but I'm telling you, Mel, he is so lucky you're Miss Nice Bitch today. Because, honey, if he had been alone in that tiny room with me, it wouldn't have gone the same way. I wouldn't have told him shit from shine-ola. I mean, what did he expect you to know? I just think it's real suspicious that they took so long to even say something foul had happened to Ava. I'm no expert, but something about that ain't sitting right with me."

"He wanted to know who would have a motive to poison Ava," Melody replied, removing her earrings.

Gary moved from her side and flitted around the room, busying himself with making Melody a drink.

"And what exactly did you tell him?" he probed, eyebrows raised inquisitively. Gary thrived off of gossip and drama, but he was the only friend she had and could trust.

When Melody had first met Gary he'd come to an open call for dancers for her first solo tour. From the minute she saw him there was just something a little extra special about him. Melody saw more than a dancer in Gary. She had hired him as her personal assistant, but when she learned that Gary could talk a person out of their own drawers, he moved up to her manager. They'd become best friends over the years. They'd had their share of ups and downs. Sometimes Melody knew she was being cruel to Gary, but he always seemed to take it in stride. They always made up. Their relationship was solid. It was the only solid relationship Melody had right now.

"Shit, I told him what I know, which is nothing. Lyric was always angry at Ava, but she couldn't have killed her. That little girl may be a misguided nutcase, but a killer she is not. And, Harmony? Oh, please. That girl is so soft she wouldn't kill a fly buzzing around her head. Murray's ass is too old. So I'm all out of suspects myself. It is curious, though. Like what you just said, I had to ask the detective why it took so long after her death for the medical examiner to rule it a homicide. I mean, shit, we buried her and had time to spare before this revelation surfaced," Melody said.

"Right. And what did Mister Fine Dimple detective say to that?" Gary asked cheekily.

"He said something about the type of poison used not being easily identified by the toxicology test. He mentioned that it's found in the body's soft tissue and the samples taken during autopsy hadn't shown the poison until further tests were run," she replied. She sighed and closed her eyes again. "I just feel overwhelmed. Ava's dead. Tour postponed indefinitely. Up and down with my sisters. One minute I can get along with them, the next minute they both hate me. They don't appreciate anything I try to do for them. Always hell-bent on punishing me for Ava's mistakes. And let's not forget a certain piece of baggage that I inadvertently picked up while I was feeling like a mental basket case," Melody lamented, picking at her gel fingernails.

"Well, I tried to prevent that one," Gary reminded her. He had tried to keep Ron away from Melody. Gary had been fiercely protective after hearing about Ron's violent outburst against Melody, but Melody had insisted on dealing with Ron against Gary's advice.

"Everything is spiraling out of control, Gary," Melody complained. "I don't know what I did to deserve this seven years of bad luck shit." She yawned and put her forearm over her eyes.

"Listen, honey," Gary said, with his signature effeminate wave, "more money, more problems, okay? I know you were upset they put you through this, but, hey, it's better than having them rush into a packed concert waving a warrant for your arrest. You know those fuckboy NYPD cops *will* do it. Those charges won't stick when your team of attorneys get through stomping all over that shit. Now, where are those charge papers? Because I'm sure the lawsuit is next. I'll get right on taking care of this bullshit. There will be a PR god that will come down and turn all of this into a million-dollar moneymaker for you. You just leave it all up to me, as usual. I gets the job done," he said boastfully.

Without opening her eyes, Melody pointed to her oversized Louis Vuitton tote bag. That's why she loved Gary. Anything and anyone who got in Melody's way, he would do *whatever* needed to be done to clear the path. With an emphasis on *whatever*.

Gary sauntered over and retrieved copies of all the paperwork the police had provided to Melody. She heard him flipping through the pages.

"Mm, hmm. So this heffa still went to the police even *after* I paid her private doctor bills, paid for plastic surgery to cover the scar, and gave her enough money to ride off into the sunset for the rest of her miserable hood-trash life? You know, some people just don't learn. She ain't no different than Ava. Look how much you paid Ava every single month, yet she *still* threatened you with going public with that story about a certain high-powered senator-turned-president and a certain disappearing baby," Gary fussed, shaking his head.

Melody squeezed her eyes tighter. She hated even thinking about the affair she'd had with a United States senator and the fact that she'd gotten pregnant by him right before said senator became president. She had quickly taken care of her little "problem." The affair ended with both of them promising never to see each other again.

It had been particularly painful to go to campaign fundraising events with Sly and watch her then lover proudly display his beautiful, regal wife. He'd even requested that Melody sing the National Anthem during his inauguration. She had wanted to tell him *hell no* but turning down a president's personal request would have been a career killer for her. During the entire ceremony, she'd felt the president staring at her, but she never met his gaze. The affair was over, and life had to go on for both of them.

It was one of those secrets that she had buried deep . . . until she'd fallen out with her mother and the blackmail had started. Melody regretted the day that she'd had a moment of weakness and turned to Ava for advice about the senator. She never thought her own mother would later use that information against her. Melody had learned the hard way, more than once, that money could drive people to do some terrible things, even to their own family.

"I just hate a greedy-ass bitch. There's a special place in hell for all of them, if you ask me. If I could wipe them all off of the face of the earth, I sure would. Especially to protect you." Gary winked and brought Melody another drink.

Melody opened her eyes and sat up a little bit.

"I agree. Thank God for BFFs that deal with all of the greedy bitches in your life for you," she joked, taking the drink.

"For sure," Gary agreed. He was definitely a lifesaver. Melody sent him to do all of the things she didn't want to deal with, including delivering Ava's stipend every month. Gary had been the one who told Melody that Ava was intending to blackmail her.

He turned around and saw Melody looking at him. "What's the matter? You don't look so good. Lie back down, chile," he instructed, patting her on the hand.

Melody stared at him for a long minute before she acquiesced.

"I . . . I just need rest. I'm exhausted," she replied, easing herself back down on the pillows. She stared up at the ceiling and felt like her entire world was falling apart before her eyes.

Detective Simpson's voice played in her head. *Whoever poisoned your mother had to have regular, ongoing contact with her. This wasn't done overnight. It took some time and planning.*

Chapter 8

Lyric

The beat from Drake's "Hotline Bling" resounded through Milk River, a Brooklyn hot spot. Lyric felt the music course through her body, but even the catchy beat was not enough to cheer her up. It was her friend Bethany's idea to hit up the club, hoping to take Lyric's mind off of Rebel. Maybe they would even cop a few Percocet and Xanax pills, Bethany had told her. With little extra prodding, Lyric decided to go along with the party plan. She had nothing to look forward to anyway.

Bethany was a spoiled child and wealthy heiress to a hotel magnate and television executive. In other words, a trust fund baby who never had to work and spent most of her time partying and getting high. She had been a lifesaver to Lyric after she had found Kim and Rebel's two-timing asses in bed together. Bethany had let Lyric crash at her loft in Manhattan's meat packing district and even rolled a fat doobie for Lyric when she got there. Bethany was rich, but she was good people when it came to helping a friend in need.

Bethany also encouraged Lyric to get fancy and find a replacement for Rebel. *Put on a hot dress and go get somebody and show that bastard you're over him.* Three ecstasy pills and a blunt later, Lyric listened to her friend and let her hair loose . . . literally. The long side of Lyric's hair fell to the left with a few curls dancing around her jawline. She dressed in a black, form-fitting bandage dress that accentuated her hips, a pair of Bethany's designer pumps that she could hardly walk in, and a full face of makeup, complete with false eyelashes. Bethany's doing and certainly not Lyric's norm. She would've preferred her usual grungy jeans, leather motorcycle jacket, and steel-toed boots.

Bethany wore something similar—the obligatory tight freak'um dress, a pair of Red Bottom pumps. Her blond hair was piled high on her head in a purposely messy top bun. They'd definitely commanded attention when they walked into the club together, arms linked. Ebony and ivory, Bethany had joked. They were beautiful contrasts to each other.

Sitting at the bar, Lyric watched the partygoers sway their bodies and move their hips and feet to the music. In a club full of humanity, she felt entirely alone. That, it seemed, was the story of her life.

Lyric pretended to belong, but deep inside, she just wanted to be holed up in a dark room getting stoned . . . alone. Lyric nursed a snifter of Hennessey, her favorite drink. She watched as Bethany jumped to the music and whirled around on the dance floor. Bethany had endless energy, the life of every party. She also had no shame. She hitched her dress up a few times and twerked like she was working for dollars. Lyric laughed and shook her head. At least her friend was amusing.

Lyric's eyes wandered to the velvet ropes that separated the regular club goers from the VIPs. She remembered a time when she received all of that special treatment and attention. She watched the female club hostess trail into VIP with $1,000-plus bottles of liquor adorned by sparklers and place the bottles on the table in front of a very good-looking man who was surrounded by throngs of women and a bunch of security personnel. Obviously, the man was someone important.

From where Lyric sat, she could see that he had a headful of close-cropped jet-black hair. He wore a full, neatly trimmed beard. Around his neck hung thick gold, Cuban Link chains. Typical, but still sexy. The old Lyric would've gotten a few more drinks in her and boldly walked over to him. The new Lyric just watched from afar, left to wonder about the gorgeous mystery man.

"Are you going to dance or what?" Bethany screamed in Lyric's ear. Lyric whipped her head around. She hadn't even noticed that her friend had danced her way back to the bar.

"Uh-oh. Wait a minute . . . Somebody is caught up," Bethany said into Lyric's ear over the music. She followed Lyric's trancelike gaze over to the VIP section.

"Not me," Lyric replied, waving Bethany off.

"Oh, yes, you! You didn't even see me standing here talking to you. That's how mesmerized you were," Bethany teased. "It didn't take that long for you to get over that loser, Rebel, now, did it?" She nudged Lyric in the ribs.

Lyric's cheeks flamed over. She rolled her eyes and took the last gulp of her Hennessey. Bethany was observant and aggravatingly persistent.

"Oh, please. You know damn well I'm not ready to be looking at no-damn-body. You're wrong.

I was just bored and started watching the little show over there. That's all," Lyric shrugged.

Bethany laughed. "Mighty defensive. I know that look anywhere. So, do you want to know who that is?" She wiggled her eyebrows. Lyric rolled her eyes and smiled coyly.

"I'm not saying that I'm interested, but sure, who the hell is he?" she asked, jerking her chin in his direction.

"I knew it. I knew your ass was attracted to that cutie over there," Bethany screamed.

"Shhhh!" Lyric hushed her friend, glancing around to make sure no one had heard Bethany's big mouth.

"Girl, that is Khalil Aziz. He's one of the young Saudi princes. Which means oil money. I'm talking, he has the kind of money he can burn. He loves to come to spots like this and hang out with hip-hop artists. He even made a few rap songs and dabbles in the industry. He pays big-name rappers big stacks to be on his records just for the notoriety. He damn sure don't need the money. I'm sure you heard like four or five of his popular mix tapes. Your sister's man, Sly, was on a couple. People say Khalil would give up being a prince to be a rapper full time, but the royal family won't have it. I guess he's fascinated with the lifestyle," Bethany filled her in.

Lyric listened intently, though she tried hard not to react to the information. Now she remembered why he seemed familiar to her. Rebel talked about him often and even pointed to him once while they were in a club uptown and said Khalil was a wannabe that threw his money around to be liked. Rebel personally hated Khalil and often referred to him as an "insecure punk." She recalled mention of some beef over a record that went sour. Either way, dude sounded like he was way out of her league.

"And one more thing. Khalil is known to always have the best dope in town. I'm talking about that primo, overseas, high-you'll-never-forget, shit. See, whenever he arrives back in New York on his private plane, those customs boys at the airport aren't even allowed to search him or his shit. So outside of the rumors that he carries over $200,000 in cash at any given time, he's also known around town to be the free dealer. Like he just gives the shit away with no cares about a price. Shit, I'd fuck him for a taste of that good dope alone," Bethany said, licking her lips.

"Yeah, okay. Shit, rapper or prince or king— either way, he's out of my league," Lyric said dismissively. She turned her back on her friend, who was distracted by an old friend passing by and ordered another drink. It was turning out to be a long night.

"I was just going to ask if I could buy you a drink," a man appeared at Lyric's side, his left hand falling to her lower back.

"Get your hand off of me," she hissed, twisting away.

Lyric noted a slight accent in his English. Her scowl softened a bit before she looked over her shoulder. Maybe he was unfamiliar with the customs of this country.

"I usually don't approach women in clubs. But my boss sent me over," the stranger said, jerking his head toward the VIP area. "He thinks you're beautiful. He says you've been staring at him all night. But he also says he is impressed that you did not come over and force yourself on him like the rest of the women here. He would like to meet you, if you please," the man bowed slightly at the waist, his hand over his heart.

A flash of shame and embarrassment lit Lyric's cheeks aflame.

Oh my God! How embarrassing that he caught me watching him like some bar wench stalker.

Her eyes darted back over to the VIP lounge, where Khalil sat smiling like a harem king surrounded by his concubines. Lyric quickly averted her eyes. Her stomach fluttered.

"Thanks. But tell your boss, I'm good. I don't accept invitations from strangers," she said flatly.

"Maybe if he came himself, instead of having his royal servant do his bidding, I could respect his offer. No offense," she quickly added.

Suddenly Bethany wedged her way between Lyric and the emissary.

"Um . . . excuse me. Hi, I'm Bethany," she intruded, rudely jutting her hand in the man's face. He took a few steps back, clearly taken aback by her blond girl bravado.

When the man refused to shake her hand, she quickly retracted it. "Shit, I forgot you guys have rules about all of this. Anyway, don't mind my friend, here. She's just having a bit of a rough time tonight. You know, a lot on her mind," Bethany chuckled, tapping her finger against her temples, as if to get her point across. It was difficult to tell how much the man understood. "In fact, she was just telling me how *handsome* she thought Prince Khalil was," Bethany said, nudging Lyric from behind. "Remember you just asked me, 'Who is that fine dude?'" she said in mock desperation.

Lyric rolled her eyes at Bethany, shaking her head in silent protest.

"And how much you'd just like to meet him. For no other reason than to get a glimpse of his royal gorgeousness up close," Bethany finished, cutting her eye at her friend.

When Lyric didn't respond, Bethany continued. "She's just a little shy," Bethany explained, playfully patting the man on the shoulder.

The man turned his attention back to Lyric.

"Prince Aziz would like nothing more than to have the company of you and your friend. No strings attached," he said. "I can't go back over there and tell him you refused. He is a man of great pride, and he does not like hearing the word 'no'—this is unacceptable."

Lyric sighed. Between Bethany anxiously bouncing on her legs like a child begging for a toy and the messenger's wary look, she finally relented.

"One drink with the royal entourage, Bethany. That's it," Lyric cautioned. "Bad enough there's a million bitches in there fighting for his attention. That shit is so gauche."

"One drink. I promise," Bethany said cheerfully. In a bold move, she hooked her arm through the flunky's and off they went to VIP.

"Thirsty as hell," Lyric muttered behind her friend. She was a handful to be sure.

Lyric felt all eyes on her when she walked behind the velvet ropes. She quickly took a seat where she could see and hear Khalil's raucous party. Khalil's man had told them to sit and wait, as if they needed an appointment to see the prince.

Women surrounded the prince as he tossed handfuls of one hundred-dollar bills in the air, laughing as they scrambled on their knees like hungry dogs looking for scraps on the floor.

"Oh, see. This shit is not for me. I would have to be high as hell to stay up in here," Lyric leaned in and whispered into Bethany's ear. Were all men, regardless of race and religion, dogs? It appeared so.

"That's just showing off. You know all of these rappers and rich entertainers act like that. Look at how Mayweather acts when he goes out. I heard he's the nicest fucking guy behind closed doors. Don't judge him before you know him," Bethany advised.

"You, I want you," Khalil slurred, pointing to a Hispanic chick with a thick ass and tiny waist.

"Ass implants," Bethany mumbled.

"Definitely," Lyric agreed.

They both watched intently as Silicone Ass rushed over and put her bottom in Khalil's face. One of his side men dumped a small hill of cocaine on the balloon cheeks. He bent down and snorted it all up in one inhale. Khalil threw his head back and laughed. Then he slapped the girl's ass so hard she squealed and nearly fell flat on her face.

"Get her out of here now!" he yelled. Two more of his side men rushed over and dragged the girl out of sight.

"These bitches ain't loyal!" he yelled. Then he picked up one of the most expensive bottles of liquor sold in the club—the gold bottle of Ace of Spades—and took it to the head. Loud laughter followed.

Lyric watched Khalil snort at least six lines of cocaine and chase it down with liquor.

"Oh, shit, he's coming over here," Bethany said, bouncing in her seat.

Lyric was trying to play it cool, but her heart was pounding in her chest. She didn't know if it was fear or excitement. She was excited about the attention, but she was afraid that he would offer her drugs. She would not be able to say no.

"Hello, I'm Khalil. And you are?" he asked, grabbing her hand and kissing her knuckles. Lyric felt flushed. Khalil was even better looking up close. She couldn't stop staring at his long, dark eyelashes and his shocking white teeth. She thought his skin was so beautifully golden.

"Lyric," she answered, somewhat breathlessly. She looked away, suddenly too nervous to maintain eye contact. She could see several envious glares from the women in the room.

"Lyric . . . That's a beautiful name. Well, Lyric, you are my special guest now. Let's talk," he said, flashing his perfect porcelain teeth. Lyric's insides melted a bit. Of all of the beautiful women in the club, he'd chosen her.

"What would you like to talk about, Your Royal Highness?" she replied, flashing her most flirtatious smile.

Chapter 9

Harmony

Harmony flexed her neck and stretched her arms over her head. She sighed as the knots in her neck began to melt. Her muscles were as tense as her life had been for the past two months. She was barely sleeping; even going to the dance school every day, something she normally enjoyed, had become a chore.

She lifted her right foot and placed it on the wooden balance bar in front of the wall of mirrors, then lowered her head to her knee until she felt the muscles in the back of her leg stretch. She did the same with her left leg. As if on cue with the end of her stretch, the musical interlude of Rihanna's "A Million Miles Away" filled the studio. Harmony put her arms up, slightly bent at the elbows, her thumb and middle fingertips together and her pinkies in the air. She stared at herself in the huge mirror for a few seconds

before she moved. Dancing helped her to relieve
her stress and frustration. So far, it had been a
lifesaver.

When Rihanna's smoky vocals filled the room,
Harmony closed her eyes and swayed her torso
from side to side, letting the rhythm move her.
She flexed her feet until she was on her tiptoes;
then she made a four with her legs and released
them again. She repeated the step three times.
Her body moved across the studio gracefully
as she completed four consecutive pliés to the
piano accompaniment in the song. She eased
into a relevé and sauté with each high note in
music. The song's lyrics about lovers growing apart moved through her soul and made
her dance with ferocity and passion. Harmony
repeated the ballet steps over and over, swaying
and pirouetting as if she was in front of a crowd
of thousands. The movement, the sound of the
piano, the dance moves all drew her back to her
childhood.

*Harmony was seven years old, dressed in
a white leotard and a wide, fluffy white tutu
made of layers of wedding dress tulle. She
wore a headband of white feathers dotted with
tiny iridescent beads. Harmony was one of ten*

little swans set to perform their version of Swan Lake. *She was excited, but slightly disappointed as she watched the other tiny ballerinas back-stage hug and kiss their mothers who were all smiling and gushing with pride.*

Ava rushed over to Harmony and started pulling and tugging at her costume.

"You have to look perfect. Bad enough you're the darkest one in this sea of white. You already stick out like a sore thumb," Ava said in a hushed tone as she turned Harmony around, adjusted her skirt, and readjusted her head-band. Harmony looked around, and then sadly hung her head. Ava was right. All of the other girls in her class were pretty with fair skin and hair long enough to make a perfect bun. Ava had purchased a fake bun and pinned it to the back of Harmony's head.

"Now go work hard. You have to work extra hard so people won't look at you like the little dumb black girl. If you make any mistakes, it will be your behind when you get home," Ava threatened in Harmony's ear. No words of praise or encouragement—just more criticism and threats.

With sweat beads lined up at her hairline, Harmony stepped on the stage. She got into her place and when the orchestra started playing,

She tried to forget who she was and where she was—she could feel the music enter her body and move through her spirit.

Harmony definitely stuck out, but not because of her dark skin. It was her innate dancing abilities. At a young age, Harmony moved gracefully and on rhythm, unlike her novice classmates. At the end of her piece, there was a big pause, followed by a thunderous standing ovation. Mothers wept and fathers cheered loudly. Her mother may not have appreciated the effort that Harmony put into her routine, but others did. Harmony was smiling brightly as she scanned the crowd, searching for her own mother. Her smile faded when she saw that her mother was the only one not standing, or waving, or wearing a proud expression on her face. Even with a near flawless performance, Harmony still wasn't good enough for Ava.

Harmony was lost in the past as she leaped across the wooden floors. Suddenly, a scream cut through the air, causing her to miss her landing and nearly topple to the floor.

"What the hell?" Harmony gasped, turning toward the sound. She raced across the expansive room to the doors and burst through them to find her staff running in a panic.

"Oh my God," Harmony shrieked, jumping back as her slippers became wet. "Where is all of this water coming from?"

"I guess a pipe burst," Dani, one of her dance instructors, grunted. She was trying in vain to lift heavy boxes of dance supplies off of the floor before they were soaked through.

"Everything is getting wet. I won't be able to save it all. This is thousands of dollars' worth of supplies," Dani yelled, distraught.

"This is all I need right now," Harmony grumbled, as she sloshed through the rushing water, searching for the source.

Her mind raced in several directions. The dance studio was her life, all that she had left. It was the only stable thing in her life right now. And she was watching her dream wash away . . . literally.

"The floors—they'll all be ruined. How will we be able to dance or conduct classes?" Kimmy cried out, perched on a chair, as Harmony rushed past. Kimmy was a college dance student that had recently signed on to teach Harmony's teeny ballerinas' class as part of an internship class offered through her college's performing arts program.

"Call the fire department. Ask if they can help us," Harmony instructed Dani. "I know they have tools to turn off pipes and stuff. There's no way we can wait to find a plumber and pray that he can come soon enough to save this place from complete ruin."

Harmony raced to the back of the studio where the utility room was located. When she opened the door to the small room, she fell backward against the rush of cold water. She flailed her arms, panicking for a few brief seconds, before she managed to slam the door closed with the full weight of her body. She'd never learned to swim so even small amounts of water scared her. She finally got her bearings and scrambled to her feet. She tried the door again, but it seemed to be stuck. There was no way she could reach the pipes to turn off the main water valve if she couldn't get safely into the room.

The studio was covered in several inches of water already. Harmony knew that meant hundreds of thousands in damages and months of insurance claims and subsequent estimates and reestimates of replacement costs. Her heart sank. She wanted to scream at the injustice of it all.

How much more can I take?

"Ms. Harmony. They're here," Kimmy called out. "The firemen are here." Harmony turned around just in time to see five firefighters enter her studio in knee-high rubber boots, armed with axes, wrenches, and large bolt cutters.

"Stand back, ma'am," the head of the pack commanded, his voice deep, and his tone serious.

"The main water valve is behind this door, but for some reason it's stuck," Harmony said, indicating with a quick jerk of her chin before she moved out of their way.

"We'll take care of it, ma'am," the leader assured.

Harmony swiped her hands over her face as she watched the firefighters axe the doorknob and hinges off of the utility room until the door swung open with a bang.

"Whoa!" she heard two of the firefighters shout as water rushed at them like a raging river.

"We need to choke off the water main. This much water can't be just an indoor pipe. Go around back. Find the manhole associated with this place. Hurry up," the leader yelled at the others.

Harmony splayed her fingers across her forehead. What did she do to deserve such a terrible lot in life?

It took almost twenty minutes to get the underground water main turned off. The dance studio was in shambles. Chairs had floated into mirrors and shattered them. All of Harmony's student files were floating around in the standing water. The hardwood floors were starting to buckle and lift.

Harmony sat in the lobby, shivering and distraught.

"Ma'am, are you the owner?" the head firefighter asked.

Harmony lifted her gaze and stared at the stranger. He had striking slanted eyes and his olive skin was smooth with just enough hair to make him look rugged but not unkempt. He stood about six feet tall and had broad shoulders.

"Yes," Harmony rasped, barely above a whisper. "I'm the owner."

"Captain Birdwell. Blake Birdwell," he said, extending his hand.

"Harmony Bridges." Harmony pulled her trembling hand from under her arm and extended it for an obligatory shake.

"I'm sorry about your place, Ms. Bridges," he offered. "Probably going to be some pretty bad water damage to the hardwood. You may have to replace it all. And you'll have to watch out for mold growth with this type of sitting water," he said looking around.

Harmony closed her eyes as she processed the information. All she could hear was money, money, and more money. That was the one thing Harmony didn't have right now.

"Can you tell what happened? How did this happen?" she asked, genuinely perplexed.

"Seems like it was more than your typical water heater bursting. Seems like an underground water main gave way. Sometimes they burst and the water flows underground, but other times, the damaged main spouts up like a geyser like this one did. Anytime we see this much water gushing, it's usually from the water main that leads to the indoor piping system. In this case, we had to stop the feed from outside or else this place would've been ceiling high with water. The entire block is without water right now. City's got to come out and do some major patching up down there before it can get turned back on."

Harmony sighed loudly. "How long will that take?"

"There is just no telling, ma'am," Captain Birdwell said sympathetically.

"So there's probably no way this can be repaired in time for me to hold classes by next week?" she pressed. Captain Birdwell shook his head. Harmony let out a tiny gasp and whimper.

"My girls worked so hard all year, and the school's big recital is coming up soon. We need to keep working on it. What will I tell all of my hardworking students and their parents?" she lamented.

"If I were you, I'd call the insurance company right away. They probably can't fix it as soon as you need it done, but at least you can get the claims process started," he advised.

"I don't know a thing about filing an insurance claim," Harmony replied, shaking her head.

"I tell you what, let me run to the truck and get my card. I don't mind coming back over and helping you fill out the paperwork. I've seen businesses fail to get what they deserve simply because the owner didn't use the right verbiage in their claims. Dealing with insurance companies can be tricky."

"Oh my goodness. Thank you so much," Harmony replied sincerely. She could use all of the free help being offered.

"No problem. I'm sorry that you lost so much today. I know it must be very difficult for you. I'm happy to help where I can," he said. "I'll be right back."

Harmony glanced at her reflection in the mirror across the room.

"Shit. I look a damn mess," she huffed, trying in vain to smooth her fuzzy hair with her hands. She noticed that her eyes and face were puffy from crying and her leotard and tights were stained and smelled like a mixture of sweat and mold.

Captain Birdwell was back in what seemed like a flash. He had taken off his heavy-duty equipment, exposing his bulging biceps and muscular chest through a form-fitting fire department T-shirt.

Her cheeks flushed. It was the first time in years that she had that reaction to a man.

Are you serious right now? You're married, and he probably is too, Harmony silently chastised herself.

"That was fast. Guess you couldn't wait to get out of that heavy gear," she said, smiling awkwardly. She hoped he hadn't seen her trying to spruce herself up. Even she didn't understand why, at a moment like this, she cared what the fire captain thought of her.

"It can be a pain to wear sometimes," he said, lightening the mood.

"All of my numbers are listed here," Captain Birdwell said, extending his card out to Harmony.

"Thank you so much." She accepted the card with slightly unsteady hands. Harmony couldn't tell if the trembling was a result of shock or the cold water seeping through her clothes, chilling her to the bone.

"I'm pretty handy too. So once you get an adjuster to come out and assess the damage, I can help you find a good crew for the job. I don't want you to get robbed by these crooked New Jersey contractors," Captain Birdwell said.

Harmony's stomach fluttered. Not only was this man sexy, but he was thoughtful too.

"That would be awesome. You know how it is once they see a woman. They think they can tell us anything and we'll believe it. Thank you again, Captain Birdwell," Harmony replied, looking down at his card to avoid blushing again.

"Blake. Call me Blake," he corrected.

She glanced up, and he flashed her a beautiful white smile. In a time of chaos, God had sent her an angel.

"Blake. Blake Birdwell," Harmony repeated, the name rolling off of her tongue like a new, happy song. "I'll definitely be giving you a call."

Chapter 10

Melody

"In today's entertainment news, a big announcement seems to have shocked the music industry last night. Diamond Records artist Terikka revealed to the world that she was expecting her first child. In true over-the-top Terikka style, she ended her performance at the World Music Awards with a tear-away shawl that revealed her noticeable baby bump. After the crowd erupted in cheers, Terikka walked into the audience and grabbed Diamond Records owner and rapper, Sly, and placed his hand on her belly and kissed him in full soap opera fashion. We have footage of the exciting moment."

Melody clasped her right hand over her mouth as she watched video footage of Sly and Terikka.

"Oh God," she gasped, feeling the urge to vomit. "I am the laughingstock of the industry and the world."

"Industry insiders tell us that everyone was shocked by the news. As you all may know, Sly was the longtime boyfriend of Melody Love. Although there were rumors of infidelity in the relationship, there was never any confirmation. For now, it looks like the couple is elated about their soon-to-be bundle of joy. Melody hasn't been seen. We speculate she may be hiding out, trying to digest this news. We will continue to follow this story closely."

Another shot of Sly and Terikka flashed across Melody's television screen. It was a freeze frame of the kiss seen around the world. This time, Melody couldn't hold it together. She darted across her bedroom and made it into the bathroom and to the toilet just in time.

When she was finished regurgitating her lunch, Melody collapsed on the cold, tiled floor and stared up at the ceiling. She squeezed her eyes shut and let the tears streak down her face.

"Honestly, Mel, I came to tell you something else," Sly said, followed by a long sigh. *"Something that needed to be said in person and not through a punk-ass text or over the phone."*

"I'm listening," Melody said, twisting her lips to the side and wringing her hands in front of her nervously.

Sly cleared his throat and lowered his face into his palms. He took off his Yankee fitted cap, scratched his head, and set the cap back on it. He repeated this three more times.

"You playing right now, Sly. I really don't have time for it today." Melody tapped her foot expectantly and folded her arms across her chest.

"Okay. Okay," Sly relented. He placed his cap on his head and lifted his head a little bit so that he stared at her chin.

"I wanted you to find out from me and not some blog or paparazzi magazine," he said, his voice unusually mousy.

Melody hugged herself. All of a sudden, she felt cold. Bad news would surely follow.

"Find out what?" she asked impatiently.

"First, let me just say this, Mel." Sly lowered his eyes to the floor, choosing his words carefully.

"Don't caveat your news with a bullshit line about how you love me and how you want to be with me. Tell me what you need to tell me now, Sly," Melody demanded, her patience wearing thin.

Sly's shoulders slumped. "A'ight. I'm just gonna come out and say it then . . ."

"*Fucking say it already, Sly!*" Melody exploded. Her nerves were already shot to hell. "*I mean, what haven't I heard before? What did you do now and with who and—*"

"*Terikka is pregnant,*" he blurted, cutting her off.

Melody's lips snapped shut. "*Terikka is pregnant? And . . .?*" She met his gaze.

Suddenly, her head jerked back like he had just thrown cold water in her face. "*Terikka is pregnant. And . . .?*" she repeated Sly's words with more urgency so that they settled in her mind.

"*And what does that have to do with me?*" she pressed, her heart racing hard. Every nerve ending in her body was tingling.

Sly lifted his cap from his head and scratched his head again. Melody recognized that nervous tick. She knew it all too well.

"*What does that have to do with me, Sly?*" she asked again through clenched teeth.

"*A'ight, man, I'm just going to say it.*" Sly paused. Melody narrowed her eyes to a pinprick and held her breath.

"*Terikka's pregnant, and she's keeping the baby. I'm the father. I had to tell you now because she's planning on announcing it at the awards at the end of her performance.*"

Melody fell back into a nearby swivel chair, sending it rolling backward a few inches. She felt like a brick had been dropped on her head. Melody bit her bottom lip so hard she tasted blood.

"Mel, listen." Sly reached his hand out toward her.

Melody leapt from the chair and charged at him, feral, as she clawed at his face with her sharp, pointed stiletto nails.

"Shit!" Sly exclaimed as Melody's nails raked down his left cheek.

"I hate you. I hate you," she yelled, flailing her arms, throwing wild punches at his face and head. Melody bared her teeth like a rabid dog and tried to bite him near the chin.

"Yo, stop it," Sly yelled at her. "You're acting fucking crazy!" He wedged his hand between her mouth and his face, trying to push her face away.

"I hate you." Melody caught Sly with a fist to the left side of his head. She was a woman possessed.

"I hate you. I fucking hate you. How could you do this to me? How could you? You knew I wanted a baby. You fucking knew all this time that I wanted a family more than anything, Sly," Melody sobbed loudly. She lifted her knee swiftly and caught him in the center of his balls.

"Oh, shit," he groaned, shielding his privates with both hands.

"You knew I wanted a baby," she cried, the pain evident behind every word.

"I hate you," Melody screeched before she attacked him again.

"Stop," Sly gritted, grabbing her wrists. Melody tried to break free from his grasp.

"Stop it," Sly demanded, roughly flipping her down on the couch. He pinned her wrists at the sides of her head and her body to the couch with his legs. Melody tried to kick, but Sly's weight held her down. He loomed over her as her chest heaved like a madwoman. Her eyes were wild with anger and grief. Sly looked down into her face, the blood on his cheek and neck painting his skin with deep red slashes.

Melody closed her eyes. She couldn't stand to look at him. Every muscle in her body was tense, cording against her skin.

"Listen to me, Melody. I didn't mean to hurt you," he explained.

Melody bucked against him. She turned her head to the left and tried to bite his hand so that he would release her.

He clamped down harder.

"Listen to me. I have been trying to tell you for years now that you needed to lower that wall

you have up with everybody. Don't say that I didn't try, Mel. I fucking tried over and over again. I tried to soften your hard heart. I tried to love you, but you were unlovable most of the time."

Sly's words were painfully true, but it didn't make his actions any less wrong.

"The only time you let yourself be a woman was when I was fucking you. You know how that made me feel? I wanted you to be my lady . . . not my fucking competition." His words stung like an openhanded slap to the face.

Melody came alive again, kicking and trying to free her arms. She moved her head from side to side and nipped at his hands like a crazy psych patient.

"I tried, Mel. This news could've been about us. The world wanted to see us have a kid and grow the record label together. I wanted that more than anything, but I couldn't do it no more. Your mother turned you into a real fucked-up, mean person. Don't be like her, Mel. Find that soft spot and open up to the next dude. Maybe you'll get the family you always dreamed of—it just won't be with me."

Melody sobbed. Sly's words cut deep into her like a surgical scalpel.

"I wish you all the best, but I wanted some-one who could let me in. Someone who didn't base her entire life on things—material things. Money and fame don't mean shit if you can't love. I wanted a woman that could be vulnera-ble, not one that always wanted to be in charge or in competition with me," Sly continued, clutching her tighter.

Melody finally stopped moving. She closed her eyes and tried to slow her breathing. Tears drained out of the sides of her eyes and pooled in her ears. She wanted to die. She literally wanted God to take all of the breath from her body. She had never felt like this before. Her spirit was dead.

"All I want is someone to love me," Melody whispered. "All I ever wanted was someone—anyone—to love me."

Melody scrambled up from the floor, exhausted from the memories. The loneliness she felt, the reality of her empty life, made her question her purpose in life. God had blessed her with so many things. But why not love? Melody needed something. She needed to fill the void. She rushed out of her bathroom and into her bed-room. She watched Ron's chest rise and fall in his sleep. He was still there, but even that was temporary, and she knew it. Ron had taken some really harsh treatment from her over the past couple of days, but she could always lure him back in with cocaine.

Without a word, Melody rushed to the side of the bed where Ron slept. She climbed on top of him. He jolted awake, his arms up in defense. Melody grabbed his wrists and pinned them down to the bed. She crushed her mouth over his, both panting heavily but for different reasons. Melody's insides burned with jealousy, neediness, and hurt. She needed someone . . . anyone . . . to make her feel whole again. She was angry at herself for showing this type of weakness when she'd always prided herself on being the tough one.

Ron groaned. "Wait," he protested. He tried pushing her off, but a combination of sleep and shock made him weaker than normal. Melody had never made this type of move with him before. She knew he was probably shocked, and she didn't care. She wouldn't stop. Her hands were down Ron's boxers, and she tugged roughly on his manhood.

"I don't make you hard anymore? Huh? You don't want me?" she whispered harshly in his ear.

"Wait. Give me a . . ." Ron started. Melody reached down and slapped him across the face.

"Be quiet and fuck me," she growled.

"What the hell is wrong with you?" he gasped, his eyes wide with shock.

"I need you to show me how much you love me," Melody huffed. "Now." She didn't stop fondling him. Her hands moved over his body in a frenzy.

"Melody . . . what . . . this . . ." Ron stammered. "Let me get myself together." He tried to push her off, but she clutched him even tighter.

"I said I need you," Melody mumbled. "I want to feel you inside of me. I want you to fuck the shit out of me. I want you to take it like you want. Want me. Love me," she pleaded. Now, Melody could feel Ron's manhood pushing against her fingers.

"Yes, that's what I want," she whispered, wrapping her fingers tightly around him. "Take it. Now."

In one easy motion, Ron flipped her on her back with her legs still straddling his waist.

"Is this what you want?" he panted.

Melody closed her eyes. She knew it wouldn't take long for him to fall in line. After all, she held the purse strings to his addiction.

"Do it. Fuck me," she whined, digging her heels into his ass cheeks like she was spurring a horse.

"I need you. I need you now," she cried, her voice heavy with emotion.

Ron responded to her prompting and finally entered her. "Why this change of heart all of a sudden?" he panted in her ear. Melody didn't answer. She grinded her hips into him and dug her nails into his back. Ron winced. That just seemed to make her dig harder.

"Fuck me like you love me. Like I'm her," Melody whimpered, her eyes squeezed shut. Ron picked up speed. He grinded into her as deep as he could.

"*Harder*. Like you *want* me," she growled. She bucked her body upward, urging him on. Now Ron slammed into her so hard he was struggling to keep his breathing steady.

"Ah," Ron cried out as Melody dug her razor-like nails into his back. Rough sex had never been his forte. He had told her before that pain and pleasure did not mix right for him. But she didn't care about what *he* wanted. This was about *her*.

"Stop it," Ron gritted. She ignored his pleas.

"Kiss me," she demanded. Ron lowered his mouth over hers, and she clamped her teeth down on his bottom lip. Ron moaned in agony. He moved his head trying to free his lip, but she wouldn't let up until the metallic taste of his blood exploded on her tongue. Melody held Ron in a death grip while he plowed into her as hard as he could.

She screamed out as she climaxed.

Ron quickly pulled himself out and raced to the bathroom, his hand covering his bleeding mouth.

As soon as he left the bed, Melody curled into a fetal position and sobbed, her entire body vibrating with grief.

Ron returned with a cold washcloth pressed against his mouth. He sat carefully on the edge of the bed and pulled her into his arms. It was the first gentle moment they'd shared since their sordid affair began.

"What's going on, Melody?" Ron whispered. "I thought you hated me. And this . . . what happened here . . . it was so out of character for you."

"I know you went to see her," Melody cried into Ron's chest. She could feel his body stiffen.

"I know you want to be with her. I know that you're only here because of the money, the drugs. I thought I could make you love me."

"Look, Melody," Ron spoke softly. "Both of us have made mistakes with this situation."

"Is that all I am to you? A mistake? A situation?" Melody asked defensively.

"Well, we can't pretend that what we did and what we're doing is right," he said.

"That's all I was to Sly, to my father. That's all I ever was to everyone . . . one big mistake. No one ever loved me just for me," she croaked.

Ron sighed heavily. Melody sobbed for a little while longer.

"All I ever wanted was to have someone for myself. Since I was a little girl, my sisters had each other, and then Harmony had you and even Lyric had Rebel, but I never really had Sly to myself," she cried. "I knew about the girl, but I was in denial. I knew about *all* of the girls, but I pretended it didn't happen. I lived every day like I didn't see what he was doing out there . . . with her."

Ron stroked her hair and rocked her against his chest like a small child.

"No one can love you unless you first love yourself. You have to really love yourself before you can receive real love," Ron said, pulling back to look Melody in the eyes.

"And no more lies between us. I went to see Harmony because I love her. I'll never stop loving her for as long as I live. I care about you, but I can't love you. I'm married to your sister,

Melody," Ron rasped, his voice cracking with his own despair.

"Get out," Melody whispered, pulling away from him. Ron's eyes were wide, as if he didn't expect her reaction.

"Get out," she said louder this time.

"This is not new information, Melody, so please save me some of the dramatics. I never tried to make you believe we'd live happily ever after. Right now, I am nothing more than a two-timing piece of shit shuffling between my wife and her sister for drugs. My loyalty is always going to be to . . ."

The sad fact was Melody knew what Ron was going to say before he finished the sentence. They both knew that his loyalty was to Harmony and his daughter, but Melody also knew that there were times when getting high trumped everything, Harmony and his daughter included.

"Get out." Her voice went higher.

"C'mon. I thought we were keeping it real," he replied, his eyebrows furrowed.

Melody stood, her chest heaving in anger. Pain was etched into thin stress lines radiating from the corner of her eyes.

Ron stood too. He knew exactly how this would go.

"I said get out! Get the fuck out!" she roared this time. "Go home to your wife and your baby and live happily ever after just like Sly and Terikka. Go home and pretend that you're not a drug addict and that you can live without this constant supply you've gotten over the past two months. Go make more children and live happily ever after. You have a family and a wife who loves you. I'll survive, like I always do. But I want you to remember something, Ron. Loving someone doesn't mean you're meant to be with them," Melody cautioned.

Ron nodded his understanding and began scrambling around looking around for his clothes.

"Go home and pretend, like me, that you have the perfect life. If you can't live in reality, then you might as well create your own fantasy."

Chapter 11

Lyric

"Where exactly are we going?" Lyric asked for the third time. She lifted her hands and tried to remove the blindfold from her eyes. Someone tapped her knuckles, and she quickly pulled her hands back. Lyric figured it was one of Khalil's servants—that's how he referred to them anyway. She'd heard of celebrities having personal assistants, but Khalil viewed his people as property belonging to him. Not so different from slavery or indentured servitude. She knew it was customary for men from his country to have similar household arrangements. When she questioned the practice, he'd told her that where he came from, it was an honor for the men to serve him. She supposed it could be worse—he could have been using poor Filipino and Bangladeshi women as maids and sex slaves, as many royal families did.

"No peeking," Khalil said. "If I wanted you to see, I would have left your eyes free."

"Why do I need to be blindfolded? Is this place top secret? Some kind of hidden castle for a prince?" Lyric pressed. She had an uneasy feeling in her gut. She had trust issues, and she hated being left in the dark—literally.

"I think this is fun," Bethany chimed in. "Fun and kind of sexy, if you ask me. The prince whisks the two fair maidens off to a mysterious place for an adventure of a lifetime," she said dreamily, in a mock fairy-tale narrator voice.

"Shut up, Bethany," Lyric retorted under her breath, her legs bouncing nervously.

Bethany purposely bumped against her shoulder. "Calm down. If he was going to rape or murder us, he would've done it by now," she whispered near her ear.

Lyric closed her mouth. Bethany, hopefully, was right. She was too optimistic for her own good.

The girls had been partying in Khalil's suite at the exclusive Waldorf Astoria Towers over the past week. Khalil had supplied them with all of the coke and liquor they could stand. The dude sure knew how to have a good time. They had partied sunup to sundown for days straight.

If not for the constant high, Lyric would've crashed a long time ago. She hadn't had time to think about Rebel's two-timing ass.

"Remove the blindfold," Khalil commanded.

"Finally," Lyric said, swatting at a man's hand. "I can do it by myself."

"Oh, shit," Bethany gasped as she craned her neck to look out of the heavily tinted windows. "This shit is really a castle," she said, awestruck.

Lyric peeked around to see for herself. Bethany wasn't lying—the place Khalil had taken them to resembled a castle. The building sat regally atop a mountain.

"We have to be far away from the city," Bethany said in confusion.

"Of course, we are. Did you not notice how long it took to get here?" Lyric snapped at her. Lyric didn't like the uneasy feeling creeping down her spine. She shivered and fought to keep her chattering teeth from making noise.

Khalil laughed. "If I didn't like you two so much, I would have thrown you out a long time ago. So much talking. Like a fly buzzing around my ear. Women should be like old men's beards . . . seen and not heard."

The Mercedes G-Wagon came to an abrupt halt in front of a tall black and silver gate. Lyric had seen mansions before, but this building looked like a small replica of the Taj Mahal. She didn't know that property like this could even be built in the United States.

Lyric and Bethany exited the vehicle after Khalil, following him to a set of huge white and gray-speckled marble steps. "What the hell?" Lyric whispered as she stood at the bottom. The steps were too many to count; they reminded her of the scene from *Rocky* where he ran up and down the steps in front of the Philadelphia Museum of Art. This place seemed unreal. She hoped the drugs were not making her hallucinate this spectacular scene.

"Good day, Prince Aziz," a tall, slender man dressed in a tuxedo approached the group. The man bowed at the waist in subservience until Khalil began to ascend the steps.

"We're about to get the royal treatment," Bethany whispered to Lyric. They were welcomed in the same way—a nod, a bow, and a gracious manner befitting of a royal household welcoming guests. As they entered the glass front doors, Lyric took note of the gorgeous, perfectly made up, half-dressed model-figured women lined up on either side of the grand hallway. At first glance, she guessed that many were from Eastern European backgrounds.

A harem? This can't be his housekeeping staff wearing fishnets and leotards. Three women in maid outfits appeared seemingly from the walls, instructing Lyric and Bethany to follow behind the men.

"Prince Aziz," Lady One said softly as she bowed. She was carrying a tray of gourmet finger foods.

Lyric recognized the expensive caviar right away. She'd seen the same food at perverted record executive Andrew Harvey's mansion. She shivered. The whole atmosphere reminded her of Andrew Harvey's place. Maybe that was why she was so uneasy. There was something eerily familiar and similar about the feeling. Lyric's mind raced.

Lyric had looked up at the beautiful, pale yellow sandstone mansion with its six regal white Roman columns, smooth white and gray-speckled marble steps, and what looked like over 1,000 windows. She couldn't get excited because fear gripped her insides like a clenched fist.

"Andrew Harvey is living like a damn king. I have never seen a fountain like that unless it was in a museum or on TV," Melody had said, still whirling around, taking in the scenery.

"And, look at the beautiful greenery. It must cost a fortune to have your bushes carved into your initials and little animals like that. This is how I want to live when I grow up." She shook her head, enchanted.

"For real. Definitely something to live up to," Harmony added. *"Right?"* She nudged Lyric with her elbow. *"Why you so quiet? You see this house? Do you understand what it means to get invited to an Andrew Harvey private party?"*

Lyric shrugged away from Harmony. *"So? Everything excites y'all. It's just a stupid house,"* she grumbled, folding her arms over her chest.

She hated everything about Andrew Harvey. From their first meeting until now, every time Lyric had to be in his presence she went into a dark place mentally.

"What's wrong with you?" Melody whispered harshly, frowning. *"You better change that mood. This party is in our honor. We finally went platinum and a big player like Andrew Harvey is throwing us a party,"* she chastised.

"Ladies, right this way." A man dressed in a tuxedo interrupted their little spat. *"Mr. Harvey is awaiting your arrival."*

"And he got his own Geoffrey like the one in the Fresh Prince of Bel Air," Melody whispered as they followed the man.

When Lyric, Melody, and Harmony crossed through the beautiful, glass front doors, Lyric felt a nauseating sense of déjà vu.

"Oh my God. The inside of this house is even more amazing," Melody gasped. "Look at these floors." She tapped her foot on the gilded floors. "You think this is real gold?"

"Plated. Gold plated," Andrew Harvey chuckled from behind them. The girls all spun around in unison like a dance routine.

"Mr. Harvey," Melody beamed. "Oh my God. We love your house. We have never seen anything like it."

Andrew Harvey laughed. "I can tell."

Lyric reached over with a shaky hand and furtively grabbed Harmony's hand. Harmony looked at her and questioned Lyric with her eyes.

"There's my special girl." Andrew Harvey stepped in front of Lyric and placed his hand on her shoulder. Lyric clutched Harmony's hand in a death grip.

"Wait until you see the cake and the spread I had made up for you girls," he said, keeping his eyes on Lyric the entire time. A small amount of acidic vomit leapt into her throat. She forced herself to swallow it back down.

"Ava said to send you her apologies. She wasn't feeling well," Harmony told him. "She told me to look out for everyone," Harmony emphasized.

"Oh, she didn't come?" Andrew Harvey asked, looking over the girls' heads as if he was making sure. "Don't worry. I'll take good care of all of you. You don't have to act as the mother. You're just a kid yourself. You need to enjoy yourself." He smiled and placed his hands over Lyric's shoulders. Harmony tugged on Lyric's hand, pulling her away from him.

"So, is the party out there?" Harmony jerked her chin toward a wall of glass doors that led to Andrew Harvey's expansive backyard, patio, and saxophone-shaped pool.

"Yes. Yes. All of you girls make yourselves at home. This is all about you and that beautiful platinum plaque you've earned," he said cheerfully, extending his left arm toward the action.

"Let's go," Melody cheered, rushing for the doors. Lyric and Harmony followed her.

The party was packed with people. Lyric, Melody, and Harmony stood flabbergasted by the attendees. There were famous actors, singers, dancers, radio personalities, and even politicians in attendance. Beautiful girls, dressed in traditional French maid outfits and high heels,

walked around serving drinks and hors d'oeu-
vres held on silver platters. The gorgeously
laid out spread of food began at the right of
the door and extended the full length of the
property. Melody and Harmony were giggling
about the ice sculpture with Sista Love carved
into it. Lyric had never seen so much lobster,
giant shrimp, king crab legs, and oysters in her
life. Seafood was her favorite. There were four
carving stations—pork, lamb, prime rib, and
venison—manned by men in tall white chef's
hats and white chef coats.

"Let's give it up for Sista Love," the D.J.
announced their arrival.

Everyone in attendance turned their atten-
tion to Lyric, Harmony, and Melody and began
clapping, whistling, and cheering. Melody
drank up the attention, waving like a beauty
queen at a pageant. Lyric's face turned dark
red. She lowered her head, shyly.

"This is so crazy," Harmony whispered, as she
plastered an obligatory smile on her face. "Like
are we really in the same party as Tiasha?" she
said through her fake smile.

"Yes, and she's a megastar. Can you imagine?
I feel like I'm dreaming," Melody answered.

After two hours of eating, drinking, dancing,
swimming, and hobnobbing with the rich and

famous, Lyric had finally let her guard down. Andrew Harvey kept his distance, and she barely saw him. Lyric began to think she had been afraid and tense for no reason.

It was just what needed to be done a couple of times, for the deal, but it's okay now. He's not thinking about me, she had finally convinced herself. Lyric had loosened up and even shared laughs with her sisters and a few other celebrities in attendance.

"Dang. I have to pee so badly," Lyric told Harmony, as they stood in the shallow end of Andrew Harvey's pool holding their virgin Piña Coladas and singing along with songs from their album.

"You better not pee in this pool. What if it's filled with the stuff that turns blue if someone pees in the water?" Harmony warned. They busted out laughing.

"Okay. I'm going to go inside," Lyric relented. "Watch my drink."

She climbed out of the pool and was immediately met by one of the pretty servants who was holding huge, fluffy, white oversized towels out in front of her. Lyric smiled at the girl, took the towel, and wrapped it around her body. She rushed toward the house, her full bladder threatening to bust.

"Bathroom?" Lyric fidgeted, doing the pee-pee dance in front of another tuxedo-clad staff member.

"Right this way." He pressed a little button on a silver earpiece and spoke some code into it.

High tech, she thought. Lyric followed the man down a long hallway that had high ceilings, a beautiful Oriental rug runner down the center, and was decorated with walls of gorgeous paintings that she could tell were probably one of a kind and expensive. The man turned another corner and walked down another seemingly endless hallway. This one was adorned with glass-encased sports memorabilia that, again, was probably worth more money than Lyric could fathom.

"Is it this far to the nearest bathroom? I really gotta pee," Lyric winced.

The man didn't respond. Finally, after six more turns, he stopped in front of two beautiful wooden doors with beautiful long, shiny, gold door handles. Lyric's eyebrows folded into the center of her face when he opened the doors to a bedroom decorated in all off-white and gold. The huge poster bed in the center seemed swallowed up in the expansive room. Lyric blinked a few times. The room seemed bigger than her entire house.

"I just needed the bathroom," she said, looking into the room apprehensively. "A half bathroom or guest bathroom would've been fine." She didn't want to intrude into someone's bedroom.

"Straight back."

"Um, really. I, um, I could've just used the guest bathroom closest to the pool," Lyric stammered, turning and pointing back down the hallway she'd just walked through.

"Mr. Harvey insists on special guests having privacy," the man said with no emotion behind his words. Lyric looked into the room again. Now her bladder was one second from truly busting open. She took a deep breath and reluctantly rushed through the doorway.

"Please wait for me. I don't know how to get back."

The man didn't respond. He simply shut the door behind her. The click of the door made her stomach twist. Lyric's heart pounded wildly in her chest. If she didn't have to go so badly she would've turned and run straight back to the party.

Lyric raced through the huge bedroom and made it to the white and gold-trimmed bathroom door.

"Is everything in this house trimmed in gold? Crazy," Lyric whispered, pushing the door to the bathroom.

"Dang." She gawked at the huge, white, marble soaking tub.

"A gold toilet? Guess when you have money . . ." Lyric spoke to herself, as she let her towel fall on the floor and pulled down her bikini bottom.

"And who had bathing suits waiting for people at a party?" Lyric kept talking to herself. She closed her eyes and relaxed on the beautiful toilet and released her overflowing bladder.

She finished and walked over to the long, marble-topped double sinks. "Fancy," she whispered, examining the sophisticated hand-engraved gold faucet. Lyric put her hands under an automatic soap dispenser. She smiled because the liquid soap fell into her hand in the shape of a heart. Lyric looked up into the beautiful beveled mirror and smiled at her reflection. "They were right. This is how I want to live."

She finished washing her hands; then she turned around, picked up her towel, and exited the bathroom singing cheerfully.

"You like my house?"

"Ah!" Lyric gasped, staggering backward off balance. She braced herself just before she hit the floor.

"Hey. Hey. It's just me." Andrew Harvey stepped closer to her with his hands out to break her impending fall. Lyric pushed his hands away from her.

"Why did you sneak up on me? What are you doing in here?" she huffed breathlessly. Her chest moved up and down like she'd run a race.

"I was looking for you. You're my special girl," he said, moving closer. Lyric took a few steps backward. Her hands started trembling.

"I thought I would bring you something to make you relax a little bit this time." He held a little pill between his pointer finger and thumb and extended it toward her.

"Please. I don't want to," Lyric pleaded, moving backward as he advanced toward her. "I just want to go back to the party. I was relaxed out there. I don't need the pill. I just want to go have fun like everybody else."

"You don't want to what? Keep a record deal? Make your mother happy? Keep performing? Be famous? Keep your sisters happy?" Andrew Harvey asked, his tone steely. Lyric shook her head.

"But we can just sing and keep—"

"That's not how the business works," he snapped.

Lyric jumped when her back hit a wall. She couldn't go any farther. He reached out and gently swiped her wild, wet hair from her face.

"You're beautiful," he said. "Here, be a good girl and take the pill."

"Please don't," she gulped, trying to move away from his touch. She could barely breathe. His cologne and sweat, mixed with the chlorine soaked into her bathing suit made her stomach swirl.

"Take the pill," he whispered, using his huge hand to clutch the back of her head so he could hold it in place.

"No." Lyric struggled. That just made him clamp down harder a handful of her hair until he was holding it painfully tight. Tears sprang to her eyes.

"You're my special girl," he murmured, putting the pill between his teeth and lowering his mouth over hers.

Lyric writhed under his grasp and moaned into his mouth. She almost choked as the pill tumbled awkwardly on her tongue. Andrew Harvey used his long, lizardlike tongue to push it into the back of her throat. Lyric tried to fight some more, but she was no match for his girth and his strength.

"Hey, you don't want to taste this good-ass food?" Bethany said, nudging Lyric and snapping her out of her trance.

"This shit is so good," Bethany said, rolling her eyes with pleasure.

"Oh . . . um, yeah," Lyric said, blinking a few times to rid her mind of the memories. She picked up a few huge shrimp from a silver tray.

After the prince sampled the food, others in the room were offered the same. Khalil finally settled himself against large silk pillows inside of a spacious room perfectly suited for entertaining. It had twenty-foot ceilings, arched entryways, and was decorated with gold leafing on the ceiling that accented the fifteen-tier crystal chandelier dangling in the center. The room literally sparkled. This sort of wealth and luxury was beyond Lyric's wildest imagination. It had topped Andrew Harvey's house, and she never thought she would see anything better than that place.

When she stopped gawking at the ceilings and walls, Lyric counted eight ornate sofas, trimmed with gold and silver. Each sofa was in a different color-coded section of the room. Red, gold, purple, and blue. The room was a dizzying kaleidoscope of colors.

"Do you see this shit? I bet those curtains alone cost more than my entire apartment," Bethany whispered. The floor-to-ceiling windows were covered by beautiful white, gold, red, turquoise, and royal blue valences. Lyric knew right away that the long, flowing drapes were made of expensive silk fabrics.

"I feel like I'm in some kind of dream . . . or a movie," Bethany continued. "Who lives like this?" she asked, gesturing to the indecent amount of wealth on display.

Even the coffee and end tables were trimmed in gold. The tables were adorned with silver trays containing expensive treats—prawns, crab-stuffed wontons, caviar-topped crostini, crown-shaped puff pastries, pistachio nuts, figs, dates, and artistically shaped fruits. Some trays really made Lyric's mouth water. She couldn't believe how much drugs were laid out for the taking.

Lyric remembered once crawling around the floor of Rebel's house looking for a hit. Now, like a dream, she had trays of coke, heroin, and weed laid before her—a true bacchanal feast.

"I think we hit the jackpot," Bethany said in disbelief.

"I bet you this is not even a quarter of the house," Lyric replied. "But why bring us to his private palace? He hardly knows us. Why pick us—you and me—out of all the beauties out there?"

"Here you go with the paranoia," Bethany chided. "We are ebony and ivory—maybe that's why! I don't know about you, but I'm about to have a good time. I'm sure he will eventually send our asses packing, but until then . . ."

Bethany waved for the servant to bring over the tray with the neat lines of cocaine on it.

Lyric's shoulders slumped. She didn't want to be a downer, but she didn't fully trust any man's intentions. Especially when it seemed so suspiciously easy. Lyric watched as Bethany did two lines and immediately became more upbeat and energetic.

"If you can't beat 'em, you might as well join 'em," she mumbled to herself before she bent over the tray to take a hit.

Within two hours, Lyric was so high she couldn't remember what her reservations were about coming here with Khalil. As more guests arrived, she got even more comfortable. The music blared, gray tufts of smoke circled the air, and bodies swarmed the space.

Lyric danced, giggling as she imagined herself being as graceful as her sister, Harmony. She took another swig of Hennessey from one of the dainty crystal glasses she'd grabbed from a passing servant. She had finally let her guard down, and the liquor had made it easier.

"Damn, Khalil. You really know how to throw a party," she slurred, lifting her glass and toasting her new friend.

Khalil perched in a high-back white chair with gold trim, much like a king's throne. He licked his lips as he watched her sway sexily to the rhythm of the music.

"You like what you see?" she asked flirtatiously, holding his gaze as she danced over, teasing him with her movements.

"Take off your clothes," Khalil said, a lazy grin spreading on his lips.

Lyric laughed and downed the rest of her drink.

"In front of everyone? Get out of here, man," Lyric chuckled, punching him lightly in the arm. "Now if we were alone, that would be another story." It wasn't the first pass Khalil had made at her. The first night they were together, Lyric allowed him to kiss her, but they had gotten too high to take it all the way. She was glad for that. She didn't like putting herself in such a vulnerable position. When she was on the party scene right after her Sista Love had broken up, Lyric had woken up several times, unable to remember who she'd slept with, but she was aware she had semen draining down her legs or crusted over her face and in her hair. She had become paranoid about mixing sex and drugs.

She continued to dance in front of Khalil, licking her lips and grinding her hips, a lap dance of sorts. Khalil repeatedly told her how beautiful she was in his eyes. He loved brown skin and the texture of her hair—he thought it was all very exotic. Lyric didn't think she was a great beauty, but she did have a nice body, and she was often complimented on her eyes and smile.

"I said I want you naked," Khalil said, this time with a bit more bass in his tone.

"What? I can't hear you," Lyric yelled facetiously over the music. She feathered her fingers through his thick, dark curls.

"I need another drink," she snapped her fingers at one of Khalil's servants.

A tall, slender man rushed over and refilled her glass. Another servant held a silver tray in front of Khalil so he could sniff the freshly poured mountain of cocaine.

After two long hits, Khalil relaxed back on his throne, his eyes hooded over.

"I said, get naked," he said in an eerily calm voice.

Lyric laughed briefly. His demands for her to strip were starting to really irritate her.

"Stop playing around, Khalil," she said. "If you want to see me, we can go upstairs," Lyric offered, taking another swig of her Hennessy.

Khalil snapped his fingers and within seconds, four of his men rushed over. He whispered something in one man's ear. The men reacted immediately, practically pouncing on her.

"What the fuck? What are y'all doing?" Lyric slurred, barely able to fight the men off.

Two men held her arms in a firm grip. Khalil nodded and the other two men began tearing at her dress.

"What the hell? Khalil! What's going on?" Lyric screamed in full panic mode. Her buzz was fading fast. All eyes in the room were on her now.

"I said I wanted to see you naked," he repeated.

Lyric stood in the middle of the floor, completely naked now. She couldn't even use her hands to cover herself. Her face reddened. She was utterly humiliated.

"Get off of me," she gritted, trying in vain to shake off the hands that still gripped her arms.

"Bring her to me," Khalil ordered, his eyes running up and down her body.

"You fucking punk. You just going to do me like this in front of everyone?" Lyric spat, the heat of embarrassment setting her entire body on fire.

"Touch yourself," Khalil demanded. Lyric spat in his direction.

"Fuck you, Prince."

Khalil nodded again, and the man clutching Lyric's left arm twisted it painfully. Lyric buckled to the floor. She searched the crowd for a friendly face. Her friend Bethany was nowhere to be seen.

"Touch yourself," Khalil commanded again in an utterly bored tone. The man was a sociopath.

With tears in her eyes, Lyric reached down and touched her clitoris, putting pressure on it until it began to visibly swell. In response, Khalil slid his hand down to his crotch.

"Now, come touch me," he demanded as he stroked himself roughly.

"Please don't do this. Not like this. We can go somewhere more private if you like . . ." Lyric pleaded.

"Come touch me. Don't answer back again," Khalil said, his voice decidedly irritated. Lyric felt the heat of everyone's eyes on her. She froze in place, unable to move.

"Crawl to me. On your knees," he commanded.

Lyric let out an audible sob as Khalil's men pushed her down on her knees. She crawled over to Khalil, her eyes gazing down at the beautiful marble floors. When she reached his chair, she glanced up. His lips parted with a wicked smile.

"Now, beg for it," he hissed, clearly turned on by her subservient position.

Lyric stared at the floor, refusing to comply with his demands.

"You don't want to beg for it? Like you begged for my drugs, huh? All of a sudden, you have pride?" Khalil stood abruptly. He grabbed a handful of Lyric's hair and pulled her head up to look her in the eyes.

"You belong to me now. Do you understand? This is what you wanted, right? Drugs, attention, to party all day and all night? That's what all of you whores want, right?" Khalil growled, yanking on Lyric's hair, snapping her head backward.

"Ow!" she hollered. "You sick fuck. What kind of man gets off by hurting women?"

"Let her go! Get the fuck off of her! You can't do that to my friend in front of everybody like this!" Bethany yelled, her blond head making its way to the front of the room. Khalil let out a loud, raucous laugh. He jerked his chin in Bethany's direction. Three more men rushed over, hoisting Bethany up and carrying her, kicking and screaming, toward another room.

"Your friend is right. I shouldn't do this in front of everyone," Khalil said, his demeanor fully composed. "Take her to the room," he commanded.

"Please, let me go. I won't tell anyone about this . . . this place," Lyric promised. Her high was totally gone now. Sheer terror had a sobering effect.

"I will let you go when I'm done with you," Khalil said. "For now, get comfortable being here. And remember, this is what *you* wanted."

Chapter 12

Harmony

Harmony groaned as she lifted the heavy bucket of mold remover paint.

"You shouldn't be trying to lift that." The deep baritone voice sent shockwaves down her spine.

"Oh my goodness, Captain Bird . . . I mean . . . Blake," Harmony gasped, fussing with her frazzled hair, trying to smooth it back from her face. "I wasn't expecting you." She used her forearm to wipe the sweat and grime from her face. Her heart was pounding. Her cheeks flushed red, and her toes automatically curled inside her sneakers.

"Your contractors should be doing this. That's what you pay them for," Blake said, flashing his perfect teeth. He walked over and lifted the bucket from her arms with ease. "I thought during our last conversation we talked about this."

As promised, Blake had helped Harmony deal with the insurance adjusters and to find a contractor that could complete the work the fastest for the least amount of money. They usually scheduled their meetings in advance, and Harmony made sure she looked decent each time they met. Today, Blake had caught her off guard sans makeup with her hair resembling a bird's nest, and no time to remedy either situation.

Harmony adjusted her raggedy, paint-stained T-shirt and tugged on the waistband of her dirt-covered sweatpants. It was no use. She looked a mess, and there was no fixing it. Blake, on the other hand, looked handsome dressed in a pair of neatly starched Dockers and a three-button Polo that hit his chest in the right places. His freshly lined up haircut accented the one patch of gray in the front of his head. Harmony thought the gray made him look distinguished.

"All you should be doing is supervising the contractors and telling them what to do," he said, arms folded across his chest.

"I know, but with everything going on here, I've been trying to do as much as I can myself to keep the costs down," she confessed. "Without being able to hold the dance and theatre classes, things are looking . . ." Her voice trailed off, and she shrugged. She had said too much already.

She didn't want him to think of her as a charity case. "I shouldn't be bothering you with this stuff," she said, rubbing her sweaty palms on the front of her sweatpants. "You've done enough already. I still think it was your report that helped me get as much as I did from the insurance."

"It's really no big deal. I tell you what," Blake said, lowering the bucket to the floor. "I'll let you hold your recital rehearsal classes at the firehouse—you can use it as a makeshift studio in the short term. I'll get some of my guys to come over during their downtime to help you with other tasks—especially ones involving heavy lifting. They can log it as community service hours. We'll make sure you get your place up and running without having to cancel the recital your students have worked so hard for all year. That's a win-win, right?" he said with a grin and wink.

Harmony's eyes widened, and she shook her head. "That's very generous of you, but I can't let you do that. We'd be putting you all out," she waved. "Besides, you must not know what it's like to have thirty little ballerinas giggling and running around. Do you *really* want your fire station being overrun by little girls in pink tutus?" she chuckled at the image.

"Listen, my guys don't care about that—most of them have young kids at home, anyway. When we're not out on calls, all we do is sit around that place and eat, play cards, and watch TV. Most don't even exercise during off time because the job keeps us in shape; the few that do work out can use the weights outside, at the back of the house. I'll clear out the recreation room and leave you the space to hold classes," Blake said.

Harmony shook her head again. "I really can't—"

"I insist," he said firmly.

"That is so nice of you . . ." Harmony replied on the brink of tears.

"I do have one favor to ask, though," Blake said.

Harmony tilted her head and raised her eyebrows.

"I'd like to take you to dinner—no strings attached. You need to take a break from all of this," he said as he gazed at the heaps of old hardwood and paint-stripped walls.

Harmony averted her eyes and shifted her weight from one foot to the other. She looked down at her wedding ring and quickly turned the tiny diamond backward into the palm of her hand.

"I'm . . . um . . . married," she stammered. It needed to be said. She couldn't have Blake get the wrong impression. The last thing she needed was more drama in her life.

Blake raised his hands, palms up.

"I understand. This is a friendly dinner, not a romantic one," he said, lifting his right hand, as if taking an oath. "If your husband is around, he's welcome to come as well. I don't think I've run into him yet."

Harmony swallowed hard. "He's . . . um . . . he's not. I mean, we are married, but at the moment . . . he's not . . . we are not . . . It's complicated." She smiled weakly. She couldn't get the right words to come out. She'd been so busy getting Dance and More ready to reopen that she hadn't had time to even think about her current situation with Ron. The state of her marriage was a mystery, even to herself.

"You don't have to explain anything to me. And I don't want you to feel uncomfortable. It was just an invitation. You can say no, and I'm still going to be your friend and help you out. I was just joking about dinner being a return favor. There's no quid pro quo necessary here."

Harmony shoved her hands deep into the pockets of her sweats and swayed slightly on her feet. Her stomach fluttered.

"Let me think about it," she said. "I have so much going on. I don't know if I'll have time for dinner."

Blake nodded. "That's fair. Take as long as you need. You have my card. In the meantime, I'll get that rec room ready for you and the little ladies." He grinned and she watched him haul the bucket across the room before heading for the door.

Her mind raced in a million directions. The man was incredibly handsome and charming. She was honest enough with herself to acknowledge that she had become very attracted to him. Maybe a nice night out for dinner was exactly what she needed. All work and no pleasure had definitely taken its toll on her.

Smiling and optimistic, she went to check on her instructors at the front desk.

"Shhhh. Put it away. Don't let her see it. Hurry," Kimmy whispered to Dani. Both girls were scrambling to hide something behind the front desk.

"Don't let me see what?" Harmony inquired, looking around them.

Kimmy's eyes were stretched so huge they started to water at the edges. Dani had both of her hands behind her back like a kid caught stealing candy.

"It's really nothing," Dani chuckled nervously. Her left eye was twitching, giving her away. Whenever Dani offered up a lame excuse for showing up late to work, her eye did the same thing.

"Then let me see," Harmony said, moving sideways so she could see what Dani was holding. "It can't be nothing because you both look guilty as hell."

"Really, Ms. Harmony, you should just pass on this one," Kimmy said, gnawing on her bottom lip. "It's kind of bad."

Dani sucked her teeth at Kimmy.

"Well, it is," Kimmy retorted.

"It can't be that bad after all we've been through these last few weeks. Now hand it over," Harmony pressed with her hand outstretched, waiting expectantly.

Dani reluctantly pulled a magazine from behind her back and handed it to Harmony.

Harmony's eyebrows dipped. "*US Weekly?* That's what you were hiding?" she asked, incredulously.

Kimmy made a mousy noise, and Dani collapsed into a chair like she'd suddenly lost all strength in her legs.

"What's the big deal?" Harmony asked in confusion.

She looked down at the magazine and flipped to the only page in it that was dog-eared. Harmony sucked in her breath as she scanned the tabloid pictures. Her entire body went cold, like someone had just injected ice water into her veins. She rubbed her eyes and silently prayed that they were deceiving her. She looked at the girls who were both staring at her with sympathy.

"I'm so sorry," Dani offered. "We wish you didn't have to see that."

Harmony's eyes roved back down to the incriminating pictures. She swallowed the hard lump that had formed in the back of her throat and read the caption under the picture.

Melody Love sneaks out with new love interest, former child star Ronald Bridges. Bridges is married to Melody's sister, Harmony, former member of Sista Love. As we all know, Sista Love had a bad breakup, but the sisters recently reunited when their mother was found dead in her house. Looks like Melody has finally moved on from Sly—but with her sister's husband. This tea is so hot it will burn down the house! Stay tuned for more as this family saga unfolds.

Harmony couldn't move. She couldn't speak. She could only stare at the picture of Melody and Ron exiting a vehicle together. Her sister's hand was held trustingly in Ron's. She felt sick to her stomach. Her sister and her husband—she didn't think she'd ever felt so betrayed—not even by Ava.

"I'm so sorry, Ms. Harmony," Kimmy said softly.

"The story is running in *People, Gossip Mag, OK!* and *In Touch* too. Just so you know . . ." Dani offered, her voice trailing off at the end.

Harmony closed her eyes for a few long seconds. She couldn't hear anything but the rush of blood from her pounding heart. Her hands curled around the magazine until the picture crumpled. She took a deep breath and opened her eyes again.

"Get back to work, ladies. We have a lot to do around here," Harmony said in a surprisingly calm tone. Dani and Kimmy looked at each other, shocked.

"I mean it. Let's get to work," Harmony repeated, trying like hell to hold on to her composure. Both girls scrambled from behind the desk and headed to the back of the studio. When they were gone, Harmony took one last look at the picture of her sister and her husband.

Melody had, once again, taken everything she loved from her.

"You won't get away with this, Melody. Not this time," Harmony whispered through her sobs. "Not this time."

Chapter 13

Melody

Loud banging roused Melody from a drug-induced sleep. Her head pounded from being jolted awake. She groaned. Who could be banging on her door? She told everyone that she was not working or handling any business issues right now.

Since Sly and Terikka's baby announcement to the world, Melody had been using Percocet and Ambien to relax and sleep. She had been careful to stay away from the usual places the paparazzi harangued her.

"Gary?" Melody called out, her voice still gruff with sleep. She'd only allowed Gary to visit her at home. Melody had given him limited power of attorney so that he could keep on top of her business dealings while she took a mental break. So far, Gary had been doing a great job of keeping everyone away.

The loud knocks came again.

"Gary!" Melody screamed louder this time, causing the pounding in her head to increase. No answer. She groaned, throwing her comforter back and forcing herself to sit up. Her head swam for a few seconds before she got her bearings. More loud knocks propelled her to her feet. She didn't bother with her robe or slippers.

"Who the hell?" Melody grumbled as she made her way to the door. "This better be fucking life or death," she hissed as she yanked the door open. Her words tumbled back down her throat like she'd swallowed a handful of marbles. Her eyes bulged.

"Harmony?" she said, her mouth agape.

"I'm probably the last person you expected to see, right, Melody?" Harmony said through her teeth, her nostrils flaring.

You damn right.

"You're my sister. Why shouldn't you visit me?" Melody replied, her voice rising and falling, the nervousness ringing loud and clear.

"Come in. Come in," Melody said, quickly gathering her composure and stepping aside to allow her sister inside. "Things are dark around here. I gave my help off for the week so that I could get some rest and go off the grid."

"Oh, this won't take long. I'm actually kind of glad we're alone," Harmony replied stiffly, stepping inside Melody's Upper East Side loft that few people knew about. The place was much smaller than Melody's other properties. It had been one of the first places she purchased when Sista Love started making real money.

"How'd you know I would be here?" Melody inquired.

"A sister's intuition," Harmony replied sarcastically.

"Well, as you can see, not much has changed." Melody opened her arms, making reference to Sista Love's two platinum plaques hanging on the walls and the first two Grammy Awards sitting on the glass shelves on the wall.

"Is everything, okay, Harm? Do you want to have a seat?" Melody asked, pointing to the sofa.

"I don't want to sit. I'm not staying long," Harmony said abruptly.

"Okay . . ." Melody's voice trailed in confusion.

"You know, Melody, I thought when I saw you, I'd be so upset that I wouldn't be able to speak. I thought I would just rush in here and tear your hair out from the roots," Harmony said evenly.

Melody's stomach began to churn. "What . . . what are you—" she started.

"I'm getting to it," Harmony cut her off.

Melody's lips snapped shut.

"Like I was saying. The fact that I am not nearly as upset as I thought I would be tells me that I am at a different place in my life. But I guess when it comes to you, I've always been at a different place in my life."

"Harmony, this cryptic speech is not necessary. We're adults. Get to it." Melody folded her arms over her chest and tapped her foot impatiently.

"I'll get to the point of today's visit when I'm ready. But first, I want you to think back to Christmas of 1997. I was ten and you were eight years old." Harmony's hands curled into fists at her side.

Melody rolled her eyes and sighed heavily. Since Ava's death, she had been bombarded by her sisters' need to bring up the past.

"Not another one of these strolls down memory lane, Harmony. I've had enough of living in the past with you and Lyric," she snarled. "We were kids, and that's all behind us now. Can't we just move on?"

"I was ten, you were eight," Harmony continued, ignoring Melody's complaints. "Ava had put up a beautiful Christmas tree, and she'd decorated it with all sorts of special ornaments—gold ones, sparkly white ones, and even those teardrop crystal ones that she claimed to have inherited from her grandmother. It was shaping up to be a very good Christmas. She told us to make a list of the things we wanted that year. *'Don't put more than three things on your list, Harmony,'* she said to me." Harmony's voice cracked with emotion.

Melody sighed. The memory was coming back to her, whether she liked it or not. She closed her eyes.

"All I put on my list that year was a Rapunzel Barbie," Harmony bit off her words. "I thought if I put only one thing on my list, it was a guarantee that I would receive it." She held up her pointer finger. "One goddamn thing is all I asked her for."

"You're angry at me because of a stupid doll?" Melody interrupted. She remembered what happened, and the heat of shame burned in the center of her chest now. But that was years ago, and she was just a child.

"When I opened my *one* gift, I was over the moon. Ava had finally done something nice for me. She had finally given me something that I wanted, instead of making me accept what she thought I should have. That doll was beautiful. My dream of owning a Rapunzel doll had finally come true," Harmony said, shaking her head.

"Oh, yes. I was so happy that if I had died at that moment, I would've been fine with knowing I had at least one happy day in my young life. As I held my *one* gift, I looked over at you opening probably your tenth gift that morning, and you were scowling and unhappy. You ripped the pretty, shiny gold and red wrapping paper and threw each new toy aside like it meant nothing to you. Nothing could ever satisfy you," Harmony said, tears falling freely down her cheeks.

"Harmony, look, I don't know what—" Melody began.

"And then!" Harmony shouted, cutting her off. "When *all* of your gifts were opened and tossed aside, even the most beautiful dolls, ones that I would never dream to even ask Ava for, you looked over at my doll with her chocolate skin, long braids, and pink lace dress and cried out, '*I want that doll*,'" Harmony said accusingly.

Melody bit down on her bottom lip, fighting back her own tears.

"And you know what?" Harmony shook her head in disgust. "Ava walked over to me with her hand extended. I turned away, screaming and begging her not to take away my doll. But none of that worked. Ava ripped that doll, my *one* and only gift, right out of my hands, and handed it over to you without a blink of an eye.

You snatched it like the greedy and selfish kid you were and danced around the room, gloating in your victory, all the while I lay balled up in a knot under the tree sobbing." Harmony's body shook with emotion.

Melody swiped roughly at her own tears.

"Well, the way I felt that day—less than human, unloved, robbed, abused, alone, and defeated—is the same way that I feel today knowing that you slept with my husband," Harmony said, letting the words drop like a sledgehammer.

Melody's head flew back as if she'd been slapped. She opened her mouth to speak, but Harmony put her hand up to squelch the debate.

"There is nothing you can say to defend yourself. I'm not asking you to confirm anything for me. I already know the truth. I only came here today to ask you why you enjoy torturing me so much. Why do you always want to hurt me?" Harmony's lips twisted in anguish.

Melody shook her head, defeated. "I told her not to say anything."

"Told who? What are you talking about?"

"I know Lyric told you. I guess I didn't meet her money demands fast enough," Melody said. "But it's not what you think. I didn't go after him because I wanted what you had. It didn't happen like that. We are not kids anymore, Harmony, and a husband is not a toy to be stolen. Love is not an object to be taken. If he really loved you, he wouldn't have even entertained the thought of being with someone else." Melody's self-defense argument, of course, placed the blame squarely on Ron.

Harmony seemed to sway on her feet. "Lyric? She . . . She knew about you and Ron?"

"It just happened, Harmony. I didn't set out to hurt you," Melody explained.

"Lyric knew?" Harmony punched her fists into the palm of her hand.

"If she didn't tell you, then how did you find out?"

"It's in every gossip magazine and tabloid paper, Melody," Harmony said exasperated.

Melody fell back on the couch. "But how?" she asked, almost breathlessly. Harmony dug into her purse and pulled out the *US Weekly* and tossed it in Melody's lap.

"It's right there—in black and white. There's no mistaking it," Harmony growled. "There's nothing you could ever do or say to make up for this one, Melody. I never want to see you again. I hope your money buys you all the happiness you clearly think you deserve," she spat.

"I have proof that I didn't make a move on Ron. He approached me," Melody said frantically. "You wait right here. I can show you."

Melody rushed to her bedroom, desperate to clear her tarnished reputation. She couldn't forget that night . . .

"What the . . ." Melody looked dumbfounded at the sight of her brother-in-law standing in her doorway, propped up by her doorman, Ralph.

"Listen, I . . . I . . . know, I'm the la . . . last person you . . . ex . . . expected to see," Ron slurred, his words uttered in an alcohol-scented cloud. "But I . . . need to say some . . . some . . . things to you," Ron's left pointer finger moved unsteadily in front of his face until it was directed at her.

"My God, Ron, you're a mess," Melody said, eyeing his twisted, untucked shirt and the big wet spot on the front of his pants. He was barely coherent.

"You are . . . you . . . fuck . . . fucked . . . up. Fucking up . . . my marriage," Ron warbled.

"You're pissy drunk," Melody said, anxiously knotting the bathrobe sash around her waist.

"You can't break up . . . no . . . break up my marriage with your stupid . . . tour," Ron said, dribble running down the side of his mouth.

"Ms. Love, I can call your security and have them remove him," Ralph said, holding Ron by the collar of his shirt as if he feared contamination.

"Trust me, he's not a threat. Look at him. He couldn't harm a fly right now even if he wanted to. He just needs to dry out," Melody replied, shaking her head.

"You need to get out. Get out . . . out . . . of my marriage," Ron said doggedly.

"Ron, just come inside and dry out. You're not yourself right now," Melody said evenly. She was running out of patience. She had no time for this drunken foolishness.

"No. I came to say . . . I love . . . love my wife. You can't do this to uh . . . us." Ron leaned toward Melody and almost fell over.

"Whoa," Melody said as she and Ralph both reacted at the same time, keeping Ron upright.

Melody's face reddened. She nodded to Ralph, excusing him. "Thank you, Ralph. I'll take it from here."

The doorman looked at her skeptically.

"Honestly, it's okay," Melody assured.

Ralph shrugged his shoulders and slowly released his grip on Ron. Melody stood aside as Ron staggered into her apartment.

"I came here . . . here. To give you . . . a piece of my . . . mind." He swayed dramatically to the right and almost fell over a nearby coffee table.

"Listen. Concentrate on staying on your feet." Melody grabbed his arm and guided him to *her white leather couch. She tossed his jacket down first and wished she could immediately disinfect her hands.*

Ron mumbled under his breath something that Melody could barely understand.

"Sit down. You are a complete mess right now."

"I . . . didn't have any place left . . . I mean . . . left . . . to go," Ron rambled incoherently. "I didn't . . . have anyone else to tell. She . . . hurt me. She . . . hurt me, bad. You caused all . . . all of it." Ron choked down a sob. He was on the verge of a mental breakdown. That much was obvious.

"Where are you coming from at this time of the morning? A bar? A party?" Melody pressed as she retrieved a bottle of water from her wet bar.

Ron closed his eyes and seemed to relax for a bit on the couch. His mouth hung open, and his breathing was labored. Oh, no, she would not allow him to fall asleep in this state. Who knew when he'd wake up, if at all?

"Does Harmony know where you are?" Melody inquired.

Ron groaned. At least he was still conscious.

"What's going on, Ron? I don't even know how you knew where to find me. I'm not even

here all that often. I only came here after Ava's death. You come here accusing me of interfering in your marriage, looking like you've been on a bender for a week. And God, you smell awful," Melody said, waving her hand in front of her nose.

Ron grimaced when Melody placed the cold bottle of water on his forehead. He cracked his right eye open.

"You probably need ten of these." Melody held the bottle out to him.

Ron looked suspiciously at the bottle before turning his head away. He closed his eyes again and seemed to have fallen asleep or passed out—she couldn't tell the difference.

"I'm going to call Harmony," Melody said, frustrated.

"No! Please. Don't," Ron shouted, the words falling heavy from his mouth.

That had gotten his attention. Melody was startled by how adamant he was about not calling her sister.

Ron closed his eyes again and spoke, carefully constructing his words.

"She can't know that I came to you. She . . . she can't see . . . me . . . like this," Ron hiccupped a sob. *"I wanted to fix it."*

Melody rolled her eyes. Ron couldn't make up his mind. Did he want to be a mad, confrontational drunk or a sad, sobbing drunk who was too ashamed of his wife learning about his behavior?

"I'm sure Harmony would understand what you're going through. She's your wife," Melody said, her voice trailing off as she stared down at Ron's handsome face. She tilted her head to the side. Something inside of her stirred. She stumbled back a few steps, dizzy with conflicted feelings. Why did he come to her house? She was still not clear about his intentions.

Ron snored loudly. The sound snapped her out of her fantasy.

Melody quickly shook off her conflicting emotions and thoughts. She set the water bottle down on the end table and rushed to her bedroom to retrieve her cell phone. Melody was tempted to dial her sister's number, but Ron had explicitly requested that she not call her sister. Melody didn't really want to call her anyway. Let him tell her.

Ron was snoring like a bear on her couch. She smiled and picked up her phone and snapped a few pictures of him.

***

"Look," Melody panted, showing her cell phone pictures to Harmony. "I'm telling you, he came to me. I wasn't trying to take what was yours."

Harmony squinted down at the screen. Her husband was asleep on Melody's couch like he belonged there. She shook her head.

"Well, you don't have to worry about sneaking around behind my back anymore. He's all yours," Harmony spat, moving swiftly to the door.

"Harmony—wait," Melody called out. Harmony stopped walking, but she didn't turn around.

"I always wanted to be you—to be as . . . . I just wanted to be as strong, pretty, and smart as you. None of this ever mattered if I couldn't share it all with you and Lyric. I wish we could have been Sista Love in truth, but it's not too late," Melody said, finally breaking down.

"It is too late. As far as I'm concerned, I don't have any sisters," Harmony said before she stormed out.

Melody's shoulders shook when the door slammed. The impending loneliness finally hit her. She had gone too far this time, and she knew it. Through teary eyes, she looked down at the crumpled magazine photo clutched in her hands. That picture probably netted the seller over a hundred thousand dollars. Melody sucked in her breath as comprehension washed over her. Only a few people could've taken that picture and sold it—Ron, Gary, or the driver.

Melody was going to get to the bottom of the photo. It seemed that someone was profiting off of her pain, and when she found out who, she would make them pay for it.

Chapter 14

Lyric

Khalil growled and panted as he reached an orgasm. It was the fifth for the night and normal for a drug-fueled roll. Lyric followed with sounds of her own, but she was faking it.

Khalil released his grip on the chain attached to the dog collar around her neck. They both collapsed on the bed.

She rolled on her side and drew her legs up to her chest. Her insides burned, and the area between her legs was raw. She felt like she'd been dragged down a concrete road naked. For the past three weeks, she had been held captive, drugged up, and abused. Every time she begged to leave, Khalil would find a new kinky form of abuse to inflict on her. She'd been so out of it most of the time, she didn't even have the strength to protest.

"I have to say, you're the best I've had in a long time," he said, sitting up on the side of his custom-made circular bed. "I'm usually bored by now, but there is something about you that I find more appealing than the others," he said, pinching her nipple. Lyric squeezed her eyes shut and fought to stave off the vomit creeping up her throat.

Khalil snapped his fingers, and the two servants posted in the corners of the room rushed over to prepare the heroin Lyric needed to keep from being dope sick. Three weeks was all it had taken, and she was hooked all over again.

"I don't want to," Lyric whispered weakly. She had come down from the last high long enough to think about her situation. If she refused the drugs and got really dope sick, maybe Khalil would be disgusted and throw her out on the street. At this point, being on the street was better than being brutalized as a sex slave.

One of Khalil's servants grabbed the long silver chain around her neck and yanked it until Lyric sat upright. The other held her arm, forcing it flat against the table.

"Please, I don't want any. I . . . just want to leave," Lyric cried, closing her eyes as she listened to Khalil laugh at her pleas.

"Now you refuse my drugs? You were very happy to accept them when we first met. This is what you like, no?" he teased.

Lyric winced as the tip of needle broke through her skin. The drugs hit her system faster than any of the stepped-on dope she normally bought off the street. Her head dropped forward until her chin touched her chest. There was a time when having this much drugs in her system would have been a dream come true. Now, it felt like a nightmare.

"Please," Lyric slurred, barely able to lift her head in Khalil's direction. "Just let me go home."

"Trust me. When I'm done with you, you'll be going home," Khalil said, grabbing the chain and yanking her into his lap so that she straddled his hips.

Lyric numbly complied.

Lyric's eyes rolled in a circular motion and she kept laughing, so high out of her mind she could barely remember her own name. Khalil had forced a speedball into her vein. He'd said he wanted to experiment with her to see how the drug would affect her.

"Bring the other one in," Khalil said, waving his hand toward the gold French doors. Lyric laughed for no reason, her half-opened eyes still rolling around.

"Lyric! Oh my God. I thought you were dead," Bethany cried out. Lyric finally got her eyes open long enough to see that her friend wore a collar and chain around her neck too.

"Dead?" Lyric slurred, fighting to keep her eyes open. "I just started living."

"I'm so sorry I convinced you to come here. It's all my fault," Bethany cried, reaching out to embrace her friend.

Suddenly, Bethany was yanked down to the floor by the chain.

"Stop all of this sniveling. It's time for the show," Khalil complained. He took a long sniff of cocaine and laughed. "Don't you bitches just love to party?"

"Please, no," Bethany shook her head. "Not with my friend."

Khalil laughed raucously. "Who better to do it with than your own friend? Who says money can't buy a man's wildest desires?"

"I like men. I . . . will do anything for you . . . just you," Bethany begged, on her knees with her hands clasped together.

"I don't care what you like. I've already spoken. And when I speak, women obey," Khalil snarled. He nodded at one of his men nearby.

Bethany screamed as she was dragged across the floor over to the bed. The skin on her knees burned.

"What's the matter?" Lyric sang in a silly tone, her eyes closed as she drifted in and out of consciousness.

"Lyric, we have to try to get out of here," Bethany whispered loud enough for her friend to hear. Lyric laughed in response.

"Start the show!"

"I . . . need something to take the edge off. I . . . can't do it without—" Bethany begged.

"No. You'll do it without being high. It's your reluctance that turns me on. If you're high, the drugs will ease your pain and embarrassment," Khalil replied, squeezing his crotch and licking his lips.

"No more delays," he warned, walking over and slapping Bethany on her naked ass so hard, his hand print remained.

"Get her up," Khalil commanded.

Lyric felt herself being yanked around by the chain. She wore a silly grin, and her head flopped from one side to the other side.

"Make believe you want it or you'll both regret it," Khalil growled at Bethany.

Lyric looked at her friend, confused.

"Why are you crying, Bethany? This shit is so good," Lyric giggled, falling down on the bed.

Reluctantly, Bethany whipped her hair around and around to the music that now filled the room.

"Crawl," Khalil gasped, his manhood growing in his hand now. Bethany got down on all fours and crawled toward Lyric like a hungry predator.

Khalil nodded at his people, and they rushed over to the bed, forcing Lyric's legs open.

"Hey. What the hell?" Lyric groaned, followed by a hysterical laugh.

"Keep your legs open," Khalil insisted. Lyric stuck her tongue out at him and mocked his command.

"What you trying to do? I don't get down with bitches," she slurred, her words barely intelligible.

"Taste her," Khalil hissed.

With tears running down her face, Bethany used her hands to part Lyric's labia.

"Get the hell off of me. I said I don't get down like this. She's my friend, not my bitch," Lyric warbled, struggling to sit up.

"Do it now or else you'll both be sorry. I have much in store for you two. This is just the icing on the cake . . . so lick it," Khalil ordered, laughing at his own joke.

Lyric covered her face with her hands as she felt Bethany's lips on her inner thighs at first. The drugs made her entire body sensitive to touch. She quivered at the contact.

"Yes. Just like that," Khalil urged. "Open wider. Let her taste you."

Lyric reluctantly let her legs fall open. Khalil slapped Bethany on the ass again. She whimpered and buried her face between Lyric's legs.

Lyric closed her eyes. At first, she was tense, but once Bethany drove her warm, wet tongue deep into her middle, Lyric slowly opened her legs wider, closed her eyes tighter, and began grinding her hips toward her friend's mouth.

"Yes . . . that's it. Exactly what I wanted. More. Go deeper now," Khalil hissed, growing harder as his sick fantasy was being fulfilled. "Act like you love it. Say you love it," he demanded, yanking Lyric's hair in his fist.

"I . . . I . . . love it," Lyric said weakly. Bethany licked between her legs, hardly able to breathe.

Khalil stood up and got behind Bethany, who was lapping away at Lyric's clit.

"American girls have no honor. This is what all of you like to do, huh? Fuck like dogs," he said, his accent thick as he forced his pulsing manhood deep into Bethany's dry center.

She screamed in agony at the forced intrusion. That seemed to make Khalil more excited. He pounded into her unmercifully, like a dog in heat.

The sound of sweaty skin slapping together filled the room, and the musky scent of body fluids wafted through the air. Lyric's chest heaved with a mixture of forced pleasure, embarrassment, and fear. She felt sick to her stomach, but would never dare voice her complaints.

"Act like you want it," Khalil said to Lyric. "Make this bitch work for it."

Lyric began thrusting her hips harder and faster now as Bethany sucked and put pressure on her clitoris. The drugs in Lyric's system intensified the sensations pulsing through her body, and she could feel herself nearing climax. This was not supposed to feel good. She was not a lesbian. She didn't even like girls . . . or so she thought.

Lyric groaned and panted, her body tingling everywhere. She couldn't fight the feelings anymore. The more noises she made, the harder Khalil slammed into Bethany. Lyric turned her face sideways and opened her eyes. Even Khalil's servants were turned on and touching themselves. It was one big orgy and freak show. Lyric's thighs began to tremble.

"Stop," Lyric slurred, her body so hot with lust she felt like she would explode at any moment.

"You better not stop," Khalil said cruelly yanking on Bethany's beautiful blond hair. "You. Come show her what we like," Khalil said, pointing to one of his men.

The man approached and pulled the chain connected to Bethany's neck.

"Please! Just kill me! I can't take this anymore!" she screamed.

Khalil roared with laughter. "You will take whatever I give you, *habibi*." He slapped his servant on the ass, prompting him forward. "Take her. Now."

The man used his foot to push Bethany down on her stomach. She screamed until her throat was raw. The man got behind her and began thrusting himself into her with no mercy.

Tears ran down Lyric's face at her friend's humiliation. These men were animals. She was starting to doubt if she would make it out of here alive.

"Stop. Please. Take me. Let her go," Lyric begged as the man moved in and out of Bethany like a jackhammer, all the while keeping his eyes on the prince.

"You want to take her place? What a stupid girl you are. When we took her away from you, she gave you up. She told us you would do almost anything for free drugs," Khalil said.

Then, Khalil signaled for another man to come join in on the fun with Bethany. Lyric closed her eyes. She didn't think she could watch her friend get raped again.

"Please," she whimpered. "Please let her go."

"Open your eyes and watch," Khalil growled.

Lyric refused to open her eyes.

"Open your eyes, you slut! Now!" Khalil demanded. This time he yanked Lyric off the bed by the chain. She crumpled to the floor and pretended to be hurt.

"You want to be difficult? Well, we will just fuck her until you stop being so stubborn and open your eyes," he said.

Bethany screamed out in pain. Begrudgingly, Lyric complied with the order.

Lyric couldn't take it any longer. She got up on her knees and forcefully pushed the men away from Bethany. Khalil busted out laughing.

"Leave her alone!" Lyric demanded. "Kill me, but let her go. I can handle it—all of it. You have to let her go!" she sobbed.

"I knew there was a reason I liked you," Khalil said, grabbing Lyric up from the floor and forcing his tongue into her mouth. Lyric groaned as she fought the urge to vomit. At least, the focus was off of Bethany for a while.

Khalil had his servants prepare another speedball for Lyric. This time, she didn't bother to put up a fight. She welcomed the escape. As soon as the drugs hit her central nervous system, Lyric fell back on the bed, and her eyes snapped shut involuntarily. In that moment, all of the pain she felt bubbled to the surface. She saw the faces of her mother, her sisters, and Andrew Harvey. Lyric couldn't process the noise in the room anymore; everything seemed to die down to a low roar—like a beach shore at high tide. She felt damn good. Her body and spirit seemed to detach from each other. She was drifting into a space that felt welcoming and pleasant.

"You ready for more?" Khalil's voice intruded. She felt her left butt cheek roughly slapped. She was so close to nirvana.

"More . . . I want more," Lyric groaned, longing for the peace the drugs had given her.

Chapter 15

Harmony

Harmony took a quick glance over her shoulder at her backside, and then switched angles so that she could look at her stomach. She groaned at the tiny bump that was still there after giving birth to Aubrey.

"There's no way I can go out. I look a mess," she murmured as she leaned closer to the mirror, second guessing her choice of dress.

Harmony looked over at the clock. "Shit. He's going to be here soon." She closed her eyes and leaned her head back for a few seconds. She hadn't been this nervous about a date in years.

After confronting her sister over the affair with her husband, Harmony had finally accepted Blake's dinner invitation. She told herself it was just an innocent dinner between friends—a gesture of gratitude given all he had done for her and the dance school. Harmony wasn't a two-

timer like her husband and sister. She was just
going to dinner—the only thing she expected
was a decent meal and perhaps good adult conversation. She had been feeling the effects of
being a single parent to Aubrey, running the
dance school alone, and being without Ron alto-
gether. She was lonely.

"Oh my God. I need to have on two pairs of
Spanx," she complained, turning around and
reexamining her hips in the mirror. Dressing
up was also something she hadn't done in a
while. She couldn't remember the last time she
and Ron went on a date that required a girdle.
She'd been wearing mom jeans and oversized
shirts so long that now she felt like she looked
crazy. Worry creased her brow as she pulled and
tugged at her outfit. She blew out an exasperated
breath, and her shoulders drooped. She felt
completely out of her element.

With only fifteen minutes to spare, she rushed
into the bathroom and applied a coat of deep
burgundy NYX lip cream. She hoped the look was
not too seductive. Blake was a nice man, and she
didn't want to give mixed signals. She smacked
her lips together and gave herself a once-over.
"Makeup, a form-fitting dress, and uncomfortable
heels? Harmony, what has gotten into you?" she
jokingly scolded herself in the mirror.

She looked over at the clock again. She had about ten minutes before Blake would arrive. She delved into her closet, grabbed her favorite red suede, fringed pocketbook and a pair of black, patent leather heels, and headed toward the baby's room.

"Sonia," Harmony called out. Sonia emerged from Aubrey's bedroom with her finger over her lips.

"Sorry," Harmony lowered her voice. "Just letting you know that I'm leaving. If there are any emergencies you can reach me on my cell phone," she whispered.

Sonia nodded. "I have it all under control. You look beautiful, my dear. Go and have a good time," she said, shooing her toward the front door.

Harmony smiled and rushed for the stairs just as the front doorbell rang. Her heart skipped a beat in her chest. She couldn't remember being this nervous, even during performances with her sisters.

Harmony stopped in front of the door, exhaled, and pulled the door open, a wide smile lighting her face.

Her smile was quickly replaced with a frown.

"Oh . . . Detective Simpson. I . . . didn't expect you," Harmony stumbled over her words, gen-

uinely surprised at his arrival on her doorstep.
His timing couldn't have been worse.

"Was kind of a last-minute visit," he said
sheepishly. His eyes roved over her body, taking
in her appearance. "Going out?" he asked, nodding at her outfit.

Harmony's cheeks flamed over.

"No . . . I mean . . . yes, but my friend has not
arrived yet," she replied, sweat beads forming
at her hairline. She hoped Blake was running a
little late. She did not want him to show up here
while the detective lingered in her doorway.

"What can I do for you? I'm really in a hurry,"
Harmony said, looking past the detective to
make sure she didn't miss Blake's arrival.

"Can I come in for a minute?"

Harmony looked at her watch and sighed
heavily. "Yes, but please make it quick," she
countered.

"Okay. I'll get to the point of my visit. Your
husband, Ronald . . . What was his relationship
to your mother?"

Harmony frowned. "My husband didn't have
a relationship with my mother, Detective. He
only met her once, when he accompanied me
to court when I was suing my mother and the
record label."

"The things you told me about her, her cruelty toward you and your sister as a child . . . Did you ever tell Ronald about that?" he pressed.

"Look, get to the point," Harmony shot back. "Don't play hide-the-ball here. Do you think Ron had something to do with my mother's death? Have you run out of all possible suspects?" she said sardonically.

Detective Simpson sighed. "There was a 911 call a few days before your mother was found dead. She called and said that her daughter's husband had attacked her. When we checked, you're the only one of the Love sisters that is married."

Harmony shook her head. "Impossible. She had to be speaking about someone else. Sly and Melody were damn near married as well. And Lyric had been with Rebel for a long time. If I were you, I'd check on those two characters before I'd even consider Ron a suspect in a murder," Harmony offered. The detective was grasping at straws. She couldn't believe he came all the way to her house to throw around crazy theories about her husband.

"Well, the information I have may point to your husband," Detective Simpson said flatly.

Harmony waved her hand dismissively. "There would be no reason for Ron to attack my mother, Detective. I would bet my life on that."

"Even if he found out that your mother was the reason his parents got divorced twenty years ago?"

Harmony stumbled. Her pocketbook slid off of her shoulder, and she didn't bother to grab it. "What?" she asked breathlessly.

"Your mother, who we now know had a history of being a mistress to many men, including Arnold Bridges—your husband's father. After your in-laws went through their messy divorce, your husband, Ronald Bridges, started on his path to booze and drugs, which eventually ruined his acting career. Oh, I can assure you that your husband hated Ava Love. In fact, he paid her several visits, I suspect, to let her know just how much."

Harmony flopped backward onto the couch. She was utterly flabbergasted.

"That's impossible. Ron hardly went into the city. If he wasn't at the dance school, he was at his NA meetings. . . ." Harmony trailed off. How stupid she had been to believe him.

"So you really couldn't account for all of his time, then? Is it possible that he told you he was at meetings, but he really snuck off into the city to take care of the woman he hated with a passion?"

Harmony shook her head slowly. She felt like a bucket of cold water had just been dumped over her head. Why hadn't Ron ever mentioned that Ava had been his father's old mistress? How had the detective even figured that out?

"You're wrong. That story . . . it . . . It just doesn't make sense."

"When you took him with you to court and he saw your mother for the first time . . . maybe he didn't know until then," Detective Simpson opined.

"He would've said something. We are . . . um . . . were best friends. He would've told me," Harmony said confidently. She looked down at her hands and sighed.

"Ron? Let's go. The court hearing is over." Harmony shook Ron's shoulders and snapped him out of a trance.

"What is it?" she asked, noticing that his jaw rocked as he stared at Ava and Murray with fire flashing in his eyes.

"I just hate what she's putting you through," Ron gritted, his eyes hooded.

"Oh, baby, don't worry about that. She'll get what's coming to her. Don't let her get to you.

I learned a long time ago not to let my mother get into my head too deep. It'll consume you."

"It's a little too late for that," he grumbled. *"She's all up in my head, and I'll never forget her now that I know exactly who she is."*

"I think we need to speak to Ron. Is he home?" Detective Simpson asked, looking around. Harmony blinked a few times, snapping out of her trance.

Before she could open her mouth to answer the detective's question, the doorbell rang. Her stomach immediately cramped up. She had forgotten about her date with Blake just that quickly. Harmony felt as if her feet had grown roots.

"Would you like me to open the door?" Detective Simpson asked, puzzled.

Harmony closed her eyes and wished that she was anywhere but here. No matter how hard she tried to be happy, Ava had a way of ruining everything. Even from beyond the grave.

Chapter 16

Melody

Melody held the headphones that covered her ears and let the music move through her. She had spent hours writing a new song on the loose sheets of paper scattered on the table; the lyrics poured onto the pages as if divinely inspired. She had finally returned to the studio after her three-month sabbatical. Music was the only thing she had left. It was her constant, most reliable companion.

Melody kept her eyes closed and swayed to the tune. The music soothed the aching spots in her heart. She remembered her mother saying to her once, *"When you can't find your voice, be quiet and listen to your heart."* Melody wanted to listen to her heart at the moment.

When she arrived at the studio, it was brimming with activity. Sound technicians and personal producers were all abuzz at her arrival.

But she dismissed them all. She was the boss, and she needed complete control of her environment when she was in her creative moment. It was a good thing that she owned the entire building and could empty it with a snap of her manicured fingers.

Melody threw her head back and swayed slightly. She hummed lightly, waiting for her heartbeat to fall in line with the music.

Melody knew that the song she had just scribbled down, just like all the rest, would miraculously turn her feelings into a beautiful, soul-stirring, chart-topping hit.

Today, she woke up feeling all alone and missing her sisters. She was so depressed she briefly contemplated ending her life. But, then, as if it were fate, Melody heard Sista Love's first hit play on the radio. She remembered the day she sat down with Harmony and Lyric to write the words to the song. She remembered how so many times their hit, "Liar Liar," had brought them back together after arguments. Melody remembered that it was always the music that had saved her when all else failed.

Suddenly, an abrupt banging sound startled her. Her eyes popped open, and the music faded. The heat from her anger rose from her feet to her face. Her nostrils flared at the disruption—she felt like someone had dragged the record player needle across her favorite old-school LP.

She snatched the headphones from her ears and glared through the glass. Gary waved at her. She sighed heavily, the vein at the right side of her temple pulsing fiercely.

Melody hung the headphones on the hook next to her and stormed out of the booth.

"Gar—" she started.

"Listen, Mel, we ain't got no time to talk. I need you to see something," Gary huffed, grabbing her arm and yanking her behind him.

"What the hell is going on?" she said, swatting at his hands. Her legs moved faster than her brain could register the information.

"Just be quiet and wait," Gary said, his voice a bit more frantic than Melody was comfortable with.

They approached the door that led to her office conference room. He punched in the passcode, which only he and Melody knew, and pulled her inside.

"Sit," he demanded. He walked around the long, mahogany table and retrieved the remote control for the large, flat-screen television mounted on the wall.

"Gary, this better be good," Melody said, exasperated.

"Yes, yes, I know. You haven't been in the mood to sing or dance or perform, and you don't want anyone bothering you and interrupting your flow. And you have a lot of shit on your mind and blah blah blah. I heard it all before. Listen, if this shit wasn't important, I wouldn't be bothering you," he insisted. "Now, sit back and watch."

He powered on the television, turned to Channel 52, and eased back into one of the conference chairs.

"You brought me here to watch the news?" Melody asked, shifting her eyes between the screen and Gary.

"No . . . It's a damn press conference. Now, watch it, please. You'll have to be ready to deal with this. I'm sure there will be a shit storm coming your way."

"What do you mean?" she asked suspiciously.

"Watch, Melody," Gary reprimanded, turning up the volume.

Melody recognized Sly's public relations representative, Maura, speaking at the podium. Melody's heart hammered against her chest, and her fingertips felt numb. Gary reached out and grabbed Melody's hand for support.

"As many of you know, I am Maura Androse, PR representative for Diamond Records. It

is with profound sadness that I share with all of you the great loss suffered by Diamond Records owner, Stephan 'Sly' Carlisle and his fiancée and Diamond Records recording artist, Terikka Felix. Last night, while leaving a late-night studio session, Terikka was attacked by a crazed fan. The man, who police are still working to identify, slipped past security and physically assaulted Terikka. The altercation resulted in her being tackled to the ground."

A collective round of gasps rose and fell over the crowd of reporters.

"Terikka was rushed to the hospital, with Sly by her side. The couple were expecting their first child at the time of the incident. Unfortunately, we are sad to report that the unborn child was lost. Sly, Terikka, and the entire Diamond Records family is grieving at this time. We all ask that you keep Sly and Terikka in your prayers and respect their requests for privacy during this very difficult time. As always, at Diamond Records, we operate as a family. As such, we will remain by their side and pro-vide them with all of the support they need. I will take a few questions from the media at this time."

"Maura! Maura!" several reporters screamed at once. Maura pointed to a short woman in the front holding an NBC News microphone.

"*We at NBC would like to extend our heartfelt condolences to Sly and Terikka. Do you know what provoked the violence against Terikka?*" *the reporter asked.*

"*All we know is what was in the police report. Terikka was alone at the studio with her security and management team. She left the midtown Manhattan building at 11:30 p.m. When she stepped outside of the building, an unidentified man charged into her, knocking her to the ground on her stomach. Terikka's security team physically detained the man until the police arrived. The report did not specify if any words were exchanged during the incident. Several witness accounts claimed that the assailant was screaming insults at Terikka—specifically regarding her relationship with Sly. I cannot comment on why it happened or what exactly provoked this man to carry out such a heinous act,*" *Maura answered carefully.*

"*Is it true that several of Melody Love's fans have expressed their anger over news of the relationship between Sly and Terikka and the birth announcement?*" *another reporter shouted.*

"*We are not speculating on why this assault occurred. We want to focus on supporting the grieving parents and helping them heal.*

This press conference was simply to announce that the Diamond Records family is asking for respect and privacy at this time. I have no information regarding the perpetrator, his affiliations, or his motives. Thank you for your time," Maura said, stepping down from the podium and quickly exiting the room.

"Enough," Melody said, her voice shaking. Gary quickly aimed the remote at the television to turn it off.

Melody closed her eyes and inhaled deeply. It was one thing to hate Sly and Terikka for what they'd done, but it was an entirely different thing to think about a baby dying. Melody shuddered and lowered her face into her hands. Once, in anger, she had wished for something like this to happen . . .

Melody stared from behind her dark shades and observed the neighborhood from her passenger-side window. Birds chirped from the trees in the yard, and the bright August sun blazed bright in the sky. The beautiful stone townhome in Park Slope was a place she'd visited together with Sly; some of their best lovemaking sessions had occurred there.

He was living here with that bitch now, playing house.

"Are you all right? We should just drive away. This shit ain't good for you," Gary said seriously.

"What do you think, Gary? I am a wealthy, multitalented, platinum-recording artist that could probably have any man that I want; yet, I am sitting outside of my ex-boyfriend's house like a stalker feeling like my world should end right this second," Melody said despondently.

Gary let out a long sigh.

"You know that I'm here for you, Mel. You're right; you can have any man that you want. So let's go home and work on a list. I bet you my list will be longer than yours," he said, trying to lighten the atmosphere.

"I'm not leaving until I see them. I want to see their backstabbing, two-timing faces. I want to see her carrying a baby that belongs to my man, when it should belong to me," Melody grinded her teeth as she stared out of the windshield.

"Mel . . . c'mon, it's not worth it," Gary replied, patting her arm affectionately.

"You don't know what it's worth to me. I gave that man the best years of my life," Melody said bitterly, fighting the tears that were stinging her eyes. She didn't know why she felt so emotionally drained. Sly had moved on. But when news of the baby emerged, it had crushed her soul. She was green with envy. That baby should have been hers.

"I made a lot of sacrifices to be with Sly," Melody reflected. "He was already established and successful when I met him. He was the king in the music industry, and he was worshipped for it. Me, I was just one-third of a struggling girl group. My sisters and I were trying to catch a break to make it to the next level. We worked every day to keep the little momentum we had. When I met Sly, I fell in love with him immediately—his energy, the way people flocked to him, and the complete attention he showed me was overwhelming. He wined and dined me. Took me places I'd never seen, bought me things I'd never dreamed of owning. And in return, I gave him my all. My music, my heart—my undying loyalty and love."

"I know the story. I was there, girl. You can't dwell on the past anymore. This . . . what you're doing . . . It ain't healthy," Gary said, pointing to the house. "It's called self-torture. You are hurting yourself just by being here."

"I thought we would be together forever. Over the years, however, I learned the hard way that he was a first-rate con artist—a deceitful liar. No better than any other man. A

liar, a cheater, a thief of hearts. But I wanted
to be with him so badly, I forgave him for his
sins. Over and over . . . until there was nothing
left of me, and everything left for him," she
said, sobbing into her sleeve.

Gary was silent. What could he say to her
after she'd just bared her soul?

Silence fell between them. Suddenly, Melody
sat upright in her seat. The front door swung
open, and Terikka stepped out.

Sweat beads cropped up on Melody's forehead, and her legs bounced with nervousness.

Terikka seemed to be glowing. Her hair was
pulled back into a neat ponytail, and her face
had spread slightly from the weight gain of
the pregnancy, but it seemed to enhance, not
detract, from her beauty.

Melody bit down on her bottom lip. Sly
stepped out and smiled adoringly at his new
love interest. He wore a smile that Melody
hadn't seen in years. It was that true bliss look
that he'd displayed with her in the beginning
stage of their relationship.

He seemed to be genuinely happy. She hated
to imagine that Terikka, an upstart singer, had
captured Sly's heart. It was easier for her to
think of the other woman as a piece of meat—a
sexual tryst that would surely end when the

passion died down. From the looks of it, Sly was in love with Terikka.

"Mel, why don't we just leave? Stop torturing yourself here," Gary pleaded with her. Melody ignored her friend, intent on watching the couple.

Sly put his hand on the small of Terikka's back and helped her into their waiting car. Melody felt the same gnawing jealously she'd felt the first time she'd seen Harmony and Ron together at her mother's funeral.

"She's a problem that I really want to disappear," Melody said stiffly. Gary looked at her in confusion.

"Are you sure about that? I mean, he's the one that needs his ass kicked. He should've been loyal and faithful to you. We already know these hoes ain't loyal," Gary said evenly.

"Did you hear what I said?" Melody asked sharply. "I wish she and that bastard baby of hers would disappear. They can both die for all I care."

Gary put up his hands to his forehead like Melody had hit him over the head with a hard object. He was good at theatrical displays in times of intense emotional situations.

"Wishing for someone to die is a bit over top, don't you think?" he asked.

"*My wishes never come true, anyway,*" Melody said wistfully.

"Sometimes it takes the right people around you to make things happen," Gary said abstractedly. "Now, I take it you've seen enough and are ready to go home?"

This mission had been too top secret to have one of Melody's regular drivers. Gary started the ignition and moved the car to take them home. The two of them never spoke about the incident again.

"I didn't really want the baby to die," Melody said, her voice barely above a whisper. "I was angry at the time. I felt betrayed and hurt when I said it, but I wouldn't really want something like this to happen."

Gary sucked his teeth and waved his hand at her. "Sly and Terikka lost their baby, and somehow, you feel sorry for them? How is that your fault? It was just a crazed fan. They are both grown adults, and they lied to you. He's a two-timer, Melody. Remember, he cheated on you. And let's not fucking forget that they publicly humiliated you. They could've just let the world see her belly through paparazzi pictures. They didn't have to make their grand announcement at a show that aired around the world. They brought the negative attention to themselves and their unborn child. Sly wanted you to feel hurt. And you know what? All of those things are choices that *he* made on his own. You are not responsible for what the universe had in store for his ass. He should know that everything we do comes back to us . . . It's called karma. Oh, yes, baby girl, I'm learning that we all better watch out, because karma is one powerful, vindictive, angry bitch. Trust me, you made your wish, and now it has come true. Don't look a gift horse in the mouth. Sly and Terikka just got what was coming to them." Gary was so riled up his face was turning red.

Melody saw something in his eyes that unsettled her. Did he actually just say that the baby dying was a gift from God?

The guilt of wishing harm on the unborn child made Melody sick to her stomach. She bolted up from her chair and rushed to the nearest restroom, hand over her mouth.

Melody splashed water on her face, still shaky from vomiting. She looked up at herself in the bathroom mirror and sighed. What happened to Terikka was weighing on her mind. Then she replayed in her mind some things Gary had said to her.

"Trust me, you made your wish, and now it has come true. Don't look a gift horse in the mouth. Sly and Terikka just got what was coming to them. I just hate a greedy-ass bitch. There is a special place in hell for all of them, if you ask me. If I could wipe them all off the face of the earth, I sure would. Especially to protect you."

A fine sheen of sweat blanketed Melody's forehead now. She had wished Ava dead for blackmailing her, and suddenly, Ava was dead. She wished Terikka and Sly's baby dead, and suddenly, the baby was dead.

Suddenly Melody felt sick again. She raced back over to the toilet to throw up again. It couldn't all be a coincidence. Melody was powerful, but she wasn't God.

Chapter 17

Lyric

Lyric sat on the gold toilet seat in Khalil's bathroom with a phlebotomy rubber tied around her arm. She slapped the center of her arm, vigorously searching for a ripe vein to hit.

She was hooked on heroin again. So hooked that she couldn't properly function without it. So hooked that she was more terrified of leaving Khalil and not having access to his drugs than she was of any abuses inflicted on her during her stay at his house of horrors.

Lyric had stopped begging to leave. With her addiction growing more insatiable each day, she accepted that life with heroin was the only way she could live. She was trapped in this gilded cage, but there were worse places she could be—like on the streets with no drugs.

Khalil told her to shoot speedballs directly into her arm. He said it would be the best high of her life. He was right.

She slapped her arm again, groaning when she didn't get a ripe vein right away. She hated that her veins took so long to find now. She knew it was because she had blown so many of them out by her repeated needle use.

Loud banging on the door caused Lyric to jump. The needle scratched her arm, causing her to bleed.

"What?" she demanded. Lyric knew that Khalil didn't play the locked doors game. "I'm coming," she yelled, just as Khalil's little pain-in-the-ass servant opened the door with a key.

"Damn," Lyric cursed. Now that Lyric was chained to her addiction, he no longer kept her in actual chains.

She sniffled back the snot threatening to leak from her nostrils; it was an early sign that she was dope sick. She needed another hit soon.

"Prince Aziz is ready for you to join him," the man said, looming darkly over her, like a personal Grim Reaper.

"I need this hit," Lyric said, backhanding the mucus from her nostrils. "Tell him I'll do whatever he wants once I get right."

The man shook his head. "He is not in a very good mood today."

A flash of panic flared in Lyric's chest. She knew what those words meant. She could tell by the look on the servant's face that he was serious. Every second of delay would give Prince Khalil Aziz more time to think of creative ways to torture her.

Lyric looked down at her syringe.

"Help me," she implored. The man looked over his shoulder first, and then back at her, torn between his boss's command and Lyric's request.

"If he gets mad, I'll say it was my fault. I'll say I demanded that you do this for me first." She quickly tied her arm, and luckily, her veins were a little more cooperative this time.

The man felt around her arm and nodded. He picked up the needle and with shaking hands eased the drugs into her bloodstream.

Lyric closed her eyes and let out a tiny sigh. Immediately, her body relaxed against the toilet seat. Her head dropped to her chin, and she almost slid down to the floor. The man caught her under her arms and pulled her upright. Lyric laughed. She needed to be in this condition to deal with Khalil. He had done many cruel things to her since she'd arrived at his "pleasure palace." Lyric knew it wouldn't be over until the prince was tired of toying with her. Frankly, she had mixed feelings about leaving now. As much as she hated her gilded cage existence, she didn't think she could live again on the outside either. A world without drugs was no place for her.

"Do I have to call for her again?" Khalil barked.

"Stop your bitching. I'm coming, you spoiled-ass prince," Lyric grumbled, the drugs giving her a false sense of bravado.

Khalil stomped into the bathroom and dragged Lyric by her hair.

"Get her ready," he said, pushing Lyric toward his female helpers.

"Get off of me. I can walk," Lyric snapped, following the women out of Khalil's sex chamber to the Turkish-style bathing area.

The women led her to a huge, gold-trimmed sunken bathtub scented with lavender oils. She was surrounded by beautiful women, some old, some young.

They stripped the clothing from her body and helped her into the steaming aromatic water.

"These flowers will clean you to Prince Aziz's approval. It makes you tight and ready," one of the girls said.

"Ready for what?" She tried to cover her body with her hands, but the women simply brushed her hands away. For the first time, she noticed that her body was covered in small bruises. She inhaled deeply and exhaled. She leaned back against a soft bath pillow and closed her eyes, pretending she was somewhere else. Like on tour with her sisters, performing in a sold-out arena.

"Please, let us clean. We no hurt, we help," a beautiful raven-haired girl no older than sixteen said softly in broken English. An older woman smacked the girl across the mouth, ordering her to stay quiet.

The women lathered her skin and hair until every inch of her body had been cleansed. After her bath, Lyric was wrapped in a plush, white towel and helped out of the bathtub and led to a small divan bed.

A bowl of hot wax was placed on a table nearby to remove the excess hair on her body.

"No, I'm good. You don't need to do that to me," Lyric swatted at their hands as they pulled the towel away from her body, leaving her naked.

"Prince Aziz asked that you be cleaned," the head female servant explained as she rubbed Lyric's skin completely dry. "If you resist, there will be consequences," she warned.

"Oh, I get it. He brought you all over here from another country, and if you don't do what he says, he will send you back," Lyric said, looking at the faces of the women to see if she was correct. When none of them responded, she sighed and leaned back as they poured hot wax down her legs and up over her pubic bone.

Expensive artwork decorated the walls, and racks of beautiful dresses lay draped over the furniture. Neat rows of beautiful gold and diamond jewelry were displayed in cases. Salon chairs with vanity mirrors were lined up on the side of the room, and counters were covered with high-end cosmetics.

The raven-haired girl spread wax on her upper lip.

"How about you show me how to get out of here, and I'll send someone to rescue you?" Lyric whispered.

"Sorry, miss. He will send me back," the girl said, shaking her head. Her eyes were wide with fear. "Please, we have to follow Prince's orders."

"Look, my sister has a lot of money. If you help me get out of here, I promise I'll save all of you from this bullshit servitude," Lyric urged.

The girl put her finger to her lips and moved on to Lyric's eyebrows. "You must be perfect for the prince," the girl said with a sad smile. There was no light in her eyes, just bleak acceptance.

Lyric decided to leave the issue alone. She didn't want the girl to get in trouble. She knew what sort of punishment Prince Khalil could exact on a pretty girl like this one.

The young girl led her over to a beautiful silver and gold vanity chair. A pretty turquoise bandage dress hung on a rack next to the chair. Lyric recognized the design as a Hervé Leger—

his brand was unmistakable. A pair of beautiful beaded pumps and several pieces of diamond jewelry lay on the glass tabletop.

"Prince Aziz chose this for you," the head servant informed her. In other words, she had no say in the matter.

"Why do I need to be dressed up? Are we going out?" she asked, eager for information.

A woman rushed over, holding out a white lace La Perla thong for her to step into. Another snapped on a matching bra. Moisturizer was applied to Lyric's legs, arms, and back before the designer dress was pulled over her head. Jewelry and shoes were added, completing the outfit.

Lyric was pulled into the chair. Her hair was brushed and pinned into an elegant side bun. They worked together to apply a flawless face of makeup. Lyric didn't recognize herself when they were done. She hadn't looked so beautiful since the last award show she attended as part of Sista Love. She tilted her head to the side as she stared at her reflection in the mirror. Why did it take her being held captive by a sadistic billionaire for her to feel like herself again? To feel like a star?

"They are ready for you," the girl smiled faintly at Lyric.

"Please, at least tell me what to expect," Lyric implored.

The girl looked around nervously, but just as she was about to say something, two of Khalil's men walked into the room. The girl quickly stepped aside and lowered her head.

Lyric was led down a set of stairs and through a series of long hallways to a room decorated in black and red. It looked like the devil's own lair. Goose bumps cropped up all over her body. Heart pounding, she walked slowly inside, balancing on the silver stilettos she'd been forced to wear. The tight-fitting dress felt like it was choking off her circulation, and the pins in her hair felt like knives digging into her scalp.

She looked around in disgust at the crowd of strange partygoers that were mingling about the room. This crowd wasn't like the rowdy, hip-hop crowd that was gathered the first night Lyric and Bethany arrived. Instead, Lyric noticed men with dark heads of hair, long beards, and white head coverings accented with two or three thick black bands at the top, holding the material in place.

Sheikhs? Princes? Is this some sort of royal gathering?

She watched as the beautiful women, sprinkled around the room, were being grabbed and groped by the men. Lyric learned that these superrich men were some of the freakiest and nastiest bastards when it came to sex. They had lots of money and deemed normal sex as a boring, low-class activity. Most of them were unhappily married to women who only had intercourse with them to create heirs.

The women in attendance tonight were primarily of Eastern European descent, with the exception of two women who looked East African. The women were highly trained, pretending to be interested in their male companions, sitting in their laps and giggling at their jokes. They wore vacant expressions, clearly under the influence of strong narcotics.

Music played lightly in the background. It wasn't the rap music Khalil usually played but light, airy, string music, like in Bollywood films. The one thing this gathering had in common with Khalil's hip-hop party was that there was plenty of drugs and liquor to go around.

Lyric hesitated when she noticed that men and women were engaged in different sexual acts on the far side of the room. She had walked into a drug-filled orgy. Lyric hadn't been a fan of most of Khalil's proclivities, but with his increasing aggression and her need for drugs, she had gone along with it.

"The singing beauty has arrived," Khalil said as Lyric was presented at his side. The three men standing near him eyed her hungrily.

"These are my friends. They've been waiting to meet you."

Lyric was burning up inside. Her high was wearing off, and she needed another hit soon if she hoped to make it through the evening's "entertainment."

"She's the one I told you about. Better than any I've had. It's like she's been seasoned to do this," Khalil announced to the men. "She's a hot piece of ass," he continued, forcing Lyric to spin around and display her every angle.

Her stomach flipped. She had to will herself not to slap and spit on him. One of the older men approached and smiled lasciviously.

"Does she like *everything?*" he asked, rubbing his hands together.

Lyric's nostrils flared; she quickly swallowed her words of protest.

"She's American, so what do you think? They love to be fucked like animals. Besides, she has no say in the matter. Have her any way you like, my friend," Khalil said, laughing.

Lyric's chest heaved now. She shot Khalil a dirty look and folded her arms over her chest. She had been forced to do a lot of things she wasn't proud of . . . but this . . . This pushed her to her limits.

"Fuck all of you," she spat, kicking off her heels, preparing to storm away. She didn't even know her way to the front door, but she knew she wasn't going to stand for being gang-raped at a party.

The three men let out a collective gasp at her defiance. Khalil's eyes hooded over, and his jaw rocked.

"Don't try to embarrass me or I'll see to it that your entire family is wiped off the face of the earth," Khalil growled in her ear. He pulled a small packet out of his pocket and forced it into her hand.

"Go get yourself together. But first, apologize to my friends," he ordered.

Lyric swallowed hard. "Don't mind me. I'm just a bit edgy tonight. I apologize," she said, bowing at the waist, a smile pasted on her face. Lyric hated herself, but she hated Khalil even more for humiliating her so.

"She will return," Khalil said, a hint of urgency in his voice. "I apologize for the delay."

He grabbed Lyric's arm and dragged her to a corner in the room. Lyric counted each step as if it were her last. Twenty-two steps and she was shooting up again. That was all it took for her to transform into a helpless female.

Khalil led her to a small pile of pillows behind a long black curtain. Incense was burning, and several candles were lit nearby. Lyric could hear the men talking about her like she was their new favorite sweet.

Khalil pushed her down onto the pillows. "This is why you're here," he said matter-of-factly. "For my entertainment and for my friends' entertainment. You are a professional entertainer, are you not?" he joked.

"I need another hit," Lyric whimpered, although she was as high as a kite.

Khalil snapped his fingers, and his people rushed in. One held her down while the other removed her clothes. Lyric tried to fight, but she was no match against their strength.

"Stop!" Lyric cried out. That just seemed to turn her abusers on more. The first man dropped down in front of her and forced her legs apart with his knee. Lyric closed her eyes, but she could feel his weight on her chest as he forced himself into her dry vagina.

Her mind raced back to the past, when she was just thirteen years old. She could see, hear, and feel Andrew Harvey touching her. . . .

"Shhh. Let me take care of you," he whispered, moving his mouth from hers and trailing his

tongue down her neck. She was shivering all over her body. This wasn't the first time he had done this to her, but it felt just as disgusting as before.

"This is the deal that your mother agreed to—this is how you and your sisters became famous," Andrew Harvey had told her while he used his right hand to loosen the string at the back of her bikini top. "If you want me to stop, you'll have to explain to Ava why you said no to the deal of a lifetime," he warned.

"Please," Lyric cried, pitifully. Her teeth chattered in her mouth. "I'm only a kid," she whined. "I'm just fourteen." She sobbed as he licked down her neck to her newly budding breasts. Lyric felt like roaches were crawling on her. Something began to tingle in her head. She saw a rainbow of colors flash before her eyes. She tried again to fight him off. "Get off me," she groaned, weakly punching at the bald spot in the middle of his head.

"I'm a kid," she whimpered. Her speech began to slur. "I'm just a kid. I don't want to do this."

"I'm going to make you a woman," Andrew Harvey breathed into her ear. He pressed his protruding stomach against her body, and roughly worked his fingers into her bikini bottoms. Lyric's body went partially limp. She

*could feel him exploring her with his fingers,
but she could no longer fight him off.*

*"I'm going to give you something to relax a bit,
baby girl," he whispered hotly in her ear.*

*She was escaping. Flying up into the sky,
away from herself, away from this world.*

*Andrew Harvey carried her over to the bed
and threw her down. Lyric smiled lazily, and
her head rocked from side to side. He licked his
lips hungrily.*

"Yes. After tonight, you'll be a woman."

"Don't I turn you on, American whore?" one
of Khalil's guests growled and slapped Lyric's
cheek, bringing her back to reality. "Now, open
up like the nasty bitch that you are." The man
didn't even last five minutes before he scrambled to his feet, pulling himself out quickly, only
to waste his body fluids on her.

Lyric flailed and kicked until she grew tired.
She was numb. She heard the excitement in the
voices of the men around her. One by one, they
took turns defiling her body. They seemed to
derive great pleasure from slapping her in the
face. She could feel her left eye swelling, and her
nose trickled blood.

"Get into it, you bitch!" one of the men jeered.

Tears flowed from her eyes. The men turned her over and upside down. Lyric thought about Rebel. He had betrayed her, let her to fall prey to this lifestyle. The first night after she'd found him with her friend, he had tried to call her a few times. She wondered if he was still looking for her or if he had given up on her by now.

Lyric hollered as one of the men plunged himself deep into her backside. She was in too much pain to even notice that Khalil had allowed several more men and a few women to partake in this sick gathering.

Lyric vowed that if she ever made it out of this prison alive, she would see that he paid the ultimate price for her humiliation and degradation. Death had been the fate of the last man that had abused her. This time would be no different.

Chapter 18

Harmony

Harmony smoothed her dress down over her hips and exhaled. She was going to try this again. This time, without distractions. Her first date with Blake had been interrupted by a visit from Detective Simpson. After she learned that Ron had a special connection to her mother and might have motive to murder her, Harmony had asked Blake for a rain check on their date.

Blake had been sweet and understanding. He ordered food for her and offered to keep her company at home instead. Harmony politely declined, her mind too muddled to be of any benefit for polite company.

Tonight she had a chance to live a little. Harmony said a quick prayer that everything would go well before she pulled open the door to let Blake inside.

"Wow," Blake gasped, an appreciative grin on his lips.

Harmony's heartbeat sped up. Damn! He looked fine.

"You look amazing," Blake said, staring like he never wanted to take eyes off of her. Harmony's cheeks went rosy, and she giggled. It was good to feel desirable again.

"Why, thank you, sir," she said, batting her long eyelashes. "You don't look too shabby yourself."

"I clean up nicely," he joked, rubbing his goatee and winking. Harmony laughed. She felt completely at ease with him. No pretenses or forced smiles.

"I realize that, aside from the five minutes that we saw each other during our first failed date night, you've only ever seen me wet or dirty. And you probably didn't even know I had this much hair," she said, shaking her head to imitate a dramatic model movement. Her newly coiled ringlets bounced flatteringly around her face.

"You could wear a brown paper bag and I'd still notice you in a crowded room. You think a pair of sweats or uncombed hair would throw me off?" Blake asked, taking in another eyeful of Harmony's sexy figure as he ushered her to his car.

"You know all of the right things to say, huh?" she laughed, swatting his arm playfully.

Blake walked around to the passenger-side door of the white Mercedes S550 and held the door open for her.

"Wow. She's a beauty. I had no idea firemen drove these types of cars," Harmony said glibly as she slid into the buttery soft tan leather seat.

"What type of car did you expect me to drive?" he replied, chuckling. "Honda Civic? Jeep Cherokee? Toyota Camry?"

Harmony shrugged, getting comfortable in the seat. "I was just kidding, you know."

"Well, that'll teach you never to judge a man by his car or his job," Blake winked. Harmony shifted in her seat. Blake made her insides feel warm.

"I've got a special night planned for us," he announced as he began to reverse out of the driveway.

Loud banging on passenger-side window startled them both. Blake slammed on this brakes.

"What the hell!" Harmony shouted, clutching her chest in fear.

"Harmony, it's me, Rebel." Harmony scowled and pursed her lips. Blake lowered the window on her side.

"Rebel? What the hell are you doing at my house?" she asked through clenched teeth.

"I'm really sorry for intruding on you like this, but I need to talk to you." Rebel shot Blake a look. "In private."

Harmony looked over at Blake. His eyebrows were raised in inquiry.

"I'm on my way out, Rebel," Harmony said flatly.

"It's about Lyric."

"I don't want to hear anything about my sisters right now. And aren't you the one who *abandoned* my sister? Why do you care about her so much now?" Harmony asked suspiciously.

Rebel sighed and shook his head.

"Look, I know everyone is upset with me, but I did that for her own good. I was, and probably still am, no good for Lyric, but that doesn't change the fact that I love her more than any other girl I've ever been with," Rebel said sincerely. Harmony's stony expression seemed to ease a bit.

"I found out she's in real trouble, Harmony. Like the kind of trouble that she might not make it out of without your help," he said, urgency underlying his words.

Harmony swallowed hard and fell silent for a few seconds. Blake touched her hand.

"Go ahead. It sounds serious. Find out what's going on with your sister. I can wait," he said, smiling.

Harmony glanced into Blake's kind eyes. She kissed him on the cheek. "Thank you," she said, before she stepped out of the car.

She followed Rebel to the sidewalk and folded her arms across her chest expectantly.

"I have proof that Lyric has been pulled into a sex ring. I've heard stories about this dude, and he's bad news. Khalil is a wannabe rapper. Originally from the Middle East. He keeps girls drugged in his house and does all sorts of sick shit to them," Rebel said, worry etched into his face.

Harmony blinked a few times, unable to comprehend. "How would Lyric get caught up in something like that? And how do you know she's even with this Khalil person?"

Rebel looked down, unable to look Harmony in the eyes. "I walked in one of my friend's cribs, and I found my boys Drew, Mark, Darren, and Rick all huddled around a laptop watching something. They were so engrossed in the screen that none of them heard me come in. They were too busy making catcalls and touching themselves, I guess. Naturally, I wanted a good look too. I cleared my throat and stepped to them and asked what's good. At first, they tried to hide the screen from me. I got suspicious and asked them to step aside and—"

"*And?*" Harmony pressed, sweat running down her back.

"At first, they argued with each other over who was to blame for allowing me inside. They were guilty and trying to cover their tracks," Rebel gritted, emotion playing out on his face.

"What were they watching, Rebel? Get to the point, for God's sake," Harmony snapped.

Rebel sighed heavily and pulled out his iPhone. "Harmony, it's not easy to watch," he warned.

Harmony's heart was pumping so hard she felt like someone had reached inside her chest and gripped it tightly.

"Play it," she said in a low whisper, barely able to find her voice.

Rebel pressed PLAY on the video, and a grainy image appeared.

"From what I was told, this video was shot at one of this dude's many properties. Few people know where it is," Rebel explained.

Harmony's eyes widened when a clear shot of Lyric's face flashed across the screen. Harmony clasped her hand over her mouth to stifle the scream she wanted so badly to let out. The vein at her temple began throbbing, and her legs suddenly felt too weak to stand.

"What the . . ." Harmony was at a loss for words. She wouldn't take her eyes off the screen. She bit the inside of her mouth until she tasted her own blood. Six men were taking turns raping her sister.

Rebel walked away while Harmony watched the video. His fists clenched and unclenched as he paced on the sidewalk.

"Is that a . . ." Harmony squinted.

"Yeah, she has a fucking black eye," Rebel said through his teeth.

"Word on the street is that she's been held there for over three months now. They are saying he is keeping her so high that she probably doesn't even realize what is going on," Rebel shared.

"Where is this place? Please tell me you know something more!" Harmony said, her voice rising with urgency.

"I'm still working on finding that out. I haven't gone to the police yet, because that might make things more difficult for Lyric. I thought maybe your other sister could—"

"She won't help us. I don't even speak to her," Harmony interjected. She started pacing too, her insides were churning.

"I'm going to try to save her, Harmony. I heard this punk prince frequents a club in the city on Wednesday nights. I plan to pay him a visit. Only thing is, he rolls with a tight band of security, so if you're not a hot woman, you're not getting near him. That's why I came to you. I was thinking that maybe your sister or one of her dancers . . . We need someone to get close to Khalil. We need someone to help us from the inside," Rebel proposed.

Blake approached them cautiously.

"Everything all right here?" Blake asked with a look of concern in his eyes.

"You should leave. This doesn't concern you," Harmony snapped. Upset, she pushed past him and headed toward her house. She had to change her clothing and come up with a plan to save her sister.

Blake spun around, stunned by her cold dismissal.

Harmony glanced over her shoulder and could see the disappointment on Blake's face. She felt terrible that she had stood him up again, but her sister's situation was dire and required her immediate attention.

Blake snagged Rebel's arm before he could follow her inside.

"What's going on? How can I help?" Blake demanded.

"It's her sister. She's in deep trouble right now, and we're going to have to come up with a plan to save her. They're pretty close. Thanks for your

help, man, but we have to figure this out on our
own. I appreciate the offer though," Rebel said
before he followed Harmony inside.

Harmony had failed Lyric once—when she let
Ava practically sell her sister to Andrew Harvey
just to get Sista Love a record deal. Harmony
closed her eyes and remembered how powerless
she felt that day and how much of a disappointment she had been to herself and her sister.

*"We got a deal. We finally got a deal," Harmony
and her sisters squealed in excitement.*

*"Lyric, baby," Ava had interrupted their little
party, "Mr. Harvey wants to show you something in his office. He sees something special in
you," Ava said, struggling with her words. Ava
looked at her youngest daughter with a strange
expression on her face.*

Lyric's eyebrows shot up in surprise. "Me?"

*Almost at the same time, all of the girls turned
and looked at Andrew Harvey, and then back
at Ava.*

"Go on," Ava encouraged, her hands shaking.

*"Can I go with her?" Harmony asked, sud-
denly fearful for her little sister. She had always
taken care of Lyric, and she didn't trust her
mother's plans.*

"He asked to see Lyric. Alone," Ava repeated firmly. "Now go," she hissed.

Harmony watched Lyric walk gingerly toward Andrew Harvey. He put his hand on Lyric's shoulder and welcomed her with a quick squeeze. "This won't take long," he assured. "You're a very special girl. I could see that the minute I laid eyes on you. You're a star."

Lyric looked at Harmony, terror dancing in her eyes. Harmony turned toward Ava, a plea on her lips. There was a clarity in her mother's eyes that had not been there before. A cold calculation

When Andrew Harvey's office door opened minutes later, Harmony saw her sister emerge, eyes vacant and lifeless. She moved like a robot, stiff and with precise movements. Gone was the lighthearted child with a gleam in her eye and bounce in her step.

"Lyric?" Harmony embraced her sister. "Are you okay?" she whispered. Lyric didn't answer; instead, she looked wide-eyed over her shoulder at Andrew Harvey in fear. Her sister trembled in her arms. Something was terribly wrong.

"Lyric, are you okay?" Harmony pressed. Her sister didn't utter a word. She was in a state of shock.

"She's fine. I'm her mother, not you." Ava wedged herself between Lyric and Harmony. "Let's go celebrate now. We must not forget you girls just landed your first deal. Today, you can have the rest of the day to yourself—no more work."

That evening, Harmony snuck into Lyric's tiny bedroom and found her balled up in the fetal position on the floor, sobbing into her knees.

"Lyric?" Harmony whispered, trying not to startle her and wake Ava. "Lyric, please tell me what happened. How can I help?" Harmony begged, trying to pull her sister's arms away from her face. "What did he do to you?" she asked, her own tears burning the back of her eyes.

Harmony scooped her sister into her arms and rocked her like a child until her sobs turned into sniffles, and then snores.

Over the years, her mother would wake Lyric several times in the middle of the night for scheduled visits by Andrew Harvey. On each occasion, Harmony died a little inside.

In the past, Harmony had been powerless to protect her sister from harm. Tonight, Harmony vowed that she would never let her baby sister get hurt again. If it meant sacrificing her own happiness to save her sister, then so be it.

Two days later, Harmony sat in the backseat of a rented SUV. The tension in the air was so thick, it was palpable. Her nerves were on edge, and the silence was making it worse. Rebel's friends, his backup crew, all seemed to be in different stages of contemplation. Even Kimmy was quiet, which was a first. Harmony had asked Kimmy to join the group as the decoy; they needed a young, attractive female to get close enough to Khalil, and she fit the profile perfectly.

Rebel barely waited for the SUV to stop before he opened the door and hopped out. He was laser-focused on finding Lyric; hell-bent on saving her.

"C'mon!" one of Rebel's friends shouted as they scrambled out of the vehicle.

"Are you sure I'll be safe?" Kimmy asked Harmony again. She had good reason to be worried. From what Rebel had described, Khalil sounded like a dangerous character.

"All you have to do is get close and tell us what's going on. I'm not going to let anything happen to you. Trust me, I can't have another thing on my conscience," Harmony assured, squeezing Kimmy's shoulder.

The scent of marijuana filled the air in the club. Rap music pounded in her ears. Harmony had never been part of the club scene. It was all too overwhelming for her senses.

Women and men swayed to the music, some close to one another and others apart. Harmony took a seat at the bar like Rebel instructed. She watched as he and his crew moved deep inside— slapping backs and pounding fists in greeting. After about twenty minutes or so, Rebel sidled up to her with an update.

"We don't even need your friend. My boy said one of his chicks told him Lyric is here," Rebel relayed. "This sick bastard brings a certain number of girls with him to parties so he can entertain his so-called friends. Sick fuck."

Harmony's eyebrows shot up into arches, and her back went stiff. "But I thought . . . you said she was . . ." she stammered, the nervous energy coursing through her body nearly rendered her incoherent.

"I'm only telling you what I heard. The girl said it seems like Lyric is here on her own free will, and that she's so high out of her mind she can't even speak clearly."

When Harmony heard that Lyric was high, her eyes narrowed in anger.

"So we wasted our time coming here trying to save her? Instead, she's here on her own free will and back on drugs?" Once again, her family managed to disappoint.

"I don't think she wants to be here. I know her better than most," Rebel insisted. "I'm going to try to talk to her and convince her to leave with me."

"Not without me," Harmony asserted, climbing down from the barstool. She was going to give her sister one chance to explain herself before she gave her a piece of her mind.

"Private party," a tall man with a barrel chest and big beer gut grunted in Rebel's face.

"I'm invited. That's my girl over there," Rebel pointed at Kimmy. She waved. The man whispered something to a smaller man standing nearby. Harmony's heart raced.

"Five minutes to get your girl and leave back out," the big man warned, cracking his knuckles.

"I'll take only three," Rebel assured, grabbing Harmony's arm and pulling her into the crowd.

"I'm going to go over and speak to that punk-ass dude. He's Khalil's flunky. You run over to Kimmy and find out if she knows where Lyric is located," Rebel whispered in Harmony's ear. "Remember, we came here for one reason, so don't lose focus. It could mean life or death—for her or us."

Harmony's entire body trembled as she rushed to Kimmy's side. Kimmy flagged her down, her hands waving urgently.

"She's here," Kimmy whispered as the two embraced. "They have her in the back."

"Then let's go," Harmony grabbed Kimmy's arm, ushering her toward the back of the room.

"Wait. No. If we go alone, they'll snatch her away. Or worse, they may try to take us. We'll have to sneak in there," Kimmy said nervously. "I don't even know what I'm doing here. These people are rich and dangerous. We are out of our league."

Harmony couldn't argue with Kimmy. She felt the same way. But every minute that went by was another minute that could be spent looking for her sister.

"Tell me where to go and you stay behind," Harmony told Kimmy. "There's no point in both of us risking our necks. She's my sister, and my responsibility."

Harmony gave the girl a quick hug. "Go act like you want to kiss Rebel and tell him what's going on. If I don't come out in ten minutes, call the police."

Harmony forged ahead, interrupting a few intense drug and grind parties that were transpiring in random corners of the room. She wasn't leaving until she found her sister. Dead or alive, she was determined to get her sister out of this hellhole.

Harmony pulled the black curtain back to reveal a door and two men standing at either side, like sentries.

"Shit," Harmony huffed under her breath. She turned to leave, but one of the men grabbed her arm.

"What the . . ." she started.

"Aren't you supposed to be at the party in the back?" the man growled. Harmony quickly nodded. She would agree to almost anything to get into that back room. The man opened the door and pushed her behind the curtain.

"Lyric," Harmony gasped, her legs suddenly weak. Lyric sat with a rubber tightly wrapped around her arm and a needle full of heroin, ready to jam into her vein.

Lyric looked up at her sister, confused.

"Hey? Who are you?" Khalil snarled. "Who let this bitch back here?" he demanded.

"Oh, shit," Harmony panted, racing toward her sister.

"Lyric! C'mon, we gotta get out of here," Harmony urged, shaking her by the shoulders.

"Harmony?" Lyric said in stunned recognition. She dropped the needle to the ground and unwrapped the tight band from her arm. She embraced her sister tightly; she would never let her go.

A thick arm wrapped around Harmony's middle, lifting her straight into the air.

"Lyric! Run!" Harmony screamed as a man carried her roughly toward the exit.

"Harmony!" Lyric cried, held down by another of Khalil's thugs.

"No! You cannot have my sister!" Harmony screeched.

Rebel burst into the room, a 9 mm in hand.

"Let her go," he demanded, pointing the gun at the man who dragged Harmony across the room.

Khalil stepped out of the shadows. "Well, well, well. If it isn't my old friend, Rebel. So you came to save your lady?" he asked. "I thought you'd never come." Khalil laughed.

"Look, dude. I don't want no trouble. I'm sure I'm outgunned. I just want to take her home," Rebel said, turning his gun on Khalil.

"Go ahead. Take her. She's useless to me now. All of my servants have fucked her. Please, you'll be doing me a favor," Khalil said cruelly.

Rebel swallowed hard, trying to hold onto his composure.

"Take her," Khalil said again. "It saves me from having to dispose of her myself. She's already done everything you can imagine."

"A'ight, then, let us just leave," Rebel said, his jaw rocking.

"I'll let you, your bitch, and the sister all leave under one condition," Khalil rubbed his chin. Rebel's eye twitched, and his nostrils flared.

"Agree to be on my next four mix tapes for *free* and she's all yours," Khalil said, a sinister smile on his face.

"That ain't about shit. Done," Rebel snarled.

Khalil put his hands up. "Good. You must really love that dope fiend whore, huh? In my country, after everything she's done, we'd put her in a hole in the ground and stone her to death," Khalil said maliciously.

In one swift motion, Rebel hoisted Lyric onto his shoulder, caveman style.

"No! Don't touch me! No!" She was kicking, screaming, spitting, and scratching at him. "You hurt me. You betrayed me. You did this to me," she hollered, pounding her fists against his back.

"Let's get out of here," Harmony barked. They all rushed toward the exit.

"Rebel, let me go! I hate you," Lyric howled in anger.

"You hate me, but I love you, Lyric. I love you more than anything in this world," he said as he deposited her into the back of their waiting SUV.

Harmony pulled Lyric's head onto her lap and stroked her hair. "You're safe now. I've got you now. I love you, Lyric. Don't you ever forget that, sister."

Chapter 19

Melody

Melody stretched her arms out at her sides and yawned loudly. Her private jet had finally landed back in New York. Those two weeks at her house on the white sand beaches in Barbados had been much needed. She looked at her watch. Gary better be waiting for her with a long list of things he accomplished while she was taking her mental health break; most important of which should be her tour schedule.

"Thank you for such a smooth ride," Melody nodded to the pilot of the small plane. She stood at the top of the portable steps that had been propped against the jet's door and looked down.

"What the hell is this?" she whispered, flashes of red, blue, and white zipping down the runway. Detective Simpson exited one of the vehicles, meeting her as she stepped onto the tarmac.

"Melody Love, we have a warrant for your arrest," Detective Simpson said, his tone serious. Melody laughed.

"You've got to be joking. Detective, I really don't have time for your shenanigans," she said, waving him off dismissively.

"Ms. Love, please be cooperative. You have the right to remain silent. Anything you say can and will be—" he began to Mirandize her.

"Under arrest for what? I have a right to know what I'm being charged with," she shouted.

"For the murder of your mother and as accessory to the assault of Terikka Felix," Detective Simpson rattled off a list of laws that she supposedly broke. Melody snatched her arm away and pushed him in the chest.

"You have the wrong person! I hadn't seen my mother in almost a year before she died! And I haven't gone near that homewrecker, Terikka! Have you lost your mind, Detective?"

Detective Simpson stepped aside and a small army of uniformed police officers rushed at her.

"Get your hands off of me! I will have every single one of your badges," Melody squealed as she was slammed to the ground and cuffed.

"Don't resist or you'll make this harder on yourself," an officer announced as he pulled her arms behind her back to place the cuffs on her wrists.

"Get off of me!" she growled, frantically twisting her arms away from the officers. "When I get ahold of my lawyer, I will *own* the NYPD! You have *no* idea *who* you're messing with."

"We got a fighter here! She's resisting," the handcuffing officer announced, his knee pushing painfully into her back.

Melody switched gears, trying to reason with the detective. "Okay, okay," she acquiesced. "Detective Simpson, I want to talk to you. Clearly, there's been some kind of mistake. You could not possibly have evidence that suggests I had anything to do with those crimes," she said, her voice quivering in fear.

"Trust me, Ms. Love, if we didn't have evidence and at least one witness, we wouldn't be arresting you today," he replied dryly.

"But I didn't do it. Get off of me. I will have all of your jobs. Do you *know* who I am? I am Melody Love. I don't lose! You have no right!" She shouted insults at the officers holding her down. They had found her guilty without trial or jury.

Right before Melody was loaded into the waiting police car, she saw Gary standing near the line of police cruisers.

"Oh my God! Gary! Please tell them that they have the wrong person! You know me! Tell them

I didn't do it," she pleaded with her friend. Gary quickly turned his body and averted his eyes. Melody's heart sank, and her entire body went cold as comprehension washed over her.

"You bastard! You lying bastard! You set me up! This is all your doing! I was so good to you. I always looked out for you. I brought you up from nothing to something! You won't get away with this, Gary! I swear that when I get out, I'll be coming straight for you. I will kill you myself— then they can rightfully arrest me for murder!" Melody hurled her threats like hard stones. She had trusted Gary with every aspect of her life, including her mother. And now Ava was dead, and she was going to jail for her murder. She should never have let that weasel into her life. He had been the one to bring her the news of Ava's death.

"It's your mother . . . Ava Love . . ." Gary stuttered.

"Ava? What now?" Melody sucked her teeth. "Is that what you interrupted me for?" Melody had told her mother six months prior that she didn't want anything to do with her, although Melody still sent Ava a monthly allowance. Melody didn't send the money out of the kindness of her heart, but to keep her away.

"Melody, I know you don't like getting emotional in front of people, so why don't we step out of the studio and talk in private?" Gary implored. His voice was high-pitched and quivery. His eyes were misty with tears.

Melody reluctantly followed him out of the dance studio doors and into the small private changing room. Her stomach churned with anxiety.

"Mel, you might want to sit down, honey," he said softly, his mouth dipping at the edges.

"Just tell me what's going on, Gary. I have a tour coming up. I don't have time for another Ava antic. How bad can it be? I mean, did she get drunk again and make a spectacle of herself in front of the paparazzi? Did she go harass some record executive, screaming about how great she once was? Or wait, let me guess, she got caught giving head to another much-younger NBA player in the back of some sports car? No, I have a better one. She went to the Ritz and asked to be put up in the presidential suite, free of charge, because she is the mother of Melody Love?"

"No, Mel. It's much worse, hon." Gary lowered his head, and wrung his fingers together in front of him. He cleared his throat but refused to look Melody in the eyes.

"What can be worse than—"

"Ava is dead," Gary said in a rush of breath. Melody's mouth snapped shut. "I got the call from Murray today."

Melody didn't move an inch. She was in complete shock.

"Mel? Are you okay?" Gary grabbed her shoulders and pulled her close for a hug. Melody kept her arms down at her sides and didn't return his embrace. Her body was as rigid as a board.

"She's dead, baby girl. I'm so sorry," Gary consoled. His words fell on deaf ears.

"It all makes sense now, Gary. Murray wouldn't have called you. He would've called me directly. But you *knew* she was dead before Murray could even get to me. You knew because *you* did it," Melody accused.

Gary shook his head sadly. "I told you she was crazy," he said to the detective.

The officers forced Melody's head down into the waiting car.

"You won't get away with this," she screamed, banging her head against the bulletproof glass.

Gary had the audacity to actually wave goodbye to her. She couldn't wait until she called her lawyer and posted bail. Gary was a dead man.

When the police car pulled out of the plane's hangar, reporters surrounded the vehicle. Melody saw Tanya Trent, a well-known gossip columnist, ready to give the world the juicy news about her arrest. Tanya had hated Melody for years; it had always been Gary's job to handle her. Unfortunately, an unholy alliance had been formed, and now Gary stood at Tanya's side like they were part of the same team.

Tanya peeked into the cop car with a wicked smile before she began her live broadcast.

"In breaking news, we are outside of the jetport here in Long Island. WKTZ is the first to bring you this story. Melody Love was pulled off of her private jet a few minutes ago and placed under arrest for the murder of her mother, Ava Love, former disco diva.

"As previously reported, Ava Love was found dead in her home three months ago under suspicious circumstances. A late medical examiner's report ruled the death a homicide. A police spokesperson confirmed that the attack on Terikka Felix that resulted in the loss of her unborn child was not carried out by Melody Love; however, there is evidence to suggest that she may have helped orchestrate the attack. No further details are available at this time.

"We at WKTZ, as well as Melody's millions of fans, are shocked by these developments. Here with us now is Melody's manager, Gary Sithe. Gary, any thoughts that you would like to share with our viewers?"

"Tanya, I am truly as shocked as everyone else about this news. As you know, I have worked for Melody for years and considered her more than a friend . . . She is like family to me. Melody had a mean streak, and she could sometimes get downright abusive toward me and others who worked for her. But never in my wildest imagination could I believe that her anger would manifest itself in something so evil. I am truly shocked; I count myself lucky that I did not become one of her victims."

"There you have it. Gary Sithe, Melody's long-time manager and best friend, breathing a sigh of relief over Melody's arrest. Reporting for WKTZ, I am Tanya Trent. Back to you at the station."

Melody didn't have a chance to scream, kick, or spit before the police car pulled free from the reporters. She hung her head and let the tears fall. She said a silent prayer and made a vow to herself. This wasn't the end of Melody Love. She would be back with a vengeance.

Chapter 20

Lyric

A sharp pain seared through Lyric's head as she struggled to open her eyes. She moaned as the sunlight filtered through the window. She wished she never had to open her eyes.

Rebel stirred on the air mattress at the foot of Lyric's bed.

"Lyric?" he called out.

"Where am I? What's going on?" she croaked out, still unable to open her eyes fully without pain. Her mouth and throat were desert dry and her lips were cracked and painful.

"Harmony's house," Rebel said, standing up and moving to her side.

"I came and got you two days ago from that crazy dude, Khalil," Rebel explained, reaching out and grabbing her hand.

Lyric shivered. "You should've just left me there," she rasped, turning her face away. The things that she'd endured made her want to give up on life. She would never trust another man again.

"I couldn't leave you there, Lyric. I know we've been through some shit together, but you have to know that I never meant to hurt you. I love you, Lyric. Always have and always will."

Lyric could see that he spoke the truth, though pain laced his words. She used her free hand to feel her hair, and then her face. She could only imagine how bad she must look.

"I need to get out of here," she said, pulling her hand back. "I'm going to be dope sick and real messed up if I stay here." She tried to sit up, but she was too weak to lift herself off of the pillows.

"You have to stay here. I got you some methadone. In a day or two, you won't need the drugs. After you get a little stronger, your sister has agreed to take you to a detox," Rebel said.

"I don't want to go to a detox," Lyric raised her voice. "Don't you and my sisters get it? I want to get high until I die. I am used up. Abused. Unloved. Can't I even choose my own ending? Let me live out my days fucked up," she snapped.

Rebel exhaled loudly.

"You think I don't know the feeling, Lyric? I always said I was going to be a stoner for life. You have been through a lot these last three months. You don't need to go anywhere. Stay right here with people who really love you," he said, stroking her forehead.

Lyric began to sob. She wanted to get high so badly. She couldn't stop thinking about the things that Khalil forced her to do and the things that others did to her as well. She hated herself.

"Why, Rebel? Why do you keep telling me to get clean, huh?" she cried, rubbing her arms like they hurt. "So you can relieve yourself of your guilt? Is that it? Because clearly, you don't fucking love me. First, you left me in the hospital crying for you to come back. And then, when I get out, I find that you were fucking my friend." She sniffled back a nose full of snot.

"When I saw what was happening to you, I couldn't stand it. If saving you meant never taking another drug, I would do it. I made mistakes, but I've always loved you. I want you to get clean for you . . . for us. Why wouldn't I want to see you living the life you deserve, Lyric? Chasing a high for the rest of your life is not living. Getting caught up in situations like this last one is not living. Taking the help, being healthy, fighting those demons from the past—that's living, Lyric," Rebel said earnestly, his voice choking up.

"I'm so ashamed of myself. I walked right into his trap and all for a fucking hit," Lyric said.

"Look at me. I'll never be anything more than a dope fiend," she said, extending her arms so that Rebel could see all of her track marks. Her arms were gouged raw.

"You can't be ashamed in front of me. I've been to the lowest points with you, remember? We used to crawl around on the floors of my crib together searching for dope. We used to shoot up together all day and night. You was the first woman that saw how dope totally wiped out my hard-ons, and you never judged me for that shit," Rebel admitted.

He slid onto the bed next to Lyric, pulled her into his arms, and kissed the top of her head.

"I'll be right here through it all, Lyric. I promise that I won't leave you this time. I'll make sure that you get clean so that you can live the life that you deserve," he swore.

Lyric's tears soaked through Rebel's T-shirt. He hadn't showed her this much love since they'd been together. They lay together for a few minutes in silence.

A soft knock on the bedroom door interrupted their moment.

"Come in," Rebel called out. He pulled apart from Lyric and sat up on the side of the bed. The door slowly crept open.

"Hey," Harmony sang, smiling. Lyric gave her a weak smile in return. Her headache was intensifying by the minute.

"I made breakfast. Are you guys hungry?" her sister offered.

The thought of food made Lyric's stomach turn over. "I can't eat. I'm starting to feel sick."

"Oh, baby sis, I'm so sorry you're going through this."

Harmony approached Lyric's bedside, feeling her forehead for a temperature.

"We'll make sure you get what you need. What about you, Rebel? Are you holding up okay?" she asked like a mother hen.

"I'm good for now. I need to make sure she's going to be all right."

Lyric looked at both of them and smiled, tears welling up in her eyes.

"Thank you," Lyric said, her voice cracking. She really meant it. She was grateful to have both Rebel and her sister back in her life. It gave her a glimmer of hope for the future.

Lyric leaned over the side of the bed and vomited into the bucket on the floor for the sixth time in the last hour. She screamed out as another wave of pain shot through her lower back and abdomen. She was drenched in sweat, and her legs stiffened with charley horses and severe cramps. Rebel dabbed her head with a cold washcloth.

"Kicking cold turkey is a bitch, baby girl. I know. I feel you," he said as he rubbed her back in soothing, circular motions. Lyric's chest heaved; she felt like she was being stabbed by millions of sharp needles. She wanted to give up. This hurt too bad. She would die if she had to endure one more day like this.

"Reb . . . just get me one hit. I promise, it'll be my last one. I swear, I won't ask again—just one hit," Lyric pleaded. "I swear . . . It will be the last one. I can't do this, Reb. I'm weak. I'll be dead by morning," she sobbed into her blankets.

"Nah, Lyric. It's been three days, and you've made it this far. You doing damned good, baby girl. Stay strong. I'm right here with you. In a few more days, you'll be well enough to go to a place your sister hooked you up with," Rebel assured her. "If I give you a hit, you'll be starting over from day one, and then what would all of these days have been for? That shit can't rock, Lyric. You got this. I know you can kick this."

"Fuck! Fuck you and my sister! Let me out of here!" Lyric screamed, using the last bit of strength she had to pull herself upright. "You don't fucking understand," she said weakly, trying to kick her aching legs like a toddler throwing a tantrum. "Nobody understands me."

"You are stronger than you know. I got your back. You're doing better than some grown-ass men I know. I always knew you were a fighter, Lyric," Rebel praised. "I know you feel like shit right now, but trust me on this one. This shit is going to be so worth it later."

Lyric wanted to spit in Rebel's face, but she was too weak to even collect the saliva in her mouth. She leaned over and dry heaved this time. She was bone dry. An empty vessel ready for disposal. She hoped they cremated her when she died.

After another three days of cold turkey withdrawals, Lyric finally felt strong enough to sit up in the bed and eat a solid meal. The sunlight was streaming though the blinds of the guest room in Harmony's house. It was a welcome sight.

Lyric swung her legs over the side of the bed and eased to the edge. She stood up for the first time in days. Her legs were still weak, so she grabbed onto the nightstand to catch her balance and accidentally sent a glass of orange juice crashing to the hardwood floor.

"Shit," Lyric hissed, feeling like a clumsy invalid.

"Lyric?" Harmony rushed into the room. "Are you all right? I heard a noise." Harmony ran to her side and offered her assistance back to the bed.

"I'm good. I just knocked over the glass by accident."

Harmony let out a sigh of relief. "You don't have to try to do too much too fast. There's no rush."

Lyric stared at her sister for a few minutes and lowered her eyes, unable to maintain eye contact with her.

"Harmony, I'm sorry I never told you about Ron and Melody," Lyric said, contritely.

"That's all water under the bridge now. Don't you worry about that. You worry about yourself and getting better." Her sister was far too generous and kindhearted. She didn't know if she would have forgiven herself so quickly or easily. Harmony waved it off, but Lyric could see the hurt glinting in her eyes.

"No, it is not okay. I was supposed to tell you right away. You have always been here for me, whether I wanted to accept your help or not. I was wrong for not being loyal to you. I wish I could blame my addiction for everything, but that was entirely my fault."

"We've moved on. We're not going to speak about the past anymore, Lyric. Ava is dead, and so is that part of our lives. We have to heal now. I've said this before, but I mean it this time. We are going to get this right, this time," Harmony said, pulling Lyric in for a hug.

"And part of getting this right is being there for each other . . . even Melody," Harmony said. Lyric rolled her eyes.

"I just don't know why you keep forgiving her. What else does she have to do to you?" Lyric said, moving out of Harmony's embrace.

Harmony looked at her with sympathy in her eyes.

"It's not her fault. It's not any of our faults. But, at a time like this, we have one more chance to try to make things right," she replied. "Baby sis, we are all we got now, and that includes Melody."

Lyric could tell her sister was struggling to say those words. She knew Harmony was devastated by the news about Melody and Ron, but Lyric also knew that Harmony was the best at rising above adversity and hurt feelings. In fact, Lyric had watched Harmony master the skill all of their lives.

"I love you, Harmony," Lyric whispered.

"I love you more, sis," Harmony whispered back.

"You have no idea how happy I am to see you on your feet," Harmony chimed, taking a good look at Lyric's healed black eye and cleared skin.

"Yeah, but I need a shower like now . . . as in *right* now. Shit, I'm killing myself with these funky pits," she said chuckling.

Rebel walked back into the room from his own shower and shave.

"That's what I like to hear," he said smiling brightly. Lyric blushed. She hadn't taken a good long look at Rebel in a while. He was still ruggedly handsome and very rough around the edges. She had forgotten how much his tattoos turned her on.

Harmony provided Lyric with some towels and soap to freshen up. Rebel stood guard outside of the door just in case she got sick or felt dizzy.

When she first stepped into the shower, the water stung her skin. After a few minutes, the warm water cascaded down her back, and Lyric was able to ease back into the shower's powerful stream and finally relax. She couldn't stop the tears and memories from washing over her . . .

"Wash me," Andrew Harvey demanded as he moved his naked body close to hers. Although

hot water rained down on them, Lyric's teeth chattered and goose bumps covered her skin.

"C'mon. Don't be shy. You should be getting used to this by now," he said, putting his fingers under her chin to lift her face toward the stream. Lyric could never get used to being in these situations with him. It was unnatural. He was an old man; she was a young girl.

"Okay, I tell you what. I'll help you," he said, forcing a soft sponge in her hand, and then guiding it to his penis. Lyric tried to back away, but the shower walls enclosed them in the tight space together. With her back against the wall, Andrew Harvey had her pinned. He flashed her a lecherous grin.

"I think you like to play hard to get because you know it turns me on," he said, reaching back and grabbing her hair. "You've been turning me on more and more lately with your protests." She whined at the pain of having her hair pulled. He laughed at her whimper.

"Tell me what you want to do to me," he said softly, kissing her face while his ever-growing manhood pressed against her stomach. She twisted her face away, dodging his kisses.

"Come here," he instructed, turning her around.

"Please!" Lyric screamed as he probed her, getting her ready.

"Shhhh," he moaned, holding her by the hips. Their wet bodies slipped against each other making a loud, slick noise. Lyric lowered her head and gasped for air.

Andrew Harvey panted like an animal against her neck as he took her with force. The shower water pelted them like a violent rainstorm. Lyric couldn't breathe. She pushed her hands against the shower wall, her face pressed against the cold ceramic tiles.

"That's right. Let me know you love it," he whispered, holding onto her with a death grip. Lyric screamed as loud as she could, but she knew no one was coming to save her.

Lyric slid down to the floor of the shower, with her knees pulled into her chest, sobbing and shivering from the nightmarish memory. When she wasn't high, the memories came almost every day. She didn't know how she would make it without the escape of her drugs.

"Lyric? You all right?" Rebel called out, knocking on the bathroom door. Lyric jumped fiercely and looked around the steamy bathroom, dazed. Before she could say another word, Rebel was standing above her, a frown marring his forehead.

"Lyric? What happened? Why are you on the floor crying?"

"No worries, I'm good." She pulled herself together enough to stand on her feet.

"You scared me to death. I thought you fell and hurt yourself," Rebel said, wrapping a large plush towel around her body as he helped her out.

"I'm fine, really. You don't have to baby me," she said, swatting away his hands.

Rebel stood back and stared at her for several long seconds.

"What? Do I still look like shit on a stick or something?" Lyric asked, feeling like her old self again.

"No, you look more beautiful than ever," Rebel said, leaning forward and kissing her softly on the lips. Lyric allowed him the intimacy. It was the first normal thing she had done in a long time. She wished she could hold on to this feeling forever. Sadly, these moments tended to be fast and fleeting in her life.

Chapter 21

Melody

Melody's heart thrummed as she sat across the visitor room table from Gary. She knew if she went wild and crazy on him like she wanted to, the correctional officers would haul her away and she'd never get to say what was on her mind. She was surprised he'd agreed to her request for a visit. He was bolder than Melody ever gave him credit for.

Melody could see that he was fighting to keep his usual smirk at bay. She could tell that he was mocking her appearance in his head. Gone were her usually perfectly coiffed locks of hair; instead, they were replaced with a messy, thick ponytail held back with a cheap, beige rubber band. Gone was her flawlessly applied makeup; instead, her natural skin was marred with dark circles and under eye bags, chapped lips, and ashen skin. She was dying for a bottle of expensive moisturizer. The cheap shampoos and soaps were destroying her hair and skin.

Gary reeked of cologne. His expensive Gucci shirt and gleaming Rolex watch made Melody feel even more self-conscious. She wanted to crawl under the table and hide.

"Melody," he said, the first to break the awkward silence. She didn't answer; instead, she flared her nostrils and drummed her fingers on the table.

"You must be thinking that I betrayed you and you can't understand why," Gary said. Melody shifted in her seat, her leg bouncing under the table.

"I'll just tell you why, then. Remember all of the times, in the beginning, that you took such great pleasure in humiliating me?" he asked. Melody rolled her eyes. She had promised herself she wouldn't say a word to him until he was finished, but she couldn't bite her tongue any longer.

"Humiliate you? I fucking picked you up from the gutter, Gary. You came to that first audition and had been out on the streets selling your ass to gay businessmen," she whispered harshly. Gary gasped, his hand fluttering against his throat.

"Oh, you thought I didn't know what you were doing to make ends meet? I knew, but I still saw something special in you. When I made jokes about your sexuality, they were just that—jokes. When I held your pay, it was because you didn't deliver. I never humiliated you. I thought you were my fucking friend," she growled.

Gary swallowed hard. "It was everything else too. The demands. The bitching. The slaps in the face. The constant name-calling. You even punched me and spat at me in front of everyone. A man can only take so much abuse. You're telling me you did all of that to 'build my character'? I don't think so," he retorted.

"You *do* remember those times, don't you?" Gary pressed. Melody sighed. She did remember that sometimes she would take her frustrations out on him.

The conference room in the midtown Manhattan building that housed Melody's recording studio, business offices, and dance studio was packed with her staff. Melody sat at the head of the table, her hair and makeup flawless, as usual.

"Well," she sighed, parting a huge smile. "I've called you all here for some big news. Gary called; he's on his way. He said he has the news. I wanted all of you to be here when it was announced," Melody said. Hushed murmurs rose and fell down the long table. Melody giggled. She loved keeping her staff in suspense sometimes. It made her job more fun.

Finally Gary rushed into the conference room in a huff. His eyes immediately stretched wide, and his lips curled down at the sight of everyone.

"Here he is," Melody cheered, standing up and opening her arms wide. Gary moved slowly, like a zombie.

"Get your ass over here. I called everyone here because you said you had the news. You said it would be better in person," Melody said, her voice trailing as she noticed Gary's creased forehead and slack jaw.

"Um, Mel, I . . . I . . . think we should talk about this . . . alone," he stammered.

"What? No. Everyone here works for me; we're a family," she waved. "My news is all of their news."

Gary swallowed hard and fanned himself with his hands. "But, Mel. I'm telling you, this news you might—"

"Stop being so fucking worrisome. Make the announcement, Gary," Melody snapped. He sighed heavily.

"You didn't get the part, Melody. They gave it to her," he blurted. Melody knew who he was referring to. There had been only one other singing diva that had tried out for the Dreamgirls lead.

Melody's face turned red. She parted a goofy smile. "Gary, stop kidding around. Don't play like that," she said. Her heart was pounding so hard she felt light-headed.

"Mel, it's true," Gary murmured. Everyone in the room seemed to freeze.

Melody's hands curled into fists at her sides. "Then why did you make me believe the news was good?" she gritted.

"I . . . I . . . didn't," he replied.

"You fucking faggot! You lying faggot!" Melody screamed, hot tears spilling down her face. The entire room erupted in whispers and gasps.

"I . . . I . . . didn't lie," he said. "I tried to—"

Before he could finish his sentence, Melody pounced on him and punched him in the face. Gary gasped and fell backward, caught off guard.

"You liar!" she yelled as she landed punches on Gary's body at will. Melody's producer, her choreographer, and her makeup artist all rushed over to break it up. As Melody was hoisted up off of Gary, she managed to get in one last kick, right to his face.

"I was under a lot pressure at those times. And, yes, maybe I flew off the handle a few times, but it didn't change the fact that your life was much better because of me," Melody shot back.

"I think being called a faggot several hundred times over the course of a friendship is more than a little 'flying off the handle.' You think my life was better with your physical and mental abuse, and then the flowers, cards, and expensive gifts afterward to win me back? You thought *that* was enough? Did you think I would just take that forever, Melody?" he snarled.

"We could've worked it out. We always did. Did you need to go this far? To set me up? Ruin me? I've had a lot of time to think, Gary. And it all makes sense to me now. That day you picked me up from the precinct . . . the constant barrage of questions about what the detectives knew about Ava's death. You were worried. Real worried," Melody said.

Detective Simpson's voice played in her head just as it had since that night. *Whoever poisoned your mother had to have regular, ongoing contact with her. This wasn't done overnight. It took some time and planning.*

"You had the opportunity, the time, and the motive. Then, you hired that man to attack Terikka. Whatever you gave him must've been out of this world, because he swore to the police that *I* hired him, and he won't budge from his story. He's going to jail, and he *still* won't change his story. Did you think I wouldn't figure out that you were the one that sold all the pictures of Ron and me to the tabloids and blogs? I have to admit, Gary, you are one cunning bitch. Urging me to turn over power of attorney to you so you could take care of my business while I took a mental break. How much money did you steal from my accounts, Gary?"

"Very good, Sherlock," Gary patted his fingers together simulating a clap. He leaned in closer to the table and squinted his eyes. "Every single thing you got was coming to you. You walked around thinking you were an untouchable diva, and I was sick of it. You can't just fucking abuse people all of your life and think karma wouldn't pay you back. I've always told you; karma is one crazy, vindictive bitch, and she always gets what she came for. I hope these years behind bars changes you for the better, Melody. I hope you learn how to be less evil and more human," he said, standing to leave.

"You won't get away with this, Gary. Just like you meted out your own form of justice on me, the universe will bring the real karma down on your ass. You just wait. Your time is coming," Melody gritted. "Enjoy my money while you can because somebody will help me. I have somebody out there that loves me."

Gary chortled. "Chile, bye. You ran all of your somebodies away a long time ago. Sly couldn't stand your spoiled ass so he went and found himself a real woman to love. Even little old me got tired of your fucking abuse. And, of course, your sisters," Gary said, laughing cruelly. "Sista Love. What a joke! After all of the years, you did them dirty and turned your back on them. You betrayed them in the worst possible way—two-timing with your own brother-in-law and paying hush money to keep the other one quiet. And those two were the only ones who ever gave a fuck about you, Melody Love. You just couldn't see it because you were too busy looking at yourself." He shook his head, and Melody lowered hers. Without another word, he walked away and signaled for the officers to let him out.

***

A week later, Melody was led into the courtroom in handcuffs and leg irons. A collective gasp rose and fell around the room. She wished she could just disappear off the face of the earth and put herself out of this misery.

The judicial system was a farce; the courtroom looked like a damn circus. The room was filled with people; everyone was trying to catch a glimpse of Melody Love, celebrity-turned-murderer. Television news reporters were jockeying for the best camera angles and the clearest shot of the infamous Melody.

"Ignore them all," Robert Agnow, one of Melody's high-powered legal team, whispered in her ear. Melody nodded, but she couldn't stop her knees from knocking.

The court-appointed sketch artist was staring right at Melody while he scribbled wildly on his pad. Melody wished she could rush over, snatch his pad, and pound it over his head.

She tried to ignore the conversations buzzing around the room, but it was difficult to tune out.

"She killed her own mother."

"She killed her ex-boyfriend's baby."

"She ruined her career."

"Who knew she was such a monster?"

"Did you know she also slept with her sister's husband? She had this coming to her."

"I hope they throw the book at her. Celebrities all think they are above the law."

Melody's head pounded. The expensive clothes that her lawyers brought for her felt scratchy against her skin. Even her orange jumpsuit had been more comfortable than this. She looked at the clock hanging on the wall to her left and shifted on the hard wooden chair. In a few minutes, the judge would hear the state's evidence against her. Melody knew she was innocent, but she wasn't going to be able to prove it from behind bars.

Last night, she had prayed for the first time in many years. She asked God to forgive her for everything she'd done to her sisters. She asked God to reveal her mother's real killer and to have mercy on both of their souls.

A small commotion erupted as the judge entered the room. A sense of foreboding came over the room as the judge slammed his gavel and told everyone to be seated. In all of her life, Melody never thought she would be in a situation like this—defending her innocence in public, like a common criminal.

"Counsel, you may approach," the judge said.

Melody's legs rocked, and her stomach flipped. All of the money in the world didn't matter at the moment. Her fate was in the hands of one man.

As the judge and attorneys went through the formalities, Melody looked over her shoulder. Her eyes went wide when she noticed Harmony and Lyric sitting a few rows back in the courtroom. Melody stared at her sisters, wondering if they were secretly pleased with witnessing her demise. Lyric parted a warm smile and mouthed the words, *"We got you. No matter what, we are sisters. We are family."*

Overwhelmed, Melody turned back around and clamped her hand over her mouth. Tears ran down her face. She never expected to see Harmony and Lyric again. Their support meant the world to her. If there was anything she should be on trial for, it should be for the way she treated her own flesh and blood. If that were the case, she would plead guilty as charged.

Melody lowered her eyes to her cuffed hands and forced herself to think of a better time in her life. A time when she was on top of the world.

The crowd chanted their name . . . "Sista Love! Sista Love! Sista Love!" By now, the girls should've been used to it. They'd sold out major

arenas around the United States, but this was
their first performance in the UK. They weren't
sure what sort of reception they would receive
overseas.

"We are all the way across the pond with
a packed stadium, and they're calling our
names," Melody said dreamily as she sat for
hair and makeup. That was another thing that
had changed. They had an entire staff waiting
on them—hair, makeup, a stylist, personal
assistants. Sista Love was in the big leagues
now.

"This gives me chills and makes my stomach
crazy every single time. I don't think this will
ever be normal for me," Harmony confided.
Her hair was already done, and the makeup
artist was adding the finishing touches.

"Why are the fans here so early? Our concert
still has another forty minutes before it starts,"
Lyric added, stepping into her show outfit—a
pair of red hot pants and a bra top.

"I still can't believe Ava trusted us with
the staff and didn't come along for the trip,"
Melody added. "I kind of miss her standing
around barking orders and making sure we're
absolutely perfect."

Harmony laughed. "You would kind of miss
her since she never yells at you or criticizes you.

I'm personally glad she sat this trip out. Maybe she's finally going to let us test our wings. After all of our sold-out shows and hit records, I think we can manage this without all of her nagging and micromanaging."

"Enough about Ava. We have to kill it tonight. I hear these fans in Europe are hard to please when it comes to American performers," Lyric said.

"Do you hear that crowd? Do you hear our names being shouted? They don't sound very hard to please to me," Melody smirked as she stepped into her red miniskirt and halter top. The showtime clock sitting in the center of the dressing room was counting down. She grew more excited with every minute that passed. She loved performing for a large crowd.

"Are you girls ready?" Lyhor, the show's promoter, stuck his head in the doorway and asked in his distinctly English accent. Harmony gave the thumbs-up, Lyric bounced on her feet, and Melody spun around Dreamgirls style.

"We were born ready," Melody answered theatrically.

"Showtime in three," Lyhor reminded them before he disappeared behind a curtain.

Lyric fanned her hands in front of her. "I am so nervous. This is crazy." Melody laughed at her.

"You say the same thing before every show."

"It's my good-luck statement. Remember, the one time I didn't say that I was nervous? Well, my damn heel broke on stage, and I had to perform in one shoe. Not funny," Lyric recalled. *"It doesn't pay for me to be cocky."*

"It's not how you start . . . It's how you finish," Harmony said, simulating her best Ava voice. The girls hooted in laughter.

"We don't need luck when we've got each other. Our talent speaks for itself. Now, let's go out there and give them a show they'll never forget!" Melody was good at the pep talk.

"I agree. Now, bring it in," Harmony said, opening her arms and summoning her sisters closer into a huddle hug.

"All we need is each other," Melody led the chant. *"All we need is each other, and all we got is each other,"* Harmony and Lyric said. After repeating it three times, they broke up and headed straight for the stage.

The crowd roared as Melody, Harmony, and Lyric positioned themselves in theatrical poses behind the transparent curtains.

"London! Are you ready for us to show y'all some Sista Love?" Melody said in a sultry voice. She bucked her hips suggestively behind the curtain and switched to a different pose. The question sent the crowd into a frenzy.

"Can we show y'all some Sista Love?" Harmony asked, shaking her hips in a belly-dancing motion. Loud roars erupted from the fans.

"All right. C'mon and let Sista Love, love up on y'all," Lyric finished, bouncing down on her legs and standing back up.

As the curtains were raised to reveal Harmony, Melody, and Lyric, the crowd went crazy. The beat to their hit song "Love Fool" cued up, and Melody took the first stanza. She hit every note; her vocals were stronger than ever. The fans in the first couple of rows were reaching out, screaming, and some were even crying. The energy in the room was electrifying; it fueled Melody and her sisters to perform at their highest levels.

There was not a single mistake made on stage that night. It was, by all accounts, a "perfect performance." Their movements were fluid, each step executed just like they rehearsed. Six outfit changes and over twenty songs later, they performed their finale—a rendition of their first hit single: "Liar, Liar." The song always took Melody back to the beginning when they were just three little girls practicing in their backyard and dreaming about becoming famous. Melody felt the emotion behind the song every time she per-

formed it. The song had special meaning to her because she had written it with her sisters when they were all just kids. They could've never dreamed of it becoming such a hit when they sat together in their little Brooklyn brownstone writing it.

She threw her head back and sang from the inner depths of her soul.

"For the last time!" Melody huffed into the microphone as she got to the last line of the song.

The crowd went wild, the sound vibrating the floorboards of the stage.

"For the last time!" Harmony and Lyric repeated.

The cheers from the audience were deafening.

"I said for, oh for, oooh, for the last time," Melody sang, tears streaming down her face. Her sisters harmonized beautifully alongside her.

Melody, Harmony, and Lyric held hands and raised their arms over their heads as they took their final bow. "We love you! Thank you!" Lyric screamed into her microphone before they exited the stage. They all seemed to feel the finality of the moment. It was the perfect ending to a perfect night.

The sisters raced back to their dressing rooms, their excitement palpable. They hugged each other excitedly.

"We killed it—slaughtered our first European stop. You ladies rocked it," *Melody said, squeezing her sisters tightly. If they only knew how much she loved them.*

"Our performance was so boss. I swear I could've performed forever out there. This crowd showed up and showed out. We got so much love," *Lyric said, bouncing up and down as she held onto her big sisters.*

"I must say. I am very proud of you ladies. This is what happens when we don't have any bad vibes before a show," *Harmony added, tightening her grip on her sisters too. Not having their mother present at the show had made a world of difference in terms of how they performed, and also how they interacted with one another.*

"I may not always be the best sister to have, and I probably irk y'all nerves more than y'all would like, but I just want both of you to know that I truly love you. I wouldn't pick any other girls to be my sisters," *Melody said from the heart. She could see that her pronouncement shocked Harmony and Lyric. They looked at each other to make sure they weren't imagining things.*

"Well, Mel. You're our sister, and we love you too. You're spoiled rotten, and the most pretentious person we—"

"Look, Harm. This is supposed to be a happy moment," Melody interrupted. They all laughed.

"I know. I was just kidding. We definitely love you too. You may not think so because Lyric and I kind of stick together at home, but that's only because we have to stay clear of Ava's wrath. There is nothing we wouldn't do for you. We are sisters forever, and we will love you forever," Harmony said.

"Don't y'all start this crying and mushy stuff. I want to keep this pretty makeup on for a little while longer. Plus, crying is for punks," Lyric joked. "I love y'all silly selves."

"We love you too," Melody and Harmony said in unison.

Melody's tears dropped onto her cuffed hands. She couldn't concentrate on the court hearing. Instead, she focused on her past mistakes. She promised herself that if she made it out of this ordeal, she would work on being a better human being. For starters, she would try to be at least half as forgiving and compassionate as her sisters. It had taken all of her life to realize that Sista Love was not just a name for their group, it defined who and what they were. That, alone, was worth fighting for.

Chapter 22

Harmony

"I thought I'd find you here," Harmony said seductively, fighting the goofy smile that threatened to spoil her sultry face.

Blake startled. When he turned around, he flashed his signature toothy smile. "Hey, I didn't expect to see you here."

Harmony walked toward his car, balancing on her heels, flowers in hand. She showed up unannounced at his work, like he did so many times with her. Blake wore his work T-shirt and a pair of grungy jeans. *Damn, if he don't look sexy.*

"Peace offering," Harmony said, holding the bouquet of roses out in front of her.

Blake laughed. "What's this? Flowers from a lady? Isn't it supposed to be flowers *for* the lady? You didn't have to do that. You're making me blush."

Harmony blushed herself. He couldn't be any sweeter.

"Well, when the lady in question has been the worst possible friend ever, I think there are exceptions to the rules. Please accept these flowers as a token of my sincerest apologies." Harmony executed a perfect curtsy.

Blake chuckled and took the flowers. "Naw, flowers for the lady." He handed them right back to her. Harmony rolled her eyes playfully and took them back. She lowered her eyes to the ground before she continued.

"On a serious note, Blake, I was an ass. I came by to tell you how sorry I am for my actions. Two tries at a simple dinner and I failed you both times. You've done so much for me and the girls at Dance and More. I didn't want to come across as selfish or ungrateful. Frankly, I'm ashamed of how downright nasty I was toward you. I let my emotions get in the way. You didn't deserve that sort of treatment."

Blake waved and twisted his lips. "Aw, it was nothing. I didn't take it personal. If anyone knows how fast life can come at you, it's me. I figured I'd give you time to sort things out with your family. I would rather wait for the right moment than rush you into something that you aren't ready for," he said sincerely.

Harmony smiled. "Thank you. That's more than I deserve. You are too kind."

"You came back to find me, so that must count for something. What's the saying? 'When you want something, let it go . . .'"

"If it comes back to you, it's yours; if it doesn't, it never was," she finished. Blake reached out and moved a stray strand of hair from her forehead.

"You came back, and that's what counts."

Harmony's insides fluttered. She felt light-headed. She cleared her throat, trying not to become too emotional.

"Don't you still owe me that 'friend-dinner'?" she joked.

Blake laughed. "Why? You got a better excuse this time?"

"I can't believe we are here at a table in a real restaurant. I think it's safe to assume that we are officially on a date this time," Blake joked.

Harmony slapped the top of his hand playfully. She would never hear the end of this. It was so good to laugh again.

"I thought you said you forgave me. It's not forgiveness if you keep throwing it back in my face," she chuckled.

"All right. I'll stop. No more harassing you about our failed friend-dinners," he said, picking up his drink and taking a sip. "This may seem abrupt, but I've been wondering about . . . about your situation." He glanced down at her empty left ring finger for emphasis.

The elephant in the room needed to be addressed. She didn't expect any less of a man with integrity.

"Oh, okay. Let's get right down to the serious stuff, why don't we?" she chuckled, not quite sure about what her answer would be. He deserved the truth, she just didn't have much to offer.

His cheeks flushed, but he continued to hold her gaze. A relationship based on lies would go nowhere fast.

"Sorry. It's just been weighing on my mind. The last time, when I asked you out as a friend, you seemed hesitant and unsure. I don't want to get in over my head only to find . . . you know what I mean." He rolled his shoulders, as if to release the tension in his body.

"Well, honestly, Blake, at the moment, there's not much to tell. My husband has been gone from our home for a total of five months. I can't really say anything other than his actions speak for themselves," she replied without getting into the specifics.

"I have a hard time believing he just left a beautiful woman like you and your little girl behind. Was there someone else? Did something happen to trigger his departure?"

Harmony shifted uncomfortably in her chair. She needed a sip of her drink to answer that question. She paused for a few long seconds, contemplating how much she should share with him. She didn't want to let her guard down too soon, but she also didn't want to lie to him either. In the end, she thought it best to opt for the truth. If she scared him away, then so be it.

"He slept with my sister," she confessed, barely above a whisper. "My husband slept with my sister," Harmony repeated, this time slightly louder. Just uttering the words out loud was cathartic. She felt as if a lead weight had been lifted from her shoulders.

Blake choked on his bread. She passed him a glass of water.

"Exactly," Harmony replied to his stunned reaction.

"Which one? The famous one?" Blake asked, then caught himself. "Well, I know you are all famous . . . but I mean . . ."

"Yes, he slept with Melody. She's the one everyone worships. Lyric and I, we were just the shiny accessories," she said without malice.

"How could your sister do that to you?" Blake threw his hands up. "I mean, if you don't mind me asking. I understand if you don't want to talk about it."

Harmony waved off his concerns. "I guess the simplest way for me to explain this is that my husband, Ron, is a recovering addict and during a relapse, he would go anywhere to find drugs. I've had a long time to think about all of this. In some ways, it was partially my fault. I put us in a situation, and he just wasn't strong enough to deal with it. I knew he wasn't on solid ground with his sobriety, but I pretended not to know. I wanted him to be perfect because it was what I had been longing for all of my life—a perfect partner and a perfect life. But he was flawed—tremendously flawed—and my desire for perfection drove him to his addiction, rather than away from it," Harmony confessed.

Blake shook his head in understanding, urging her to continue. Confession was good for the soul.

"Ron and I never had time to really date. When I met him, he was a washed-up child star, and I was a washed-up former girl group member. We were both broken people trying to make each other feel whole. We spent most of our relationship trying to fix each other. He tried, and I tried.

But two broken people can't fix one another—
they have to fix themselves. It was too late in
our relationship before I realized that. When
my mother died a few months ago, I dragged
Ron back to the city—back to his old stomping
grounds, where temptations abounded. I did
this for my own selfish reasons, not thinking
about if or how he would cope. I needed to be
there with my sisters to deal with my mother's
death—this was more to alleviate my own guilt.
Ron couldn't handle all of the pressure of being
back in New York. It broke him and, in return, it
broke us."

"I'm sorry," Blake said, squeezing her hand.

She exhaled. If only she and Ron had made
time for each other to work through their
problems together, things may have turned out
different. Life in the rearview mirror was always
so much clearer.

"Don't get me wrong. I'm not excusing his
behavior, but I am certainly woman enough to
own up to the role that I played in our failed
marriage. He tried to tell me more than once
that he was hurting—slipping—and I didn't
take heed. I was too focused on my own needs
to listen. I was so selfish," Harmony lamented,
lowering her face into her hands.

"I've been listening to you," Ron raised his voice. *"All I hear out of your mouth is things that you've kept from me. All I hear is that you made a commitment to someone other than me and Aubrey."*

"I was going to tell you. I just have to make sure Lyric is going to be okay. She's really not doing well," Harmony said worriedly.

Ron palmed his head. *"She's a grown woman, not a little child! You don't need to go running to the rescue every time she gets into trouble."*

"Ron, I have to save her. I feel responsible for the way things are with her right now. I feel responsible for her . . . especially now," Harmony said, her voice trembling with emotion.

"So after everything that happened—turning their backs on you, leaving you broke and in the cold, cursing you out—you're really considering going on Melody's tour and being away from the life we've built because you think you can save Lyric?" he asked incredulously.

"It's not that cut and dry. I made a promise," Harmony swallowed. She felt like she was being ripped apart, like each of her arms were being pulled in opposite directions.

"You know damn well you can't save someone who doesn't want to be saved," his eyes narrowed to a pinprick. *"And what about that promise you made to me on our wedding day?*

Does that promise mean nothing to you?" Ron pointed to where Aubrey slept in their bed. "What about our life together? You want to abandon us for two sisters that didn't give a fuck about you these past three years?"

Ron started putting his pants on in a fury.

Harmony stood up. She tried to grab him, to make him listen to reason. "Wait," she cried. "Please, Ron. I can make this work."

"Don't touch me," he gritted, moving out of her reach.

"Where are you going?" she called as he roughly yanked his T-shirt over his head. He snatched his jacket from the back of the chair and grabbed his car keys.

"You don't care where I go. You only care about yourself, remember? Harmony's needs come first. Always," Ron accused, his chest heaving. "Well, I have a confession too, Harmony. I had a drink today. There. I said it. All of this bullshit made me want to run back to my old ways, Harm," he spat.

Harmony felt like she'd been slapped in the face. She opened her mouth to speak, but no words would come out.

"Don't," Ron growled, holding his hand up. "I had my first drink in three years. And you know what? It made me feel good. The house, the *party, the music, all of the rich folks gathered at your sister's place—I felt like my good old self again. That one glass of whiskey took my mind off of you and your so-called priorities. So now you know the ugly truth about me. I'm not hiding anymore," he proclaimed.*

Harmony shook her head. What had she done? How had they grown so far apart?

"I have you all figured out. You want to take care of other people so that you feel needed. You want me to be the old Ron again so that you can take care of me too? That's what it takes to get your dedication, right? You were only happy when I was a project—a drug addict that needed saving. If I'm not broken, you have nothing to fix," he spat cruelly.

Harmony doubled over in pain. Ron hit the nail on the head, but the truth was difficult for her to accept. She was losing everything that she fought so hard to keep. How could she have let this happen?

"Go ahead on tour with your sisters. You deserve it. You deserve the money and the fame. Go live that life again and let me know how happy it makes you," Ron's voice cracked. "Despite everything, I want you to be happy. Maybe we were just not meant to be." He put his hand on the doorknob.

"Wait," Harmony cried out. "Ron, wait!"

"I've waited long enough," he said, his voice hoarse. "I'm tired of waiting."

"Look, if this conversation is too much we can—"

"No, I'm a big girl," Harmony blinked, trying to refocus her attention on her date. She forced a smile.

"Okay, so enough about me. Now, it's your turn. What's your situation?" she said, turning the tables for a change.

"Well, I'm not married, if that's what you're asking," Blake replied.

Harmony palpably relaxed.

"At least, not anymore," he added for clarification.

Harmony's interest was piqued. She nodded for him to continue.

"My wife left me three years ago," he said honestly. Harmony's mouth sagged at the edges, but her heart leapt in her chest. He didn't sound too upset about it.

"She left, but it wasn't entirely her fault, either. I wasn't exactly the Perfect Husband," Blake said honestly. Harmony raised an eyebrow at that.

"I didn't cheat or anything, but I didn't give her what she needed, either. We were young when we got married—both in our early twenties. We weren't ready. I guess you could say that we had conflicting priorities in life. I wanted a career, and she wanted a white picket fence and little ones running around. I became a firefighter two years after we got married, and that took a toll on our marriage. Those overnight shifts, leaving her to sleep alone at nights, made the early days of our marriage difficult. It didn't bode well for family planning either. It was tough on her. She was always crying and complaining about my job. In turn, I was angry and downright passive-aggressive. I was glad that she had the courage to leave. I didn't want to be pegged as the bad guy, so I had convinced myself to stick it out and wait for things to get better. One day, I came home to find the house empty. I was initially upset, but in a way, I was glad that she took the decision off my hands," Blake confessed.

Harmony was hanging on to his every word. She drank in his features. She knew he was handsome, but at this moment of vulnerability, as she stared at his dark eyes and full lips, she was overcome with lust.

"So where is she now?" Harmony asked, balling up her toes in her shoes. "Did she ever come back? Did you ever try to reconcile?"

Blake released a breath he had obviously been holding.

"We saw each other a few more times during the divorce proceedings, but that was it. She moved on. She's married with the most adorable twin boys, and I'm genuinely happy for her. We don't speak regularly or anything, but there are no hard feelings there. She finally got the life that she wanted. We were both good people, just not good for each other," he said.

"All's well that ends well, right?" Harmony quoted the title of the Shakespearean play. "This is a lot of heavy stuff to discuss on a first date."

Blake lifted his wineglass in salute and took a gulp. "Now that the heavy stuff is out of the way, we can focus on the light stuff."

He grinned over the top of his glass, until she blushed a becoming pink.

"Like what?" Harmony giggled, taking a sip of her drink. She needed some liquid courage to get through this evening.

"We'll start with the basics, of course. What's your favorite food? What's your favorite thing to do? That sort of thing," Blake said nonchalantly.

"We should also talk about the weather," Harmony chimed in. "That will help us make it through dessert, at least."

"I don't care what we talk about, as long as it's not exes or sisters," Blake joked.

"Agreed! Well, I'm not sure if I have a favorite food . . . I have several favorite foods, in fact." Harmony tapped her right temple in deep thought. "Man, I guess that makes me really greedy. But you'll figure that out soon enough," she said, laughing.

"Okay, good to know. I'll make sure our next date is at one of those all-you-can-eat buffet places. Don't worry, I'll pick one of the classier places, like a Brazilian steakhouse." He winked and raised his glass in a toast.

Their glasses clinked, and they both took a celebratory drink.

Harmony shook her head. "My turn now. So what's your favorite food?"

He twisted his lips and looked up and to the left. "Steak. I love a good, well-aged rib eye with just enough pink in the middle," he explained.

"Steak, hmm? Why doesn't that surprise me? I love a man who knows exactly what he wants."

"And your favorite thing to do? We are going down the list, right?" Blake jested.

"My favorite thing to do is teach at the dance studio," Harmony said truthfully. "There are so many talented young girls out there. I love finding those little diamonds in the rough and polishing them until they shine."

Blake nodded. "I love your dedication, Harmony. It's what really attracted me to you in the beginning."

"Thanks, that's sweet." She didn't know how to respond to his compliments. They made her feel slightly uncomfortable. She wasn't used to so much attention and praise.

"The day you had the flood at your place I could see you were more devastated about the girls not being able to attend class than you were about the cost of the damage or your profit margins. You're a giver, a soul put here to help others. You show others, even during their darkest hours, that there is still some light."

Harmony exhaled. She had never heard herself described in such angelic terms. She was no saint, to be sure. But she did feel like her greater purpose in life was to serve others.

"Thank you, Blake. No one has ever so eloquently put into words how I feel." It was unnerving how much this man could read into her. Was she such an open book?

Blake smile, his heart in his eyes. "Thank you for coming back. For your honesty tonight. And for the beautiful flowers, of course," he added.

Harmony shook her head at his playful banter. "You are not going to get over the fact that I brought you flowers in front of the other guys, are you?" she teased.

"Trust me, I will never hear the end of it. I'm expecting to get prank flowers from my men for the next two months. They'll leave them in my bed, on my desk, in my shoes, in the truck. You have no idea what you've started." Blake said, his voice going low and sexy.

"Good. It's not every day that a man gets courted by a lady. You should enjoy it while it lasts," Harmony winked suggestively, blowing a kiss in the air.

Blake picked up her right hand and kissed the top of it.

After dinner, Harmony was on cloud nine when she agreed to go back to Blake's place for a nightcap. Things were progressing at warp speed, and she didn't want it to slow down. Blake was such a welcome distraction. It was finally time to put her needs first. Over the past five months, she had learned that if she didn't take care of herself first, she would never be able to take care of anyone else.

"This is my humble abode," Blake announced, opening his arms wide as he ushered Harmony inside.

"Blake, this . . . is gorgeous," she said, awestruck. "This view is amazing. I could look out this window all day long," she gushed. The wall of floor-to-ceiling windows displayed the full night's sky, like an in-house planetarium. Harmony looked down at the city in wonder and amazement. She felt like she was on top of the world, standing next to him. Harmony didn't know what good she had done to deserve him, but she silently thanked God for sending him her way.

"I'm glad you like it," Blake said, placing his hand on the small of her back. "I'm glad I could share this with you," he said, gesturing to the view below. His hand moved lower down her back, stroking her lightly.

Harmony's pulse quickened. The sexual tension between the two of them was palpable. She wasn't sure if it was the candid conversations at dinner or the wine that was making her feel so relaxed.

"What is it?" Blake asked, noticing her silence.

"Nothing. I'm fine," Harmony lied, turning back to the windows. She was thinking about Ron and how badly he'd hurt her. Revenge was never something Harmony practiced; however, the fruit of temptation was being dangled right before her nose, and she desperately wanted to take a bite. It had been five long months since she last had intimate relations with her husband. Standing in the sexy glow of the moonlight with a gorgeous man at her side, she realized just how easy it was to take the plunge and become a two-timer like Ron.

"Penny for your thoughts," Blake said, his smooth baritone sending prickles of desire down her spine.

Harmony grabbed Blake's head and pulled his six foot two frame close, until their bodies met at the hips and chest. She pressed her lips against his, their tongues instantly tangling together.

He sucked on her tongue softly, which caused a jolt of electricity in her southern parts. Blake gently placed his hands on each side of her face, tilting her head slightly for better access to her mouth. Harmony moved her body suggestively against his, rubbing her erect nipples against his muscular chest. His iron-stiff erection throbbed against the top of her pelvis.

"You feel so good," he whispered in her ear. "Are you sure about this?"

Her body tingled with desire. She wasn't going to fight it. She wanted to be loved. She wanted to be appreciated. She wanted to feel more beautiful than her sister Melody. Most of all, she just wanted to be wanted.

Blake grabbed her hand and led her to his bedroom.

Harmony eased down onto his bed, and he climbed on top of her. Their hands explored each other in a frenzy of passion. The only thing that remained between them was their clothing.

"Are you sure about this?" Blake asked again, his hands poised above her breasts. Harmony didn't answer; instead, she pulled his shirt out from his pants and hoisted it above his head.

Blake followed her lead and began to unzip the back of her dress. He smiled down at her—part wicked, part sensual. Harmony ran her hands slowly over the curves of his perfect muscular chest.

"Damn," she huffed, her fingers lingering over the ridges of his abdomen. "You're perfect." She never thought she'd say those words to another man. She could feel the tears welling up in her eyes. She fought hard to keep them from falling. Her marriage was over, and this was proof of it.

"No, I'm far from perfect," he said, his voice gruff with lust.

Harmony moved from under Blake and signaled for him to lie down. She stood in front of his prone figure and let her inhibitions fall away. She wanted to be different with him than she'd been with Ron. She was always shy and inhibited with her husband; they never had sex in the daylight, for example, and the room always had to be dark.

She slipped out of her dress slowly and quickly unsnapped her bra. Her breasts sat up taut and perky, seemingly winking at Blake.

He groaned. "You're so sexy," he whispered. "Come here, before I die," he beckoned with his finger.

Harmony's body quaked with nerves and anticipation. She slowly shimmied her hips, pulling her sexy, black lace panties off, and letting them drop to the floor. Without a word, she climbed onto the bed, pushed Blake back down, and leaned over him.

For a brief moment, she saw Ron making love to Melody in her mind. Harmony gasped and shook off the image. *He's not the only one who can do it. I can do it too.* She licked Blake's neck. Again, flashes of Ron and Melody invaded her mind. This time, Harmony arched her back and slithered a little farther down, trailing her tongue over Blake's pectoral muscles and gently biting the right one.

Blake hissed in pleasure. His reaction combined with the wine she consumed at dinner was an intoxicating mix. She continued down his abdomen, taking special care to run her tongue over every ridge on his sexy, firm six-pack. He moaned in pleasure. She smiled mischievously and bit her bottom lip seductively.

Blake sat up and flipped Harmony over onto her back before she could react or protest.

"Wait," she whispered. A pang of fear gripped her chest. It was too late for second thoughts now.

2 Timers: Love Sisters Series   345

"I won't hurt you. I won't ever hurt you, Harmony," he said. His manhood was large and throbbing.

She closed her eyes, trying valiantly to fight off the tears. *Fuck you, Ron! Fuck you! Fuck you!* Whatever Ron could do, she could do too.

Blake slid a condom on. He used his knee to gently part her thighs; then he slowly guided his manhood into her deep, wet center.

Harmony let out a song of soft moans and groans as he grinded into her.

"Oh," she cooed, digging her fingers into his gluteus muscles. He felt so good. They fit together perfectly.

"Damn," Blake huffed, picking up speed from the excitement. After a few minutes of pumping, she suggested that they switch positions.

"Let me," she whispered gruffly. Harmony wanted this to be on her terms. She wanted to feel empowered that she'd made the decision to take it to the next level with him.

Blake flipped onto his back, pulling her on top of him. She lowered her body over his stiff tool and grinded down until the angle was just right. He grabbed her hips and helped her move up and down until she was riding him with abandon. She felt the tension building inside, almost to the point of pain.

"Oh God," she yelled. "Oh God!" Her whole body was tense and focused on a release that was sure to be most pleasurable.

Harmony thought no other man could ever make her feel like Ron had—at least when things were still good between them. She never imagined she could feel so wonderful and desirable.

"Yes," he growled, clutching two handfuls of her bottom. She rocked back and forth, swirling her hips. The movement caused Blake's pubic hairs to rub ever so slightly against hers. The combination of deep penetration and the friction against her clit made her body buck. She screamed and clutched onto Blake's shoulders as small fireworks exploded in her head and squirms of light filled her eyesight. She didn't want the good feeling that flooded her body to stop. She rocked harder and faster now. She leaned down slightly, close enough for Blake to lick her rock-hard nipples. Another explosion erupted in her loins. Her entire body shook with her release. Blake's body tensed at the same time, and his climax followed.

Harmony collapsed on top of him, out of breath but utterly sated. She closed her eyes in total relaxation and peace. She was right where she belonged. *Maybe this was meant to be.*

***

Two weeks later, Blake pulled his car into Harmony's driveway. She had started out the door, saving him the trouble of ringing the doorbell. Still, he was a gentleman, so he got out of the car to meet her.

"Beautiful as usual," he said, kissing her cheek.

"I'm in jeans and a T-shirt. Hardly beautiful. Cute maybe, but not beautiful." She still had difficulty with accepting compliments.

"I know what you look like under those clothes. You can't fool me," he pretended to leer at her. She laughed and swatted at his arm.

"Here you go, sweetheart . . ." Blake said, opening the car door for her. His smile quickly faded. Harmony's eyes followed his gaze. She gasped in shock.

"Harm?" Ron said, walking slowly up the driveway toward them. Harmony's heart thrashed against her chest bone. Her breathing became labored.

"Are you all right?" Blake asked her, concerned. Harmony swallowed hard.

"Harm . . . It's me. I . . . I'm home," Ron said nervously. She could tell that he'd cleaned himself up.

"Ron," Harmony finally found her voice. "What are you doing here?" she croaked.

"I came home. I needed to see you and Aubrey," he replied. "I went to detox. See, I'm all cleaned up. I'm back. The real me is back."

Harmony shook her head and closed her eyes for several seconds. She stared at her husband, and then at her lover. Heat consumed her entire body. She felt sick to her stomach. She was both angry at Ron and embarrassed at herself for being caught with Blake.

"I came back for you, Harmony," Ron moved closer, ignoring Blake's stony expression.

Blake let go of the door handle and stepped aside. Harmony could see disappointment wash over his features.

Although Ron had hurt her in the worst possible way, she didn't want him to find out about her and Blake like this.

"It's me, sugar," Ron said, calling her by the familiar endearment.

Harmony looked from one man to the other. She was stuck between her future and her past. She never thought she would find herself in the middle of a love triangle.

"I . . . I . . . need some time," Harmony stammered, rushing away from Ron and Blake in a hurry.

What now? What now?

To be continued . . .